Evanescence

To my mother, who told me to dream.

To my father, who told me to make it happen.

To my friends, who believed...

R.J. Rogue

Contents

CHAPTER ONE: DREAMER

"She hasn't told you, has she, Evan? She hasn't told you what you *really* are."

I am alone. Standing below gray clouds looking down from a cliff. The violent waves below are a disservice to my comfort, and this lump in my throat is as bitter as medicine. Goosebumps spread across my skin, not caused by wind, but from fear. *I will not jump into the water below. I will not kill myself. I am strong.*

Thunder rumbles, and a heavy presence falls upon me: the kind of heaviness like someone standing over your shoulder. I turn to face the consequence. Doors. They are my only exit from this cliff and the falling sky. Its blood colored body has no handles, no chips or cracks in its wood, no house, nor dwelling. Nothing but the moss-filled forest behind them.

The doors open and a blinding light escapes. As my legs command to step forward, I fight to stand still and frown at their disobedience. I walk, unable to see what is before me, the same trait darkness itself possesses. The doors slam behind me, and for a moment, all is still and quiet. I continue to walk, and when my surroundings become visible, I stop.

A red carpet is beneath me. It runs throughout a vast lobby. The marble ceiling is high, and golden chandeliers hang above. A gray fountain of cherubs splashing buckets of water are centered beneath them. The walls are murals of Heaven like the Sistine Chapel, and not far from where I stand is a golden-railed staircase which leads to a second floor. I find a smile, but then that fragment of fear I was sure I defeated returns to the pit of my stomach. *Why does this place look familiar?*

"Tag, you're it!" yells a little girl when she touches my leg.

I chase her as she runs in her white dress. Her giggles echo through the long halls and opened doors. We run through empty rooms then back to the lobby and up the staircase. Her golden-blonde head full of hair dances with each step she takes and when we reach the top, I hear a

7

piano playing and wonder who else is here. I stop, listen, and hope to find the sound, better yet the musician behind the keynote, but no luck.

"Evan," she calls, now standing in a doorway.

How does she know my name? I recognize her but can't remember from where or when. She stands patient and peaceful, but when she smiles, I flinch. Her smile is rich in white fangs, two that are much larger and longer than the others. *Like a vampire,* I think to myself. Again, my legs disobey as I meet her at the door.

We walk into a dining room. Sitting at a white-clothed table is a group of four. Each face is pale and familiar, like hers. A silver platter rests in the center of the table and before I can find words, one of them stands.

"Be polite," the man says as his eyebrows form wrinkles above his nose. "We have been waiting for you long enough. Why don't you have a seat?"

His sharp tuxedo could cut a finger by the touch and his gelled salt and pepper hair matches. His eyes, however, are not as welcoming as his appearance. The red around his pupils are piercing and burn with hatred. A look I am foreign to receiving.

"Well, --"

I begin to respond, but a chair pushes beneath me before I accept his invitation. In what felt like a second, I am sitting on the opposite side of the table, next to the little girl, facing the doorway which is now closed. My eyes search for answers, but do not find them over their glare. They clock my chest with each breath I take and my lungs won't gather the amount oxygen I need to remain calm and comfortable.

"See? We don't bite now do we, Evan?" The man says with a smile.

They join in a sudden hysterical laughter as I sit silent, still, and afraid. I dry my hands across my lap, but almost immediately they moisten again. He too knows my name and he too has a mouthful of fangs like the little girl, only his are larger. The boy across from me has yet to move an inch. One of his eyes stares behind black strands of hair. Each breath he takes blows the hair away from his lips exposing his bottom row of fangs; hundreds, sharp, and glossed of saliva.

"On this special night," says the man in the tuxedo. "My son shall become one with his destiny. A destiny in which he will accept and fulfill. To become who he was born to be."

The boy continues to stare. I wipe my forehead with the back of my hand and try to keep myself from shaking.

"He will die," he continues. "And from his own ashes he will be reborn like a phoenix bird to be reunited with this family who loves him so."

"Are you alright?" asks the man with long black hair interrupting. "You don't look so well."

I want to respond, but I feel like choking. He too has fangs. Ready to take a bite and hopefully, not of me.

"I'm fine. Just a bit…hot," I say.

I don't see, but hear him smile.

"But it's cold outside for your kind, yes?" he asks leaning across the table. I gulp. My lie did not succeed.

"Shhh…" says the woman. "Have some respect. This night is of great importance to this family."

"Indeed it is. My apologies," he says to her bowing his head. "Continue, brother."

"Yes, as I was saying," the man continues. "Let us move forward and prepare the way for my son. We have been waiting much longer than anticipated and so tonight, the wait shall be no more."

They are vampires, but a figment of me wants to stick to popular belief that vampires do not exist. Their existence goes as far as myths, books, and movies. Another part of me is trying to piece together where I have seen them. Sometime long ago.

"It is the final hour," he says removing the lid. "We shall eat to stay strong and unified. We are timeless on the timeline. Leave not a drop for immortality is a privilege. Not a right."

Their eyes widen and their lips peel back exposing mouthfuls of fangs. They hiss and begin to rise from their chairs. My heart pounds against my chest and a drop of sweat slides down the bridge of my nose. Afraid of what is to come, I stand and shout which may also be my last.

"Stop!"

They turn to me and hiss. Frightened, I fall back into my chair, its legs snap from beneath me, and the back of my head dashes the cemented wall. I shatter like glass and blurry vision leaves me defenseless. Everything is cloudy like being underwater without goggles. Almost like a dream. The thought crosses my mind and becomes salvation. *Yes! A dream! I am asleep, imagining all of this. These people. This place. It is all just --.*

"A dream?!" the man yells. His nose is just a lips distance away from mine. He shakes his head.

"This is no dream, Evan. This is far more than that."

I want to run for the door, but apart from not being able to see, I'm sure he would catch me. He steps away and a head full of blonde hair appears. Her small hands press over my eyes. After a few moments, she removes them and I can see.

"Why aren't you eating, Evan?" she asks. "You have to eat. You have to or everyone will be sad again. Remember? Remember what daddy said would happen if you don't eat?"

"Remember what?" I ask as I rub the back of my head where the wall connected. "What are you talking about?"

Tears sit on her bed of eyelashes. Her face blushes.

"Who's going to play with me? I never sleep alone," she says. "Who's going to protect me?"

"Wait. I don't understand?" I say sitting up. "What do you mean? Where am I and who are you people?"

"You won't believe me," she responds. Her face hugs the floor.

"Yes, I will," I say placing my hands gently on her shoulders. "Tell me."

A bang on the table frightens us. Eyes hover above me; angered, frustrated, and impatient. The man in the tuxedo has his fists clenched, but his expression is disappointed. He takes a step to the side of his chair, his eyes not leaving mine.

"Daddy, no! Evan, will do it right this time! Don't make him go!" yells the little girl as she wraps herself around my arm. "Evan, daddy's gonna..."

"Silence, child!" he yells as the dining room doors slam open from a strong wind. The suction pulls me beneath the table and towards the door.

"What's happening?" I ask her.

"I won't let you go, Evan!"

The wind's suction becomes stronger. Darkness awaits. Everyone besides the little girl steps away from the table and the table and chairs are sucked into the black hole.

"Stop! What are you doing?!" I beg.

The wind pulls me to the doorway and try to stop myself with my feet, but fail. The suction is fierce and unforgiving, and the little girl's grip is weak. I cling onto the wood with one hand as she hangs onto my other.

"Evan, you can't go! Stay with me!" she yells.

My body lifts from the floor and I try to hold on. My shoes leave my feet and are swallowed.

"I can't!"

"Since you can't cooperate, Evan, you have to leave!" the man yells. "I told you what would happen! I told you!"

"Don't make him go!" the girl yells. "Give him another chance!"

Evanescence

"No more chances! He's had far too many already!"

The room falls silent. The suction continues and the girl hangs onto my hand, fighting her tears.

"Someday, Evan, you will change," he says. "Someday, you will come looking for answers. Someday, you will come home."

I fail to hold on any longer and fall into the darkness. The little girl extends her hand out to me with tears flowing down her cheeks. The others watch and wait.

"Goodbye, Evan," they all say.

"We'll meet again," says the man. "When the time comes, it will be you who shall find us."

"Evan!" I hear the little girl cry. "Come back! Evan!"

~

"Evan! Evan!" I hear my mother's voice. "Wake up. I'm here."

I gasp for air, rising to a sit. I am in bed and my mother sits at my side.

"I'm okay," I say breathless.

15

"Yes," she says. "You are safe."

I take a deep breath and lay my head back. My pillow is damp from sweat.

My mother looks around the room, a heavy thought crosses her face before she speaks.

"Were they in your nightmare, Evan?"

I knew that question was coming. The conversation is more like a script between us by now.

"No," I shake my head. "They weren't."

She exhales deeply.

"You haven't been getting much sleep lately," she says caressing my cheek. "You scream throughout the night. You have bags under your eyes. You—"

"I'm fine," I say. "Really."

She stares. My lie did not succeed.

"You weren't one of *them* this time -- were you?"

"Mom, please. Don't do this."

"Do what, Evan?"

I shrug.

"Worry so much."

She presses her lips together.

"You can't tell a mother not to worry about her child."

She leans forward and kisses my forehead. Her long brown hair touches the sides of my face.

"Be sure to write it down as soon as you can."

"Mom."

"Please?" she asks, though I know it is not a question.

I nod.

Ever since I was a child, when something happened, *'write it down, Evan.'* If I've had a bad day, *'write it down, Evan.' 'Oh? You haven't written at all today? Write, Evan.'* I have notebooks on top of notebooks, journals on top of journals covering almost every day and aspect of my life and don't let me miss an entry and she find out about it.

I remember when I forgot to write about the day I graduated from middle school. She was upset for weeks and was adamant about how important it is that I write every day. It wasn't that I didn't find my middle school graduation important. It just slipped my mind from all the festivities that had taken place afterwards. Now, I can never forget that day because of her.

I guess I can't blame her. She's mom and the only family I have. She always says "It's me and you against the world, Evan." I do have a father, but he left us long before I can remember. I can't remember his face, his voice, or how he dresses. I've tried searching for him before. Such a dreadful failure. His name is Kaius Macrae. An interesting name if I do say so myself. I barely have any matching physical qualities with my mother besides peach skin, but she says I resemble my him; short brown hair, lean, and acorn eyes full of ambition. I've always had an infinite number of questions about him and my childhood, but my mother never wanted to answer any of my questions. I just wanted to learn more about myself through him I guess. Over time, I stopped asking.

"I love you. Try to get some rest before school, okay?" She rises from the bed.

"Okay, I love you too mom."

She gave in easily this time and closes the door. I listen as her footsteps become faint. I clasp my hands behind my head thinking about the nightmare. I've always had terrible ones as a child and for the past few weeks, they have returned. There have been times, like tonight, when it is difficult to determine if I am asleep or awake and unlike other nightmares in my past, this nightmare felt the most realistic. It was like one big déjà vu. And those people, if that's what they are, are always in them.

I reach under my bed and grab my composition notebook. I will do as I was told and write it down; however, that nightmare will be difficult to forget. When I dot the last period, I place the notebook and pen on the nightstand and close my eyes. *Who or what are those people? Why are they in my dreams? Why do they look so familiar?*

CHAPTER TWO: CRUSHING

I can't stand sunlight. My mother would joke and say, *like a vampire*. I rise from my bed and tuck my notebook into my book bag. My room has bins of notebooks filled with poetry, short stories, and screenplays that I've written since childhood. The walls of my room are covered in my artwork and I have a few portraits of famous works. My favorite? Salvador Dali's *Persistence of Memory.* There's something about those melting clocks. I also have an easel for painting, a small coffee maker for those 4:00 am writing muse sessions, and a small desk covered in book outlines, crumbled papers of poor ideas, and books by some of my favorite writers like Ernest Hemingway, Edgar Allan Poe, and C.S. Lewis.

I love all forms of art. I remember my mother taking me to the Munson-Williams Proctor Arts Institute when I was younger and I would stare painting after painting. I also remember her reading me poems and going to Shakespearean plays. "What a genius," is how she describes him. Before I knew it, I was creating my own works of art. Not to say I am as good as Shakespeare, but I must be exceptionally well to receive the recognition I have achieved from the awards I've received in poetry, short story, and art contests. One day, I'll hopefully write a novel, but life is a novel in itself.

"Evan?" she calls from downstairs. "You awake?!"

"Yes. I'll be down in a sec'!"

"If you'd like a ride to school, you better hurry!"

After the daily bathroom regimen, I get dressed wearing my black casual shoes and glasses. I sling my book bag over my back and head downstairs. My mother is in the kitchen dressed in her white work clothes and name tag which reads, Sarah Foster. Her and dad was never married.

"Took you long enough, sleepyhead," she says before kissing my cheek. "Good morning. Breakfast is right there on the counter. I'll have to leave now to make this delivery. I waited as long as I could."

"It's alright. I can take my bike," I say. "No biggie'."

"Be careful on that bike," she says putting her lunch into a shopping bag. She then grabs the orange juice from the fridge.

"Thanks for the breakfast. Hope you didn't get any blood on my food."

I take a bite into a Morning Star veggie sausage biscuit. She smirks and pours a glass of orange juice, then slides it in front of me.

"Well, Mr. Vegetarian, my job does pay the bills around here," she says smirking. "I'm surprised you haven't turned into a vampire by now."

I flinch and think about the nightmare from last night. Their eyes, pale skin, and fangs. *It was only a dream*, I tell myself. *Vampires aren't real.*

"Could say the same for you I guess, but I have no shame in my diet," I shrug. "Have to accept me for who I am, right?"

She's frozen and unreadable. I wait for her punchline, but she doesn't deliver.

"Mom?" I say hoping to defrost her.

"And I most certainly do, Evan," she finally responds. "Sorry, must be the pain medication. I'll see you when I get home, sweetie. Don't be late for school."

"I won't be."

"I love you."

"I love you too, mom."

She slings her purse over her shoulder as her lunch bag hangs from the wrist. She closes the front door behind herself.

My mother makes deliveries for a blood donor company stationed just outside our city in Rome, New York. Sometimes she'd have to make *emergency deliveries* that almost seem routine, but I never questioned her. I learned to live with it.

I had to be about five or six years old when she had the accident. The one that left her in pain to this day. She told me it was one of the worst ice storms of the century. She was on her way back into town when she lost control of the work van and broke through a guard rail. The van rolled several times before a tree stopped her from rolling into the Mohawk River. Now, she's left with taking pain medications and a permanent scar down her right cheek as a reminder, but who would forget such a tragedy? My father was gone by then and to think how different my life would be right now if I had lost her too. I am blessed.

I've never had to rush to school, but this morning might be the first. Sometimes I use my mother's car, but majority of the time I ride my bike. I don't mind because Utica, New York is beautiful. Most disagree and believe there isn't much to do here. Others would say that the city is small, so what is there to enjoy? People move away, never here. Most of us attend Thomas R. Proctor or Norte Dame high school, but they are quite similar rather than polar opposites.

I believe Utica's small size masks its treasures. Our winters can be brick cold, but thanks to The Great Lakes, the lake effect snow makes skiing and snow tubing worth-while. Our summers are hot and humid, so building sand castles and the smell of barbeque are common activities. Right now, we have the best of both worlds. The end of March brings sunny days and thunderous rainy weather which helps with my writing.

I live just off the coast of the Mohawk River Valley named after the Iroquois confederacy. There are many forest green trees, bike paths, hiking trails, high hills, and the air is fresh. Sometimes it has this mixture of pine and mint I love. Behind my house, there is a sea of tall trees before you hit the water of the Mohawk River, which stretches for one-hundred fifty miles or so through Rome, Utica, Little Falls, Canajoharie, Amsterdam, and Schenectady. From my bedroom window, it looks like a rainforest, and I call it that.

I look down the slope road and decide to race the wind. The school is a short distance away and before I know it, I am looking up at the school's sign which reads, "*The Reason. The Skill. The Observation. The Spirit.*" Many students are conversing in the front of the school and in the parking lot. Others step off of the yellow buses that run throughout Oneida County. I chain and lock my bike on the rack, and sling one strap of my book bag over my shoulder.

"Hey, Ev!" a familiar voice calls from the buses.

My best friend, I consider him a brother, Mike Druin, steps off of his bus. Mike is a bear in size. He's not huge, but he's well-built and athletic -- more than me to say the least.

"Had fun with the hair gel? Looks all porcupine."

He runs his fingers through his thin black strands, then shrugs.

"Shower, almost missed the bus."

I smirk.

"You really should have gone to that party man," he says.

I shake my head and laugh as we head up the steps and into the school.

"You know I'm not much of a party goer," I remind him.

"But really," says the party animal. "That was the first one of the school year and almost everyone at least goes to the first one. You could've listened to music, danced, talked to Essence— "

"What?"

"Danced?" he says with a guilty smile. "I'm just saying. You would've enjoyed it."

"Can't say I disagree. I'd be lying if I said I didn't clock my closet a few times, but I needed to be alone."

Evanescence

We pass through the slams of locker doors, the chatter of students and teachers, and the zombies who faces are buried in their phones before I reach my locker. I open it with the combination.

"What's been going on?" he asks leaning on a locker.

"Well, I'm having those nightmares again. You know? The ones I've had since we were kids?"

Mike has always known about my nightmares. I use to get picked on because of them, but ever since the day I met him at the swimming pool rec center as a kid, he's always had my back and defended me.

I was being picked on by a few of the other kids when I told them about my nightmares. I was trying to make friends. I didn't know anyone. When everyone was getting into the pool for a game of Marco Polo, I refused. Regardless of how shallow the water was, it looked too deep for me. I wanted to go find my mother to ask to leave, but before I could, the kids grabbed me by the arms and tried to toss me into the pool. I still hear their voices from time to time. "You're scared of water?! Haven't you ever taken a bath?! Don't be such a scaredy-cat, weirdo!"

I begged them not to toss me into the water, but they refused to listen. The tips of my toes were over the edge, almost how they were on the cliff in my nightmare last night. I yelled for help, but didn't see my mother nor lifeguard. I begged again, not to throw me into the pool, and before the heels of my feet left the ledge, Mike pushed them aside and told them to go away. They respected Mike. Even back then, Mike was a bear and since then, Mike has been my best and only friend.

"The nightmares that half of the kids used to pick on you about? Yeah, hard to forget," he says.

"Right," I say. "Well, the past few weeks, they've come back. Almost every time I shut my eyes now. And last night's felt so different than ever before. It felt...real."

"That's the thing about nightmares, Ev. They feel real, but they aren't," he shrugs. "Your mom knows they've come back?"

"She makes it difficult to hide. She still does the whole, *'write it down, Evan,'* thing," I shake my head.

"Soon she'll have you write your biography."

"Or my obituary when I'm on my death bed."

"Have you tried sleeping pills? Nyquil?"

"Nyquil?" I say. "You drink Nyquil to sleep?"

"Who doesn't? It works every time. I know *I* sleep well every night."

"I'll pass," I close my locker. "I just hate that my mother thinks I'm as fragile as a wine glass."

"She's being protective. I'm sure she's scared just as much as you."

I nod my head and see the faces of those people at the table again, their pale skin, sharp fangs, and red eyes.

"This is going to sound weird Mike, but do you believe in – in things like," I pause.

"--Things like?" he asks as I try to find a way to not sound stupid.

"Vampires?"

He scoffs.

"No, do you?"

"I do," I shake my head. "I mean I don't. I mean, well I don't know to be honest. That's what those people seem to be in my nightmares."

"That's the thing, Ev. They're nightmares."

"But they even look familiar like," I think to myself. "Like I know them from somewhere or a long time ago. All of them. It felt much more than just a nightmare it was more like," I drift off.

"Like what?"

"Like a memory."

He shakes his head and chuckles.

"Do they try to suck your blood in any of the nightmares?"

"No actually now that I think about it. And it kind of bothers me that they didn't. They just send me away as though I had done something wrong. And this little girl, she gets so upset when I leave and she wants to tell me something, but says I won't believe her."

"What do you think that might be?"

"I don't know," I shrug. "But all five of them, I know I've seen them before. I just can't put my finger on it. One of them said, '*someday, you'll come home.*'"

"Come home? Ev, this is crazy. Listen to yourself. You are home. Utica is your home and you may not have a big family, but you still have one. Your mom, Sarah, *is* your family."

"She never answers any of my questions about my childhood besides talking about you, and she doesn't answer anything about my father. What about aunts, uncles, cousins, et cetera? Where are they? Why doesn't she want to talk about family or anyone else related to us? Why haven't I met any of them or even heard a name? There aren't even any baby pictures of me around the house. It's like, my childhood never existed and that all other relatives are either dead or don't exist. I think she's hiding something from me. Sometimes I just feel like I was dropped on her doorstep or something."

Mike places a hand on my shoulder.

"I'm sorry you're going through this and I'm willing to help you through it all, but you can't start second guessing where you come from because of a bunch of ridiculous nightmares."

"What if it's the truth?"

"What if what's the truth?"

"What if I'm adopted?"

"Ev," he sighs dropping his hand. "Stop. You're not adopted, just confused. Besides, things could be worse I mean, who would you rather live with? Sarah, your mom? Or some vampires?"

He's right. I couldn't live with them. Vampires. I shouldn't consider that they are real. Then my eyes then lay upon her. Her flawless skin and curly, dark-red hair sitting on her shoulders and collarbones. Some of her hair shades one of her eyes. Her pink lips, rests on her symmetrical thin face.

I watch as she opens her locker. She takes a look into a mirror that hangs on the inside of her locker door. Her fingers stroke through her hair from root to tip. She stops and our eyes meet in her mirror. I avert and regret dazing in front of Mike.

"Essence LaRoux," he grins.

"What about her?" I say struggling to breathe.

"You should go talk to her. She was at the party."

"Eh, no can do. I'll pass."

"Oh come on, Ev. Don't tell me you find her that intimidating."

But I do, ever since grade school. She was always the girl with a head full of dark red hair. We never actually talked to each other. Perhaps I blame myself for being shy. There were times where I would watch Essence drink from the water fountain. She would push her hair back and away from her face and purse her lips to drink. When she'd finish, she'd catch her breath, fix her hair, and smile with perfect white teeth.

I also watched her during class and when called on to answer a question, I would ask to have the question repeated only to be told to focus and pay attention. On the bus rides home, she sat right behind the driver. Mike and I would sit in the back. He would talk about Bianca, but I would be in a completely different world staring at Essence who seemed to never look back or at me -- except once.

When I was being bullied in gym class, I was pushed to the floor and wouldn't dare look up at the boys and girls that laughed. But Essence never did. At least if she did laugh at me, I did not see it. When they walked away to gossip about me being weird and having no friends, I was searching for my glasses. That was the first time she spoke to me. That was also the first time she looked at me. Essence held my glasses in her hands above asking if I was okay. I found it hard to respond, but I took the glasses and ran to the bathroom. I remember placing my back against the wall and feeling angered about not being brave and not having Mike around to save me. Worst of all, Essence felt sorry for me. At least that's what I had believed.

I look at Mike and shake my head. He raises his hands surrendering.

"Fair enough, fair enough. Don't talk to her. Just saying you should try man before someone else takes that opportunity."

That would be heart breaking, and I can feel

my stomach tying into a knot just thinking about it. Feeling this way about her is ridiculous, but then again she isn't just your average girl, at least to me she isn't. I watch her more often than I should, and she moves different from everyone else. My feelings for her are knitted deep inside my veins, her name stitched across my heart, and as extreme as it may sound, if such a procedure *is* possible, I'd secretly have it surgically performed. *Why am I so attracted to someone I barely know or talk to?*

Just another part of me I don't understand. My feelings are like instinct, undeniable, indefinable, and unconditional. But how far would I get with a girl like her? I can picture myself saying, "Hey, want to look at my finger paintings and read my short stories?" Yeah, right. I'm just an ordinary guy with the gift of being ordinary. Simple as that.

"One of these days I'll try to talk to her in class or something," I say trying to sound confident and convincing.

"Who knows? Maybe you can make *her* the addicted one."

35

I laugh hysterically in my mind. Like *that's* possible. The first bell rings and a locker slams nearby and books hit the floor. It's Cedric, the bullied, dark haired, mysterious, Adam's family relative. Well, not really, but he would blend in with them. He has always been bullied like myself which is the reason I only know his first name and probably the reason he too doesn't have any friends. Lucky for me, I have Mike.

"Idiot!" yells one of the students stepping over Cedric as he stares at them through his hair. He begins to pick up his books then our eyes meet. He glares at me like a predator sizing up its prey before attacking. He shakes his head then brushes the black hair from his face. Bianca walks by and exchanges a look with Cedric. He mumbles something under his breath and Bianca scoffs, but I miss what is said. As she passes my locker, I glance at Mike who of course is admiring her with drool. I tap his cheek with my hand.

"Is your jaw broken?" I ask trying not to laugh. He shakes his head.

"No, I'm not how you are with Essence.

"Yeah, okay. Your eyes disagree with your mouth."

Bianca has been Mike's crush almost as long as Essence has been mine. Years. Her long blonde hair dances atop her head with each step she takes. She smiles at us, but almost immediately averts her eyes and picks up her pace. Cedric is gone. Slipping away must come easy for him.

"You saw that?!" Mike asks with a cheesy smile. *And he says he's not how I am with Essence.*

"Yeah," I say. "Now it's my turn to say, 'go talk to her.'"

"I will. You'll see. One of us has to make our move. How much longer will we procrastinate?" The second school bell rings. "And it ends today. We don't live forever. Only once."

CHAPTER THREE: HICCUPS

The smell of the locker room is repulsive. Sweaty gym shorts, socks, and sneakers cover the floor. I rush into my gym clothes and hurry out. Some students shoot around the basketball and some talk and giggle on the sidelines and bleachers of the gym. Mike comes out of the locker room and meets me at the three-point line.

"There she is," he says. Bianca sits on the bleachers talking with her friends.

"You're going to go over there?" I ask.

"Not with all her friends over there, kiddin' me?"

"Where's all that confidence now?" I ask smirking.

"Just waiting for the right time. You're talking to a pro here. Besides, I think she's diggin' me."

I try to hold back my smile. Failure. My laugh escapes.

"What makes you so sure if you've never spoken to her?"

"At the party," he begins. "It seemed like everywhere

I went, she was following. Staring at me. She's obviously interested."

"Go on," I say holding another laugh.

"And I did talk to her. When I was getting something to drink she comes over and asks me to pour some punch in her cup." He pauses and stares at me. Did I miss something?

"That means she wants me!" he says almost too loud catching the attention of nearby classmates.

"Or she just wanted some punch," I say feeling embarrassed by Mike's obnoxity.

"You're just jealous that I have a little lead on Bianca," he smirks.

"Hey, Mike," calls one of our classmates. "We need an extra player."

He passes Mike the ball. Mike looks over at Bianca who watches him from the bleachers. She smiles which I'm sure is enough to do more than boost Mike's ego. He turns to the hoop, shoots, and sinks a three-pointer. He looks back at Bianca and smiles as she returns one.

"Show off," I say shaking my head with a smirk.

"Yeah well, it's a start." He pats my shoulder and joins the other students in playing basketball.

I look over to Bianca, and she looks at me as though she wants to say something. She waves shyly, and I wave back. We've never spoke in the past, but there have been times we had the opportunity for conversation and it just never happened. It always seems as though something is bothering her. I could ask, but I wouldn't know how or where to start. There have been times where she would walk up to me and instead of saying anything, she would walk away with this embarrassed expression. I've also caught her watching me plenty of times at school. I wonder how long she would keep this up before actually saying something to me or maybe like everyone else, she thinks I'm weird.

I go into the hallway for a quick drink at the water fountain before class starts. I gulp to my fullness then hear someone coming. I turn and cause a collision.

"Watch it!" Cedric yells stumbling back.

"Sorry, my mistake."

"You're right, it was your mistake," he says. "Now what do you plan on doing about it?"

"What do you mean?" I squint my eyes in confusion.

"Well you bumped into me."

"I know and I said that I was sorry."

"What are you going to do to make sure it doesn't happen again?" he says stepping forward.

Is he challenging me?

"I guess I'll be more careful."

"You guess?"

What is this guy's problem? Is he really getting mad? I've apologized. What more does he expect for me to do?

"Hello?" he calls snapping his finger.

"Look, it was a mistake. I've never done anything wrong to you. I've never bullied or pushed you around. I don't threaten you –"

"You don't threaten me? How sure are you about that?"

He stares with disgust. He looks down at my sneakers and gym clothes.

"Just forget it. You're harmless, Macrae."

Well he certainly knows more than just my first name.

"Whatever, Cedric. I'm sorry I bumped into you." I begin to walk back to gym, but he steps in front of me. I back off.

"Okay, what would it take?" I ask. "What do you want from me?"

"What do I want from you?" he asks. He takes another step forward closing the distance between us. "If I were to decide right now, I'd want you dead."

"Excuse me?"

He steps closer with his face holding a grimace.

"You. Dead." Red bleeds around his pupils and I back off staring into his eyes. Then, nothing. His eyes are dark brown making me think I was hallucinating. He chuckles and I attempt to walk past again, but this time, he shoves me.

"Stop."

I try once more to leave. He shoves me again with more force causing me to stumble.

"I'm telling you to..."

He does it again.

"Cedric," I say through clenched teeth. My tongue then rips across something sharp and blood splashes in my mouth. I touch my mouth with my fingertips confused. I feel fangs in my mouth and I jump back covering my mouth with my hand. Cedric stands silent and still, staring with a grin on his face. A painful crunch hits my head and a deafening ring fills my ears. I drop to my knees and clasp my hands to my ears. The pain intensifies. *What's going on with me!* I begin to shake and place my forehead onto the floor trying to fight the pain. Cedric stands above me. Pain leaves my throat.

"Oh well lookie here," he says with a laugh in his voice. "Don't be afraid. With time, you'll get used to it."

"Cedric!" I groan through the pain. "Don't just stand there help me!"

"I am," he says. "I'm being forced to."

"What are you talking about?" I say through my pain and aching teeth.

I yell in agony again.

"One step at a time, Macrae," he says with another laugh. "We're watching you. For now. How's the nightmares going? Dream of us yet?"

I clench one of my hands into a fist and punch the floor. The linoleum crumbles, but felt as soft as tissue paper. *What's wrong with me?* I think to myself. I place my hand on my chest to feel how fast my heart is beating, but I don't feel anything. Something's wrong. Something is completely wrong.

"Evan?" calls Mr. Wallace the gym teacher. "What are you doing out here? What's going on?"

I open my eyes and everything is quiet. The pain is gone and I can think straight. I bring a hand to my chest. My heart is running wild, but at least it is beating.

"Evan?" Mr. Wallace calls again.

I look up and a few students and teachers are watching from the doorways of classrooms. Mike comes out of the gym and stops just behind Mr. Wallace. Cedric is gone and my agony left with him. I run my tongue across my teeth. Nothing sharp. I look at the crack in the floor I left with my fist. No broken hand, bruise, nor pain.

"You alright?" Mr. Wallace asks. Mike helps me up. "What happened to your nose?"

I feel around my nose and mouth and warmth touches my fingertips.

"I-- I fell, Mr. Wallace," I say. "I'm sorry."

He nods his head looking both confused and worried.

"Well, alright," he says. "Need to see a nurse?"

"No, no," I say. "I'm fine."

"I'll look after him for a bit, sir," Mike says to Mr. Wallace.

"Alright. Hurry on."

Everyone goes back into their classrooms as Mike helps me to the bathroom to clean my bloody nose. Every bully has a motive. What is Cedric's and what did he mean by, *you'll get used to it?* What was that about him being forced to help me and asking about my nightmares and asking of I dreamed of *us* yet? He knows something. I have questions and I feel that Cedric has answers. After what just happened to me in the hallways, I'm desperate to know what he knows and what's happening to me.

After telling Mike what happened, he too is confused and insists that I talk to Cedric and see what he wants, but Cedric did tell me what he wants. *Me. Dead.* Maybe an exaggeration, maybe the reality. Would I want to know? Cedric has always made me feel uneasy and uncomfortable. His words and actions should not surprise me.

My Science and Math classes that followed blew by. Painting class is the verdict. I'm usually anxious to go, but after a rough morning, I've been far too distracted to be excited. The best part about Painting class, I am able to see her. Essence LaRoux.

Each time I see her feels like the first. The butterflies. The lump in my throat. The sweat in my palms. The skips in my heart. It never gets old and always feels new. If only there was more of myself to give. Something to offer, but I have nothing and she is the kind of girl who deserves everything.

My heart leaps into my throat. I gulp. I have been walking in autopilot and decided it would be a good idea to stand in the front of the classroom. Essence tends to have that effect on me quite often. My painting teacher, Ms. Brooks calls my name and I have a feeling she has been calling me for quite some time. I hope that those thoughts of Essence LaRoux were only thoughts and not a presented monologue.

"Evan?" Ms. Brooks calls again. "Do you mind taking a seat, please?"

Before I'm able to answer, I notice the only seat left available in the classroom is next to Essence. She smiles and my heart jumps into my throat again. She should not have done that.

"Evan?" Ms. Brooks calls again looking over the frame of her glasses.

"Um. Yes, I'm sorry."

The classroom giggles are embarrassing as I take my walk of shame to the seat next to Essence. Ms. Brooks begins class and instructs that we will continue to work on our spring project. We grab our easels from different areas of the classroom and return to our work stations. I have been working on a portrait of the woman from my dreams which is different from the woman *of* my dreams who sits next to me. I have yet to see Essence's work, so I peek in the corner of my eyes and wish I hadn't. Curiosity truly does kill the cat. She isn't working on her in-class project. She's looking at me. *Why is she looking at me?* I try to focus back onto my work and find myself scanning over the different colors of paint losing my train of thought. *Okay, um. I had a great Morning Star breakfast. Confusing mommy problems. Bike riding, bike riding. Pine trees and mint smells. Stupid Cedric.*

"Evan?" She says.

I never heard my name sound so clear and theatrical. It was like music--a symphony. I refrain from looking in her direction.

"Yes?" I answer and choke on the word.

She scoots closer. My heel begins to tap on the bar of my stool. Her face leans close to my cheek and I follow her eyes to my easel.

"Who is that?" she asks. She smells obsessive like a free-spirited lavender floral garden. Her aroma forces my eyes to close and follow the scent. I inhale, giving into temptation, but exhale with caution. I open my eyes and she stares into mine. I should reevaluate my sanity. *What am I doing?* I turn back to my easel trying to cover my new addiction that needs rehabilitation.

"It's -- just some woman," I finally answer. That long walk in her garden was exquisite.

"Just some woman," she repeats with a nod and soft smile. "Is that why she doesn't have a face?"

I refrain from bursting into laughter.

"Well, I seen her before. In my dreams actually. She doesn't have a face because it was hard to make out, but--"

I think about the short blonde haired woman in my dreams sitting at the table next to the man in the tuxedo.

"-- now I can finish it."

"Some dream, huh?"

"Yeah," I nod flexing the corner of my lips into a wrinkle. "Nightmare actually."

"Want to tell me about it?"

"You're interested in hearing?" I ask in disbelief.

"Only if you're interested in sharing," she smiles with her perfect rows of white teeth.

I can't move. Flowers bloom and her sweet scent illuminates the classroom. She brushes some of her red hair away from one of her eyes.

"Well," I begin regaining sanity. "I was on this cliff. Standing in front of these red doors. I went inside and the place looked like some mansion. Very rich with marble floors, art covered walls, a fountain, and gold railings. Then, there was this little girl I start chasing around. We get to this room and these people are at a table staring at me."

"Do you know these people?" she asks.

I shake my head.

"No," I say. "But the mansion, the people. They look familiar like -- I know I've seen them before. At least that's what it feels like."

"What happens next?" She adjusts herself in her chair listening.

"I find myself sitting at the table with them and they're celebrating -- something. The girl starts to freak about me leaving her and the next thing I know I'm pulled across the floor and sucked into darkness. I don't understand it, but it felt so real."

"That is quite some dream," she says. "So, she was one of them?"

I look at my painting.

"Yes."

"She looks pale. Almost like she's dead."

"That's how they all looked and had fangs. Hundreds of fangs with two of them much larger than the rest like some --"

"Vampire?" she finishes.

"Yeah. Vampire."

Such a thought of people being vampires is nonsense. They don't exist, but if that's who these people are, then why do I feel I've seen them before?

"So you know vampires?" she chuckles. I smile.

51

"Maybe or at least they know me."

I should be afraid of that.

"Want to look at my project?" She asks. "Not as good as yours nor anything from a dream, but I'm sure you can still relate."

"Sure."

I scoot closer as she makes room. I look at her painting and see strokes of green, blue, and gray.

"It's Utica," she says. "See? The Mohawk River, downtown, bike trails in the Valley, the school, houses, everything. It's all here."

"I thought I was the only one who loves it here," I say.

"Nope. I love it here too. Utica is beautiful."

"Not as beautiful as you."

My heart flat lines and the world stands still. *Why did I say that?* I facepalm myself and my throat feels like I swallowed a jawbreaker. She stares at me speechless. Her eyes trail away and she gasps.

"Essence, I--I'm sorry, what I meant was-- I really like your painting."

"Um, thanks," she says with a weak smile. She turns back to her painting and prepares some of her brushes. *Nice job, Evan. Nailed it.* I can't leave everything hovering above us like this. I have to learn to control myself around her, but now, she probably wishes there was another seat in the classroom I can sit.

"So um, Essence--"

She turns back to me and I almost regret continuing a conversation.

"What do you like to do?"

"I play violin. Religiously," she chuckles.

"Really?" I say excited. "I play piano."

"Seriously?" she smiles.

"Yes. But I've always wanted to learn how to play another instrument. Violin would be amazing."

"I'm sure I can teach you a thing or two. Maybe you show me piano?"

"I'm pretty sure I'll be terrible at learning violin though."

"I doubt that," she says. "With playing piano you must be coordinated already to play an instrument. I bet you're good with your hands."

I blush and sink a bit in the stool.

"Well, I should probably finish this," she says. "A few more touches and I'll be done. Can you pass me some of that red?" She asks.

I look at the paint case that rests on our work station. I open the case and pull the red paint cup from its holder. I turn back to Essence to give her the paint cup and it fumbles in my hands.

"Careful!" Essence says, but it was too late. The paint spills on my hands and onto the floor.

"I'm sorry, I--" I begin to say, but then my ears begin to ring.

"Evan?" I hear her say distorted, but I cannot respond.

I look at her, and she calls again, however no sound leaves her mouth. I look at my hands and the paint looks like blood. My heart begins to race, my stomach cries with an unexplainable hunger, and my mouth salivates. *What is happening?*

A smell meets my nose. A metallic or copper-like smell. What I would imagine blood to smell like yet oddly appeasing. I begin to lick my fingers and my hunger intensifies.

"Evan? What are you doing?" Essence says.

I stop and look around the room. Everyone stares.

I smell paint and taste it in my mouth. Bile builds in my throat.

"Evan?" Essence says once more.

"I have to go."

I rise from my stool and hurry out of the classroom. I don't know what should I worry about more. The fact that I ate paint or the fact that if it really was blood, I liked it.

CHAPTER FOUR: CHANGING

I hurry down the hallway to the bathroom. My walk soon turns into a light jog, and the air becomes as suffocating as black smoke. The hunger returns. That unfamiliar hunger. Not for fruit. Not for vegetables. Not even for meat.

A crunching sound pains my head and agony leaves my mouth. I grab onto my head and fall against a locker door. It crumbles like a piece of balled up paper. I drop to my knees and try to fight this painful throbbing, but it only intensifies. I crawl on the floor, one hand on my head and the other feeling for the bathroom door. When salvation meets my hand, I fall into the bathroom trying to catch my breath. All that remains is a migraine.

A student hurries past to leave as I struggle to pull myself up using the white marble sink. I take off my glasses, place them on the sink, and turn on the faucet to drown my hands with soap and water. I watch as the red paint sloths off of my hands and swims down the drain. When the paint is gone, so is the migraine. I splash water onto my face, dry it with a paper towel, and look into the mirror. I stumble back as a horror reaps within me. My eyes are black coated, then a dim red bleeds around my pupils like the people in my dream.

"What's wrong with me?" I ask. I step closer to the mirror staring into my eyes. They glow and my eyesight appears to be perfect without my glasses. I then hear a heartbeat and listen. It begins to slow. Then stops. I place my hand onto my chest. Nothing, and my skin is as cold as ice. I feel around desperately for my heartbeat. Still, nothing.

"This isn't happening to me," I say. However, I don't even know what *is* happening. I close my eyes, place my hands on my head, and pace.

"I'm dreaming. This is all just a dream. My mother will wake me up soon and all of this will be nothing, but another dream."

I stop pacing and take a deep breath before looking in the mirror. Brown eyes and blurry vision. I exhale and relax over the sink. I pray I am okay now. I grab my glasses, put them back on, and head back to class. When I walk into the classroom, everyone is gone. I had not noticed how much time I must have spent in the bathroom, but I'm sure Ms. Brooks is going to let me know.

"Evan?" She says rising from her desk.

"Ms. Brooks, I apologize. It was an emergency and won't happen again," I promise.

She studies me for a moment before nodding.

"Everything alright? Never seen you like this before, Evan," she says.

I nod.

"I hope so."

"Well, I accept your apology. You should hurry. Next class already started a few minutes ago. I'll make you a pass," she assures.

I grab my books, meet her at the door, and she hands me a late pass.

"Thank you."

She smiles softly.

"You're lucky you're my best student," she smiles. "Now go. Hurry along and feel better."

"I will," I say.

~

I was in autopilot the rest of the school day. I could not focus in any of my other classes and cannot piece together what's wrong with me. What happened earlier with Cedric had been similar, but slightly different from what happened to me in Painting class. What I hate most is the impression I left on Essence. Did I scare her away? Will she ever speak to me again? I mean, would I if I was in her shoes? I shake my head. I have to apologize. I have to make it clear to her that I obviously wasn't myself. I don't want her to think I'm weird especially after eating paint in front of her.

The final bell rings and I am at my locker before most. I know if there is chance to apologize it'd be now. I'll wait until I see her go to her locker, approach her hoping I won't choke on my words again, and ask to start over. My apology cannot wait until tomorrow. It *must* be today.

"Evan!" Mike yells from the wave of people that start

to fill the hallway. He has the biggest grin on his face. What
is he up to now?

"What are you smiling about?" I ask him.

"Hmmm, let's see, I have Bianca's number *and* we
have a date on Friday," he says.

"How'd you manage to do that?" I ask.

"I honestly winged it," he laughs. "I just talked about
the party, asked about herself, school, etcetera, etcetera,
and then I just -- asked."

"Nice," I clock around the hallway. No sign of her
yet.

"And what about you? You make a move on
Essence?" He asks.

"Yeah, I did, but it didn't go as well as you and
Bianca. Kind of had a moment in class."

"What you mean?"

"Well, everything was going great. We were talking
about our projects then when all that paint got on me, I
blacked out and did some -- weird things. Think I scared her
away."

Mike shakes his head.

"I'm sorry, Ev. Did you apologize? What'd she say?"

"That's why I'm waiting for her now. She put herself into a shell and then I ended up getting out of my chair and went to the bathroom. When I got back, class was already over."

"If you plan on apologizing to Essence, Evan, I think you should really hurry like right now right now," he says looking down the hallway.

"What you mean?" I ask not following.

"Essence LaRoux has left the building!" He says in an announcer tone.

"What?"

I turn to the exit doors and see her walking out with her belongings. Without hesitation I start for the exit doors zig zagging through people. I toss and turn through the constant rush then push the doors open. I run down the steps and I look around. She's gone and that only meant the worst has happened. My apology would have to wait until tomorrow, far from today.

My bike is not far from where I stand. I unlock it and shake it at the thought of a missed opportunity. I exhale the tension, pull my bike from the cage, and start to make my way home. As I pass the sea of people, Cedric is nearby. He watches with a maniacal grin until I am off campus.

The bike ride home is long. I'm not thinking about Utica and its beauty. I'm not thinking about the Mohawk River Valley, its trees, nor its smell of fresh mint and pine that blows across my face as I pedal. All I can think about is what happened in school and Essence. What does she think of me? That I'm some weird, paint eating creep? Clearly I have been correct all along. I really do have nothing to offer her.

When I get home, the car is in the driveway. I put my bike in the garage and go into the house. To my surprise, my mother isn't resting in bed from driving all day. Instead, she is still in her work clothes moving about the house.

"Hey, sweetie," she kisses my cheek.

"Hey, mom," I reply and meet her in the kitchen. I take a seat at the island, place my bag on top, and exhale.

"How was school today?" She asks as she studies me. "What's wrong?"

"I just had a rough day."

"Well, did you get a chance to write down the dream? You've had it so many times already, Evan I think --"

"YES, I wrote down the dream, mom, and I'm really not trying to think about that right now."

"I think you should."

"Well I don't."

"I'm just saying--" she raises her hands in defense.

"Stop! Just stop! You can really be inconsiderate sometimes. You don't know what I've been through today."

"Then talk to me."

"No. How about I just go write about it in my notebook?"

I rise from the stool and my legs give. I barely catch myself before my face smacks the floor.

"Evan!" She hurries over.

I struggle to prop myself against the island. My ears begin to ring again and I cup my hands to my ears to block the noise. It doesn't work. I then see flashes of red around

63

me. Blood. I shut my eyes tight and feel my
mother's hands firmly grasp my wrists pulling me. I
fight back keeping my eyes closed and my hands to
my head.

"Evan! Evan!" she yells.

I stop fighting and open my eyes slowly. I catch my
breath and she brings me to her chest wrapping her
arms round me. It just keeps happening. My mother holds
me out in front of her.

"Are you alright, Evan? You scared me half to
death."

I nod. "I--I'll be okay. Really."

I look up to her face and can tell she knows I
am unsure.

"Mom don't look at me like that." I look away.

"Like what Evan? Like what?" She starts to get upset with crack and cry in her voice.

"I'm scared for you."

"Are you sure not *of* me?"

I watch as a tear sits upon her eyelash.

"You pushed me away earlier," I mumble.

"Evan, what are you talking about?"

"I tell you to accept me for who I am and I had to practically call out your name to get you to answer."

"Evan, you know I accept you for who you are. Of all people I accept you," she says cupping her hands on her heart.

"I'm just worried about you," she says. "You're...changing."

"You don't have anything to worry about. I promise. I'm okay."

"You can't tell a mother not to worry about her child," she says shaking her head.

I sit quiet. Even I am unsure about what I just said. I

can hope this will pass over with time. I refuse to see a doctor. I hate being examined. Makes me feel like some experiment.

"I'm sorry. I love you," I say and hug her tight.

"I love you too," she says hugging back. She places her hands on my shoulders and holds me in front of her. Then cups my face with her hands. Her scar creases within her smile.

"You're growing up. I can understand that," she nods.

She wipes her tears and finds a smile over her blushed face and looks into my eyes as though she had an epiphany. Her face is frozen again like this morning.

"I knew the day would come."

We sit quiet for a moment before she begins to stand.

"Well, I have to go, " she says returning back to earth, "But I'll be right back. I have to make a stop by the cliffs in the Valley. They've been sending me all over the place lately. We need more drivers. Maybe you can work."

"No thanks, mom," I smile and stand. "I'll pass."

"Okay," she laughs and caresses my cheek. "I'll be back." She brings my forehead to her lips and kisses before she leaves.

Today has become one of many days that I would go into the rainforest and meditate over the many things haunting me: my nightmares, the altercation with Cedric, the bad impression left on Essence, arguing with my mother, and these on and off periods of mental breakdowns. As much as I disagree with my mom at times, she may be right about something. I am changing. But not changing how I would imagine puberty to be. This is something different. It feels like there's something inside of me that won't let me be *me*. I don't like it.

I grab my backpack from the island. I run up to my room, kick off my shoes, and step into my running sneakers. When I go into the bathroom, I feel like cringing thinking about earlier at school. I throw water on my face. Do I dare take a look into the mirror? My curiosity wins and I take a glance. I sigh of relief. I am okay.

I head back downstairs and open the back door. I look out to the rainforest of the Mohawk River Valley and step outside. The gray sky rumbles of thunder, and I can smell rain in the air. Right on time.

CHAPTER FIVE: THE VISITOR

What we long for most is the most difficult to attain. Whether it's stability, passion, love, or for me, understanding. How do we cope when the road is fogged? Where do we go? I know what it is like to be hungry for these things. Writing has become my saving grace. My way to keep myself stable, my passion, my love, and my cry for understanding. Nature too helps me cope. It acknowledges its past of once being nothing, and accepts the mystery of its future. How I wish to learn the secret of acceptance.

I walk through the rainforest attracted to the moss covered trees, bushy shrubs, and ground-bound rocks. The trees stand tall in the sky, their shadows hugging me below, and their large branches of arms, grip vast green leaves on its fingers. It makes a great umbrella when rain is heavy.

I follow the trails that are familiar to me, gripping the straps of my backpack with my hands. Dark brown aisles of ground, curves and dips throughout the rainforest as I step into its damp mixture. The roars of thunder in the clouds are

R.J. Rogue

music to my ears and the wind whispers between the torsos of the trees. Out here, the air is thick with pine and mint and the relaxation that I have longed for since my day had begun, welcomes me.

I have become quite familiar with the Mohawk River Valley. At least in parts that are fairly close to home. Not often would I make discovery and explore new routes, but I can't say I'm not interested. I go to the same place every time. A place where I can focus on myself and reflect. It's a great feeling knowing that you can go to that one place and no matter what emotions are attacking you, you're given an extra defense that I call a smile. Today, I didn't have many of those. The odds were against me.

I push aside a few shrubs and step out of the crowded green to meet my counselor. And there it stands. In the middle of an open, grassy meadow with beds of yellow and white flowers at its feet. My tree, which is wider than the rest. Bigger than the rest. More dominant in its stance. Its branches thick and humble. Broad shoulders in which I can stand and walk without cautioning for balance.

"I'm here," I say placing a hand on its wooden body.

Evanescence

I adjust my backpack more securely on my back and begin to climb up the wooden planks. Branch by branch, plank by plank, I climb to the torso and walk along the arm. I remove my backpack from my back, and sit with my legs crossed for meditation. I close my eyes and with one deep breath, the negative energy leaves.

"Things may not be where I want them to be or how I want them to be, but I am content," I say in a low whisper.

I repeat these words to myself over and over and focus on breathing until my head is clear and free from tension. I slowly begin to open myself to the world again, starting with nature. I listen to the small drops of rain smack onto the leaves, smell the moist air, and continue to sit silent and still, reconnecting and aligning peace within myself. I open my eyes, breathe, and now ready to write something in my notebook different from all the nightmares:

To Whom My Heart Beats for,

Essence LaRoux. What a perfect name and character for a love story or fairy tale, but she is all too real. Too great

71

of an existence to recognize mine. Calling her perfect, beautiful, or a goddess, seems more like an insult than a compliment to match her every trait. None of those do her justice. The best adjectives of the English language wouldn't leave a dent in her crowd of perfections. The best love poem couldn't impress her heart with adequate iambic pentameter of emotion. The best man, Romeo himself, has no chance of holding her hand in holy matrimony.

…If so, I would have killed him myself. Poison from a cup would have been mercy.

I've come to the conclusion that becoming her friend alone would be quite a task, especially now for what I've done. It hurts me. It weakens me. Not knowing how she feels about me. Not knowing how she feels about anything. Not knowing her favorite color, food, or hobby. Not knowing if she eats her eggs scrambled or sunny side up. Not knowing if she drinks her coffee black or with two creams and two sugars. Not knowing if she drinks coffee at all. A bit extreme? No.

The smallest things to know about a person may not concern many, but it concerns me. We should care for the

Evanescence

small things about a person because it means you are paying attention. Giving caution to what others overlook is what makes you stand out. But...I have yet to stand out to her. And it's not that I want to know all these things. I HAVE to know. I want to be a part her life in any way possible. If she decides, after my planned apology, to never speak to me again, it'd be my funeral.

No one likes being left, ignored, nor forgotten...especially by a girl such as Essence LaRoux.

With Love,
Evan Macrae

I sit staring at those last few words. I hope she speaks to me again. I hope she doesn't think it'd be best we remain strangers to one another. The rain quickens and thunder roars much louder than earlier. I begin to pack my notebook into my book bag, then hear a twig snap followed by a rush of air. I look below, but no one's there.

"Hello?" I call out. No response.

I finish packing and sling my book bag over my back and the sound returns, but is in the trees making me flinch.

"Hello?" I call out again looking around the rainforest. Nothing.

I stand to my feet and the huge gust of wind hits my tree and knocks me off balance. I try to grab hold of something to break my fall, but I fail. I fall down the tree from trunk to branch trying to stop myself. When I reach one of the planks, I hang on with my hands, but my fingers begin to slip. *I have to hold on,* I tell myself. My feet kick one of the planks from beneath me, and I cling onto the plank above with one hand like in my dream. I try to stop the momentum from swinging me away, but it is too strong. *No, no, no!* My fingers leave the plank and I fall to the ground. When I connect, I hear a snap and pop.

"Aahhh!"

I curl into ball holding my wrist to my stomach in agony. My fingers on my right hand immediately go numb, my wrist, the origin of the damage. My cheeks fill and exhale air as I try to take the pain, but it's excruciating. It's broken.

Evanescence

My mother guides me through the rainforest and talks about how worried she was and how she called Mike who didn't hear from me. All I can think about is that man. *Who was that man?* I can't see his face in my head and didn't recognize his voice, yet he didn't seem to mean any harm. I felt protected and cared for, by a stranger. If I was to see him now, I doubt I will recognize him, but I feel I will see him again. *He told me something. But what was it? What did he say?* I can't seem to remember. I slip in the mud.

"Careful, Evan," my mother says. "Watch your step."

'We're watching you.' That's it. *'We're watching you.'* But who is *we*. I slip again, but mother catches me. There was only him. No others. But wait. *He knows my father.* Goosebumps spread across my skin, not just from the cold, but from the thought of someone knowing my father, having answers about leaving me and my mother years ago. I have to find him. I have to find that man.

I scan the trees once more, remembering the noise I heard earlier. *Was that him?* Impossible.

~

79

My mother and I get back to the house free from any strange visits. Our clothes are soaked to the bone and each step I take squeezes water out of the soles of my shoes. The rain has not let up one bit.

"Take a seat and let me take a look at your wrist. May need to go to the hospital if it's broken."

I hate hospitals. They're cold. Smell of latex. Bright white lights in every room and hallway, but worst of all, the pullover nightgowns that fail to hide the butt. I take a seat at the kitchen island and show her my wrist, careful not to budge the bone and cause any pain. Been doing well with that so far.

"Hmmm, doesn't look bad at all," she says as her hands avoid my wrist area.

I inch closer for a look myself. There's no swelling, punctures, nor discoloration.

"Yeah, no kidding," I say tilting my head to the side.

"Can you make a fist?"

I lick my lips and hold my breath. With caution, I begin to make a fist. Nothing.

"Okay, now try to rotate."

"I don't know, mom."

"Try, Evan."

I nod and begin to rotate my fist expecting for agony to strike. When I complete one full rotation, I attempt another, but faster. Then, I try a third time almost hoping it would hurt so I can confirm I am right. That I broke my wrist.

"Looks to me that you didn't break it," she smiles. "Or anything at all for that matter."

"But I know I did. I heard it snap. I felt it."

I rotate my fist again. Nothing.

"Do you feel any pain now?" She asks.

I don't.

"No, none at all actually," I say perplexed. "I just could have sworn it was broken."

She shrugs.

"You're stronger than most of us regular people."

"No, I'm human just like you."

She smiles and shakes her head standing to her feet.

"I hate hearing you downgrade yourself."

I quirk a brow. She opens the freezer.

"Hungry?"

My stomach growls.

"Starving."

"Vegetable lasagna?"

"My favorite," I smile.

She nods and takes out the frozen rectangular goodness.

"Want to talk about what happened out there? Not trying to make you think I'm worrying like I usually do, but would be nice to know," she says.

Guess I blame myself for lashing out at her earlier. I fiddle with my fingers as she preheats the oven. She takes a seat across from me.

"So?" She says as she taps the table with her hand.

"Well," I clear my throat.

"Would you like some water, Evan?" She says rising to her feet. I feel like I'm being interrogated at a police station with the two way mirrors.

"Here you go."

She places a tall glass of water in front of me, takes a seat, and goes back to watching me. I take a sip of water.

"Well, I did some writing," I say avoiding her question.

"Oh yeah?" She smiles, "what'd you write about?"

Essence, but that's private.

"I wrote about today."

"And what happened today?"

"I -- it was an okay day."

"Oh?" She responds. "Well, I thought it was far worse than an 'okay day.'"

"Um. I made a new friend during gym class."

Enemy is more accurate. My stomach ties into a knot and for a moment I don't feel as hungry.

"Who's your new friend you made at school?" She gets up and puts the vegetable lasagna in the oven. I drink more water.

"Umm, Cedric."

She closes the oven door and stands still. I await a response, but none is given.

"Mom?"

She doesn't respond.

"Mom?"

"What did you say his name is?" She says still having her back to me.

"Cedric."

She nods forever, then turns to me and sits.

"Careful of the friends you make, Evan."

"What do you --"

"JUST be careful," she says cutting me off staring into my eyes. "You don't know him."

I don't know Cedric that's for sure, but what I do know is that he doesn't like me and what I also know is that he probably never will.

"Okay," she says with a much more positive attitude. "Go up, shower, and get into something dry. Your food should be ready by then."

I exhale relief from the twenty-one questions. The interrogation is over and I am free to go. I head upstairs with my book bag and a thought crosses my mind. I turn to an open page on my notebook and draw the symbol I had seen on the 'visitor's' hand. I stare at it for a bit recording it to memory. What does it mean? I've never seen it before. I close the notebook and take a nice hot shower killing the goosebumps that covers me. I dress into something comfortable for the night and head back downstairs to the kitchen.

My plate rests on the counter, but mom is nowhere to be found. I walk into the living room and there she sits in the rocking chair asleep. I take the cover that hangs over the couch and put it over her to keep her warm. She curls the covers up to her neck as she exhales deeply. Sleep is something I crave myself.

I head back into the kitchen and devour the meal, barely taking a breath. It wasn't satisfying enough. I want more. I'm still so hungry. I open the cabinets. Nothing I want. I open the fridge and then the freezer searching for something to eat as my stomach cries. Nothing. I clench my jaw, ball my hands into fists, and squint my eyes. I glance at the plate I placed in the sink. I stare at the residue and begin to lick. I stop and put the plate onto the counter. *What am I doing?* I think to myself.

I look around and try to fight my hunger pains, but a scent catches my nose. A warm, rose garden goodness. My mouth salivates and my teeth begin to ache. I look through the doorway of the living at my mother. I take a step and the next thing I know, I am standing over her, looking down and into her neck. The smell is strong and irresistible. I place my nose into her neck and inhale as deep as I can. It's her. *What is this feeling?*

The sound of a branch snapping echoes inside of my head. I crack my neck and it goes away. I lick my lips, my heartbeat beats ecstatically, and I place a hand over my chest hoping it would calm. It soon stops. I feel nothing there. My eyes race for answers as I try to feel for my heart, but still. Nothing, but my now cold skin. I take a step back.

"Evan?"

I jump out of my skin.

"You okay? What's wrong?" She asks. "You look afraid."

I try to catch my breath and feel under my shirt again. Warmth returns and my heart delays before beating again.

"Nothing…um…just tired," I say. "I'm going to get some sleep. Goodnight, Mom."

I head up the stairs and into the bathroom. I look in the mirror trying to collect myself. I blink and soon after, red surrounds my pupils, then slowly disappears.

"What's happening to me?"

CHAPTER SEVEN: NIGHTMARE

Gentle hands tuck beneath my armpits and bring me to their owner. She is beautiful. Her eyes have a calm glow against her peach blushed face and short blonde hair. She smiles and kisses my face then places me down next to a sea of toys on the ocean sized rug. A long blonde haired girl wearing a white dress and stockings takes my hand. She smiles and I return the gesture by doing the same. Our eye levels match.

"What's your name?" I ask her.

She giggles.

"A new game, Evan? I'm Beebee."

Beebee.

"Let's go!"

She grips my hand and begins to run. I struggle to keep up and soon she lets go. She's quite fast as we turn corner after corner, rounding the cream covered walls and portraits, and trotting across the red carpeted floors. I wish to stop for a quick look, but Beebee continues to run as I try to pick up the pace.

"Come on, Evan. Keep up!"

We run through a huge Romanesque room that has a large piano in the center. We then run down another hallway in which the distance between us begins to grow. She turns a corner and when I do, she is gone. I stand before a dark entrance. Cold air escapes and cuts across my skin. I hold my shoulders and hug myself.

"Beebee?"

No reply. I take a step back.

"Beebee?!"

"Come here, Evan!" She calls out from the dark.

I gulp.

"Don't be afraid," she says almost in a whisper. "You can do it. Never let anything scare you. Not even the dark."

I stare into the darkness and take a deep breath.

"Okay."

I walk with caution and fight to see what is before me.

"Beebee, where are you?"

I extend my arms to feel for her or anything that can save me, but only feel the cold of the room.

"Focus, Evan," she says. "And you will see."

My heart pounds against my sternum. I close my eyes and try to control my breathing. When I open them, I can see. The darkness is not as thick and much more bearable.

"Beebee?" I call out. "I still can't find you."

She doesn't not respond back. Each step I take, the floorboards squeak. I hear footsteps behind me and turn to face it. Nothing. Then I hear it again, but this time it almost knocks me to the ground. I cover my face with my hands and feel goosebumps spread along my skin.

"Beebee, where are you? I'm afraid."

"Up here," I hear her whisper.

I remove my hands from my face and look up. A small figure sits high on what looks like a chandelier. A faint glow of ruby red emerges from the darkness. I gasp. A bright light fills the room and her eyes are normal, human. I turn to the door and the young boy with the black hair covering his one eye stands in the doorway with his hand resting on the light switch.

"What are you two doing in my room?" He asks with a frown.

"Umm, we were just --" I look up to BeeBee, but she's gone. The chandelier swings back and forth.

"We were just playing," she says making me flinch and jump away. "Evan was trying to find me."

How did she get down so fast and without hurting herself?

"Don't play in here," he asserts.

"But we're bored and you don't play with us anymore," she says with a pout, puckering her bottom lip.

He stands silent, then rolls his eyes.

"Hmm..." He finally says. "I have something we can play."

"Really?!" Beebee exclaims jumping and clasping her hands together. At least one of us is excited.

He nods and a smirk spreads across his lips as his eyes leech onto mine. He walks past parting us and approaches the large see-through glass doors that stand from floor to ceiling. It leads to an outside black-stoned balcony. He opens the doors and a gust of wind almost knocks Beebee and I to the floor. We shelter ourselves with our arms and hands as he stands like a solid brick wall. He looks over his shoulder at us.

"Come."

We don't budge; we remain silent.

"You're not afraid are you?"

I am. I look at Beebee and she shakes her head.

"Then come."

He walks out and onto the balcony and places his hands on the ledge. My palms moisten and I brush them across my laps. He stares out to the sky and ocean. Beebee and I await our next order.

"Let's play, 'jumper,'" He says turning to us. "Beebee, you go first."

He motions his hand to the ledge. Beebee balls her hands into fists and stomps her foot.

"Why do I always have to go first?" she says. "It isn't fair!"

He folds his arms across his chest and scoffs.

"Alright, alright. Don't cry about it," he says. "Evan, you go."

My heart leaps into my throat and I raise my hands in defense. He doesn't actually mean to jump does he?

"Sorry, I don't think I--"

"Fine!" He says dropping his arms. "Since you babies are too scared, I'll go."

He pushes us aside and goes to the windows. His eyes turn red as he squats down placing a hand on the black rocks. Beebee and I step further apart and he begins to run. He places his foot on the ledge and I cover my mouth with my hands firmly. He leaps into the air with his arms out like a bird's wings and disappears over the ledge.

We rush to the ledge and look over. Only clouds and raging water against the cliff. *He killed himself!*

"Beebee! Why did he do that?!" I ask still looking over the ledge for him. "Why did he jump?

She doesn't respond.

"Beebee?" I say now turning around.

"Your turn!" The boy yells as we meet face to face. A blow hits my chest and I flip over the ledge. Screams escape my throat as I plummet through the sky and gray clouds as weightless as a feather. The sky is falling with rain, with myself within it. Soon, I will hit the water below, yet I know it will feel like cement. I cannot swim so my best hope is that the blow will kill me and not the drowning. I manage to turn myself in the air as the ocean rises exponentially. As I get closer, the water turns into bedrock. I gasp as I brace myself for a blow I know I will not survive. I throw my arms forward believing it would help cushion the impact. As soon as I connect, I'm jumping up in my bed drowning in my own sweat. I was dreaming.

Deep breaths leave my lips. I place my hands on my chest. My heart delays before it begins to beat. At least it was only that, a dream. It felt real and I'm not sure if what my body feels now is a rush of imaginable pain from adrenaline or if pain was really inflicted. That little girl, her name is Beebee, and the boy, nothing but an enemy to me. Why do I keep having nightmares about them? What do these nightmares mean and why are they always in them? I place my head back onto my wet pillow and decided to stare at the ceiling until the sun rises.

Evanescence

R.J. Rogue

CHAPTER EIGHT: SECOND IMPRESSION

I look to my window, and morning had come. I look over at the time, and my stomach ties into a knot. First period would begin shortly. I hop out of bed almost falling to the floor and shuffle through my drawer for clothes. After changing, I grab my book bag from the floor, stuff my notebook inside, and head downstairs. My mother is gone and on the kitchen island is a note.

"Was called into work early. See you when you get home. Love you. P.S. Don't be late for school. -Mom.

"Already am."

I crumble the note and toss it into the trash, then grab a Naked drink from the fridge before heading out the door. This will be breakfast.

~

It must have rained throughout the night. The pavement is wet and the sky is gray like it was in my nightmare. I wipe the seat of my bike and head for school. As I race down the streets and slopes of Utica, NY, I am unable to enjoy my favorite weather, the smell of mint and pine from the trees, and the toasted bread from the local bakery. I soon reach the school campus and lock my bike on the rack. I race up the steps and pull the doors open to find an expected empty hallway.

I unintentionally shift into autopilot unable to focus in any of my classes, thinking about all of the nightmares I have had. They are linked together and though they make me afraid, they seem relevant and more like distant memories. But memories are real, dreams are not. When I was younger, these people didn't have faces, but I could tell they were the same people. How come now I can see them for what they really look like? I use to dream about playing with the little girl, Beebee, and fighting with the little boy. The woman was always holding and kissing me, but I could say it wasn't my mother Sarah. It was someone else. The man, he sometimes was comforting as well, but I feared him. He seemed upset with me about something quite often. And the man, with long black hair, he was always in my dreams too, but I didn't fear him. He seemed like a perfect older brother or uncle.

A tray of food slams in front of me and I wake up from my daze.

"You look dead," Mike says with a half-worried smile. He takes a seat.

"Yeah, well, not yet I guess," I respond with a deep breath.

"What's on your mind?" He asks taking a bite from his apple.

"Not sure where to begin honestly."

"I'm listening."

"Well, I was in the woods yesterday and saw -- something."

Mike takes a bite out of his sandwich and shrugs.

"What was it?" he asks with a mouth full.

"It wasn't an 'it' it was more of a 'who.'"

"Okayyy, so who was it? What'd they look like?"

I shrug my shoulders.

"I'm not too sure. I couldn't get a good look at him, but he was running in the trees above me."

How stupid did that just sound? Mike's eyes squint as he shifts his head to the side.

"A man was chasing you? Running in the trees?" He asks as though I am telling nonsense. I don't blame him.

"Yes," I answer.

Mike laughs and shakes his head.

"Mike, I know what you're thinking. This wasn't another nightmare. I'm telling you this man chased me, I ran into a tree, fainted, and my mother finds me laying there with a broken wrist."

He clocks my wrist which of course did no justice in anything I was saying.

"Your wrist looks pretty fine to me," he says.

I sigh. He stops eating and puts his sandwich down on his tray. He swallows the bite he had taken.

"Okay, I'm sorry. I believe you. But Ev, if you ask me he sounds a bit like a Tarzan or something. Not a threat. Just some crazy guy scaring the living," he says.

"I did have a nightmare last night though."

"Oh?"

"I was chasing that little girl, BeeBee. We got to this room and the boy, pushes me off a cliff. It was, weird. Not just the dream itself, but the two of them. They are always in my dreams. Any thoughts?"

"I think dreams are just ways of telling you something important that you probably don't know you neglect."

I nod my head.

"That's the same thing Essence said." My heart drops. I have to apologize today. It can't go another day.

"And how am I supposed to find out what it is that I neglect."

Mike stops eating and thinks for a bit.

"Maybe you should ask yourself what's always in your nightmares that never change."

I nod my head agreeing and approach an epiphany.

"Maybe it's more of a who."

"Exactly," he says holding up his apple then taking a huge bite.

I have to find out who these people are, but I guess the only place I can start looking are my nightmares alone which haven't been much help. Do these people really exist somewhere in the world? If they do, what if they are right here in Utica? What would I say to them?

"I have yet to seen Essence today to apologize."

"She's here though," Mike assures.

I look over Mike's shoulder and across the lunchroom sits Bianca. She smiles and raises her hand as a hello. I return her gesture with a smile. Mike follows my eyes and meets Bianca's. She blushes, but then taps her hand besides her for Mike to sit.

"Evan, you'll be alright here?"

"Yeah, I'll be fine. Go to her. She's waiting for you," I force a chuckle.

"And that she is. Nice hair by the way," he says.

"What do you mean?" I ask frowning and feeling atop my head.

"You dyed it. Black," he says.

"Black?" I try to look up, but can't see for myself.

"I see you ditched the glasses and even look a bit swollen. Been hitting the gym for Essence, huh?" He laughs.

I feel my face and realize I must've left my glasses at home rushing out of the door. Although, I have been able to see perfectly fine today as if I had them. Even more confusing, Mike says my hair is black and --. I look down at myself. I guess I do look a bit more fit than I usually do. Not to mention, I feel strong.

"It's okay, Ev," he says. "I'm not judging. Digging the look. Keep it up and she'll be wrapped around your finger bro. Catch ya' later."

He grabs his tray and tosses his garbage before going to Bianca's table. I glance down into my hands flipping them back and forth. I exhale deeply and reject trying to solve yet another mystery. To my left are my books piled on the table. My writing book on top. I then realize that I have yet to write down the nightmare or a journal entry today. Mom would be upset, but it isn't like she would know anyway if I don't mention the nightmare. I smile at my carefree sense of humor, but then it dissolves. If I don't write it down, guilt will surely eat away at me.

I pull out a pen, open my notebook book to a clean page, and write down every detail that I can remember. As I dot the last period to my writing, a seductive, relaxing scent hypnotizes my sense of smell. It's a vanilla almond mixed with a dose of apple cinnamon. An aroma that makes me hungry. It is addicting. It is genuinely romantic. It's Essence LaRoux.

"Mind if I join you?" she asks. Her red hair is heart melting and her voice is that of music.

"No," I respond with a shake in my voice. "Please do."

She smiles and places her tray onto the table and takes a seat across from me.

"Nice hair by the way," she smiles. I blush yet haven't seen my own hair for myself.

"Thanks."

For a moment we sit in silence. Mike is across the lunchroom mouthing for me to talk. I turn my eyes back on Essence as she bites into an apple.

"Essence, I--" Searching for how to begin my apology.

"What made you become a vegetarian?" she asks as she examines her apple.

Didn't see that coming.

"Uh, well," I begin. "I've been this way since as far as I can remember. I don't know personally, but I can say I have no idea what meat tastes like."

"Oh wow," she says. "Had no idea. I've tried to be a vegetarian once, but failed."

"How long did you try?"

"I lasted about a week. Once July 4th came, my father grilled chicken, shish-kabobs, ribs, and burgers," she laughs. "I guess the best time to become a vegetarian wouldn't be in the summer especially before July 4th cookouts."

"I can see how that can be difficult," I smile.

"Do you ever have any urges to eat meat? Like when it's around you?"

"No, not really. It does smell good though, but I know if I eat it, I will probably get sick."

"Really?"

"Yes," I laugh. "My body won't accept it."

"I see," she says nodding. "I'm sorry."

"It's fine. I'm not use to it any other way."

She bites into her apple and sips on her soda. Speaking of I'm sorry --.

"Essence, I apologize for the way I've been acting. It has nothing to do with you at all. I swear."

There. I said it. Now for my punishment. 'Evan I hate you.' 'Evan you're such a jerk.' 'Evan, how do you sleep at night?' On the contrary, I don't. At least not without having a nightmare.

"It's ok, Evan," she smiles. "It's no big deal. We all have bad days."

YES!

"Yeah, and I've been having many of those," I respond shaking my head.

"Those nightmares, huh," she says. "Talk to me. I'm listening."

I have to say I hate it already when she stops talking. I begin to tap my foot on the floor repetitively.

"Well, I had another nightmare last night."

"What happened in this one?" She asks as she pushes her tray aside giving me her undivided attention.

"I was a child. The little girl, Beebee, was there again."

"How do you know her name?"

"She told me."

Essence nods and continues to listen.

"So, I'm chasing her down these hallways and she leads me through this empty room that's huge, but has nothing, but a piano. Then we run down another hallway, and I lose her. When I find her, she's in this dark room, sitting on a chandelier."

"A chandelier?"

"Crazy huh?" I chuckle. "But yes, a chandelier. The boy from my other nightmares comes in and is upset that we were in his room, and he makes us play this game called, 'jumper' with him. So Beebee and I follow him onto this balcony and he jumps from the ledge and into the water. What felt like seconds, he comes back up, and pushes me over the ledge. Before I hit the water, which actually turned into rock, I woke up."

"Wow," she says sitting up in her chair. "And you still can't figure out where you might have known them from?"

"Not the slightest," I shake my head. "I have no idea at all."

"I'm sorry, Evan. Maybe it will all go away. It happens sometimes. Nightmare after nightmare."

"Well, that's it. I've been trying to convince myself the same thing but it just seems like they are only getting worse."

I sigh and stretch my arms across the table placing my forehead on its cool surface.

"Hey," Essence says as she places a hand onto mine. I almost jumped out of my skin. Her touch sends an electrical surge through my body. Goosebumps infest across my arms, but I didn't care to give the remedy of calming down. I like her touch. I just can't understand why she makes me feel this way about her. I look up from the table.

"Don't be discouraged," she smiles showing her perfect, straight teeth. "I'm sure you'll figure out more as time goes on and before you know it, you'll be sleeping peacefully. I can help where I can."

I feel better already. Essence makes it easy to relax and she certainly sounds convincing in that I'll figure things out. Her eyes squint at my books.

"My writing book," She says to herself before returning her eyes to me. "You write them down?"

I look over at my notebook and then back to her unsure if that's a good thing or if it makes me weird.

"I write everything down pretty much."

"You mind if I--" her hands start to go for the book. I protect its cover with my hand. She stops, but then I remove my hand and Essence slides the notebook in front of her keeping her eyes locked onto mine. I watch as she turns page by page. Squinting here, then her eyes widen a bit there, then some small smiles, and even some facial disappointments. I fiddle with my thumbs and then my stomach growls. I take a few bites out of my apple, but then a thought crosses my mind and forces me to drop the apple. It rolls across the table to the edge slowly, then falls forever.

I snatch the book and the page she was reading crumbles into a wrinkle.

"Evan? You--?" She asks a bit shocked. "Changed your mind?"

"I'm--sorry, it's just that--"

I try to think of some lame excuse to explain yet another breakdown. If she only knew the thoughts that are going through my head she would understand. She wouldn't be shocked. She wouldn't be upset. She sure would not have asked to read it in the first place.

"I have to go."

That was the only escape from this embarrassment I can think of. I grab the rest of my books and leave out the cafeteria without looking back. I hear her call my name, but I pick up the pace. I hope she didn't read that entry. The one about her. The one proclaiming her perfections and my deep knitted feelings of her. I press my back against my locker and slide down to a sit. I open the notebook where the page had crumbled into a reliable bookmark of where she read.

Phew!

Just a couple more turns and I would have been exposed. It was never my intention of having anyone read my notebook, especially Essence. But her compelling beauty would not allow my lips to form a *no*. I had surrendered myself, becoming a mere puppet to her ventriloquy.

From down the hall, I hear someone approaching. Do I dare take a look? No. I already know who it is. I should maybe walk away now, act as though I don't see or expect anyone coming. But I can't. I can't be a coward. I have to face my problems head on and learn to stop running.

She is close and now I have to find a way to explain my actions once again without using the same lame excuse. I take a deep breath almost sure that she was right next to me and turn to face --. Mike.

"You alright, Ev? I saw you talking with Essence and it looked like something was wrong. What happened?" He asks.

I sigh.

"I apologized for yesterday which she did forgive me, but I think I made an even worse impression on her when she asked about my notebook."

"The one you write everything in?"

I nod and press my lips together.

"Yeah."

"And I'm assuming you said yes."

"I had no choice, Mike."

"I mean you could've said no," he assures.

"She doesn't exactly make that easy," I say shaking my head. "I would assume Bianca would make you feel the same."

He coughs up a smile, and nods as he folds his arms across his chest.

"I guess I have to agree with you on that," he says shrugging.

"Right. Well anyway, I let her read it, but there was something personal that I didn't want her to see."

"Do you think she read it?"

I look down the hallways hoping not to see her. I shake my head.

"No," I say. "But had I let her read just a bit more, I would have been too late."

"Good thing she missed it," he smiles as he pats my shoulder. "So what are you stressing for?"

"I snatched it out of her hands. I scared her."

Mike stares at me for a bit before exhaling deeply.

"Yeah," I say acknowledging his deep sigh. "I've been doing plenty of that lately."

"Try not to stress over things too much," he says. "Anything is fixable, just have to make the right approach."

I hate when Mike goes all shrink on me, because then, he is always right. I can fix this. It will take a lot out of me, but I can fix it. I have to. I just didn't know what to do in that situation. It was the only way, in my opinion, to save my world from ending. My feelings for her must remain a secret and I would never let the whispers in my book reveal that secret.

"You're right," I say. "I can fix this."

"I know you can."

"I was afraid she would read it, tear it out, and throw the paper in my face or something," I exclaim as I start to grab my books for the next few classes.

Mike leans against a locker.

"Well, that's a thought. What if she didn't? What if she likes you too and just isn't saying anything?"

It takes barely a second to figure out the possibility of that was quite minuscule. That's bizarre. *Not in any of my dreams would that happen. Essence LaRoux with mutual feelings?* However, instead of feeling upset about how slim of a possibility it is, her feeling the same about me, I find laughter. Maybe I shouldn't be so negative though. Maybe for once I should look at the other end of the spectrum and consider, *'what if she does? What if Essence LaRoux really has feelings for me?'*

"Noooope," I say to Mike shaking my head.

"Oh come on, Ev. Even after what happened yesterday she sat with you at lunch and without an invitation."

"Yeah, well, I just screwed that up right?"

I close my locker.

"I see you and Bianca are a bit friendly," I add. I wish Essence and I were like that. Growing in friendship.

"I'm going over to her place today after school. Knock out some homework and just relax. We may hit the pool later at the rec center. Care to--"

I frown.

"Oh-- Sorry, man," he says as his head slouches. "Forgot."

I nod.

"It's fine. We probably wouldn't be friends had you not save me from those kids when we were younger."

"Yeah," he says, his lips forming a small smile. "Well, if you're up for it later tonight, we may grab a bite to eat. Think about it. It can help ease your mind by having a calorie loaded meal."

He laughs and pats my shoulder. I force myself to join.

"Yeah, I'll think about it."

"Well, I'll catch ya' at the end of the day. And umm," he frowns a bit and looks me up and down. "If you *do* decide to come with us, think about getting a tan."

I quirk my eyebrow.

"Looking a little pale there, buddy. See ya'."

He jogs off as the hallway begins to fill with students. I head to the bathroom in a hurry wondering how much of me has changed since last night. From my hair, to my glasses, to my physique, and now, the surface of my skin. Before I reach for the door handle, Cedric comes out and stands in my way.

"Problem?" I ask.

He looks me up and down and smirks.

"Looks like you have plenty of them already, Macrae."

He bumps my shoulder with his as he leaves. I scoff and shake my head.

I approach the bathroom mirror, stop, and think to turn back around to leave. I take a peek and slowly step into the spotlight. My heart skips. I am pale, practically clear. I step closer to the mirror bringing a hand to my face. I gasp at the coldest of my skin. I run my hands through my black hair. Not a strand of brown can be found. I take a deep breath and examine my chest and flex an arm. I feel no swelling, but my body is noticeably bulk.

"How is any of this possible?"

I can't say I don't like the new look, but I am perplexed on how it happened. *Something is happening to me.*

~

As the day comes to a close, I have not seen Essence in the hallways. I'm not avoiding her, but I am ashamed of my actions during lunch. How much can she take from me and my random outbursts of crazy? I decide to wait for Mike at my locker as the hallways begin to fill with students and teachers. A group of girls look my way and smile, holding their books to their faces. One of them waves a hand of hello. I wave back with a smile and blush as they continue down the hallway looking over their shoulders at me giggling to each other. I'm not use to such attention.

Five minutes go by. Then ten. Then twenty. Still no sign of Mike. The hall begins to empty and soon, Essence is at her locker grabbing her belongings. I prepare to shape my lips for the word 'sorry.' She closes her locker, throws her backpack over her shoulders, and heads for the exit doors.

I try to fight against my frozen state which feels as cold as my skin, wanting to go after her, but I couldn't budge. My legs disobey often and such a time as this, I need to fight this fear of her. I find myself standing alone in the empty hallway. No voices, rattling of papers, roars of laughter, or girls flaunting at me. Just me, myself, and I. The way we are in the womb, the way we are when we die.

CHAPTER NINE: MISSING

Dear Journal,

Essence has given me the cold shoulder at school. We've barely made eye contact or spoke to each other, and I have yet to apologize. Plenty of times I came close but bailed. I'm sure it would've been excuses to her.

I have tried to keep myself busy by writing and drawing at home and have spent much of my time in the rainforest, free from any visits, but neither of those seemed to have helped me cope with feeling alone. My mother noticed the changes, which has not let up one bit, but she has been distant from me as well. She's also been working double time and is barely home. Each walk I took in the rainforest; I have to say, I hoped to see that man again. I have questions and want to know where my father is, but don't know where to start on my own. Why hasn't he shown his face all these years and what did the man mean that my father would be proud?

Evanescence

Apart from this, there are two things at the top of my list of worries. Mike is gone and my heart hasn't beaten since I woke this morning. It's been almost a week since I've seen or heard from him. We've never gone a day without talking to each other. I have to find out what's going on with him, but I fear something happened. Something bad. I can't explain how might I know this, but I FEEL it. Today, I'm going to head over to his house and see for myself. I've tried calling his house phone, but no one answers. His grandmother is hard of hearing, so my best hopes were to hear Mike's voice answering. Even if his grandmother did answer and I find something to be wrong, family tends to hide things for you as well as hide things from. Both I am not fond of at all, yet understand.

With hope,

Evan Macrae

-

Mike has lived with his grandmother for quite some time. When we were in middle school, his father had to relocate for work somewhere in Florida. His mother decided it would be a great place to move, but perhaps they were running away from Utica. People move away, never here. When Mike didn't want to go, his grandmother stepped in and insisted to take care of him, but of course his mother was unsure because of his young age and she would only be able to visit so often. It was his father who was okay with the idea of him staying. His father was always lenient about everything, whereas his mother was quite the opposite. At least he has them both.

I head down the front steps and to the garage for my bike. It would have been nice to drive, but my mother is gone, doing the usual, making deliveries. I pedal up the road. The smell of rain fills my nostrils. The sun is hiding behind the clouds and tries to peak through the trees above me like a game of peek-a-boo. I ride past many businesses, such as day bars, pizza shops, and bakeries which fill the air with a toasted bread aroma. The wind begins to blow a bit, so that can only mean it won't be too long before it rains. A short-cut will be needed.

Evanescence

I ride past a small convenience store, a bookstore, and around the back of an old abandoned pawn shop. I pedal down the road which soon turns into forest green ground. I whip past towers of trees as I ride my bike leaving tracks in the mud. As I pedal deeper into the forest, branches snap beneath me and small drops of rain begin to smack the leaves. Just a distance away, I hear the water of the Mohawk River along the rocks and cliffs. I follow the sound and soon skid in the mud to a stop. I drop the kick stand and walk past a few trees and bushes and overlook the horizon from a high vantage point.

The gray ceiling of clouds tumble atop each other, the dim sun meets my eye level above the endless water, and the trees are planted on my left and right, riding the hills of the valley. I take a step closer to the edge and close my eyes inhaling the smell of rain and allowing the moisture in the air to hit my face. When I open my eyes, in the distance is a large building that sits atop the tallest cliff not far across the water. My mother always makes deliveries by the cliffs. I wonder if she has ever gone there. I have to admit, the longer I stare, the more familiar it becomes. Even this scenery. I've never taken this trail to Mike's before. I know I haven't, but something says it isn't this first time I've been here and this isn't the first time I've seen that building.

I pedal up Mike's driveway and stand my bike in front of his house. As I walk up the front steps, his grandmother peeks through the blinds, which makes me chuckle. She's hard at hearing, yet can predict someone's arrival. She opens the door.

"Hello, Mrs. Druin is--"

"Have you seen Mike, Evan?" She interrupts.

"...No, I thought he'd be home," I respond. "That's why I'm here. I was going to ask you the same thing."

"Oh, dear," she says walking back into the house.

I step inside and leave my shoes at the door. I meet her in the living where she sits in her rocking chair with a few clothes for knitting. Picture frames sit across a fireplace. A small coffee table with unopened mail is in the center of the room, and an old television set sits on its stand in the corner. I sit in the loveseat across from Mrs. Druin.

"Um...When was the last time you spoke to Mike or seen him?" I ask.

She exhales and begins to rock and knit.

"The police are looking for him," she responds. "Mike has been missing for over a week."

Her face holds firm, but her blushed cheeks and swollen, glossy eyes tattle that she's been crying. It is exactly what I feared. Mike is missing.

"I'm so sorry to hear that, Mrs. Druin. I hope he's okay."

"I hope so too, Evan. His mother calls every ten minutes and she's built quite a hatred towards me. I blame myself for not being more careful with him on where he goes."

"Don't blame yourself. We'll find him. I'm sure of it. No matter where he is or what has happened. Mike is strong."

I've never seen him fail at anything and nothing ever seems difficult for him. His disappearance must be temporary. I have to believe that much.

"That he is. Thank the heavens for you, Evan. Always being so positive."

I smile.

"He never hinted to you about where he possibly could have gone or anything of the such? I just hope he didn't run away. Mike was happy here...Wasn't he?"

I can tell by the look on her face she was undoubtedly unsure. I'm positive Mike was happy here. He never wanted to leave Utica even as a child when his parents left to Florida. He couldn't have ran away. There has to be another explanation.

"He was happy here, Mrs. Druin. I'm sure of it."

Now that I think about it, last week, Mike said he was going to be meeting up with Bianca after school. Not to mention, he was supposed to be meeting up with me and never showed.

Mrs. Druin sighs.

"In this small town someone has to have seen or know something."

And I have a major clue. I just realized that Bianca has not been in school neither. They both are missing. They both could be in danger, but I should not think negative thoughts. They have to be okay.

"Mrs. Druin...Mike was supposed to be meeting with someone after school last week and she hasn't been in school neither."

She quirks her eyebrows and leans forward a bit in her rocking chair.

"Meeting with who? Do you know?"

"This girl. Bianca. I don't know her personally, but she's someone he has a crush on."

The phone rings.

"Hold that thought, dear."

She rises to her feet, careful not fall, and answers the phone.

"Yes?" she says holding it to her ear. "No, I have not heard anything yet....I'm sure he is somewhere out there safe...I understand...We will find him...okay my dear....I love you and I'll be sure to let you know if anything comes up..." She hangs up the phone.

"That was his mother."

"I feel so bad for her. For all of you."

"I should have let him go to Florida with his parents when he was a child," she says returning to her rocking chair shaking her head. "This would have never happened. He was in my care. Care that I fought his parents for."

"Mike made his own choice and you were doing what you thought was best for him. There's no shame in that."

"Yeah, well. At least he would have been more safe."

"There's no way we could have predicted that this would have happened," I assure her. "We have to keep hope that Mike is alright and that he will return."

"Yeah, you're right, Evan. I thank you for that. You truly are his best friend. He's lucky."

She rocks in her chair and thunder rumbles.

"Now, you better get going before it starts pouring out."

"Yeah, you're right," I respond rising to my feet.

"If you hear anything, Evan--"

"You can trust me that I'll let you know, Mrs. Druin," I promise.

She smiles weakly and nods.

"Thank you, Evan. I just want him home," she hugs tightly.

"Me too, Mrs. Druin. You take care."

Evanescence

We let go of each other and I step outside of the house with an emptiness. I hop onto my bike and head down the path in which I had come. Mike is out there. Somewhere. Somewhere he is breathing and he is okay. Bianca too. The idea that Mike ran away I do not consider as a possibility. Not one bit. I have to believe that he is okay. I can't allow that voice in my head to convince that there is a possibility he was taken out of his will. I can't succumb to that. If Bianca is missing with him, it must be relative. And I agree with Mrs. Druin, in this small city, somebody knows something.

~

I park my bike in the garage and head inside.

"Hey, sweetie. Dinner's ready," my mother says as she cleans off the counters in the kitchen.

"I'm not hungry," I respond.

"Not hungry? What's wrong? Did you go to Mike's house to see what's been going on?" she asks.

"Mike is gone, mom."

"Gone? Gone where? To visit his parents in Florida?"

"No," I say taking a seat at the island. "He's missing. He hasn't been in school in over a week and when I went to see him, his grandmother thought I knew where he was."

"Oh God, that's awful. I can only imagine the pain his family must be feeling."

I place my head on the counter and exhale.

"I'm sorry sweetie," she says rubbing my back. "I know he's your best friend, and I'm sure we will find him."

"Think so?" I say into the white counter with a muffle before looking at her.

She smiles.

"I know so, Evan." She kisses my forehead.

"I'm going to head upstairs and get ready for bed," I say stepping off the stool and heading out the kitchen.

"You sure? It's still kind of early, Evan," she calls after me.

"I can use the sleep," I respond making my way up the stairs.

"If you change your mind your food will be in the microwave," she yells.

I head into my room and close the door behind me. I plop back onto my bed and place my hands behind my head and stare at the ceiling which feels like forever. I take a deep breath and exhale hoping Mike is doing the same. Breathing. I place a hand on my chest and search for a heartbeat. Still, nothing. I throw on my headphones and close my eyes to drift away from today.

Mike. Where are you? Are you safe?

CHAPTER TEN: THE SUSPECT

A car horn beeps outside. I rise out of bed and head downstairs and find my mother in the kitchen.

"Good morning, sleepy head," she says smiling in her work clothes.

"Good morning," I yawn.

"I have to make a delivery by the cliffs and head to into work. You can take the car today if you'd like."

She caresses my cheek and I nod.

"Please try to have a good day."

"No promises."

"TRY," she says with a smile.

"Alright, alright. I'll try mom."

She gives me a kiss on the cheek and opens the front door.

"Remember to write. It will help. Trust me."

"I will."

"And don't be late for school," she points.

I find a smile. She always says that.

"YES MOM."

"Love you."

"Love you too." She closes the door and I sit alone in the kitchen.

The cliffs? She never says 'the hospital' or anything of the sort it's just, 'the cliffs'. It makes me think of that mansion sized building I seen yesterday. Could that be where she goes? From where I stood, it looked creepy, but familiar. I head upstairs, get dressed for school leaving my glasses behind, eat a quick breakfast, and hit the road making it to school just before the first period bell rings. I wasn't late.

Everything feels different today. I'm sure it's because of Mike and Bianca. There's photos of Mike all over school. I noticed the ones of Bianca aren't up anymore. Could that mean they found her? What does that say about Mike? Is he still missing? There's even an article of Mike, in the *Utica Observer,* titled, *"Missing Teen, Mike Druin, Possible Runaway?"* But what are their sources? I know Mike. He doesn't run away from his problems -- like I do.

He confronts them. And I know him well enough to know he didn't run away. I won't even consider that a possibility.

Mike is practically my only friend. Of course, I did know names and faces, but that's as far as that story goes. As for Essence, I had seen her this morning and as usual, I watched her until she left for class. I would hope around lunch I would have a chance to speak with her. I still have an apology to give.

And Cedric. I saw him in the hallway a few times. He just held a smile which looked innocent, but his eyes told me something different. That he didn't like me, but more importantly, he was hiding something. Normally when I see him, he's standoffish and easy to anger, but not today. He seems to be in a good mood. Perhaps because he has front row seats to my suffering. If it is because of Mike, Cedric is more evil than any demon. I have to admit, there's something oddly familiar about him too, and not just Bianca. In a chilling sort of way. Whereas with Bianca, it's more of a comforting feeling.

I take a glance down the hallway and my eyes bleed. Speak of the devil. I catch her eyes through the crowd, but she averts as though she didn't want to be seen. Bianca. She's not missing. That would explain why her photos were removed around school and the city. But if she is here, where is Mike? She must know something.

She stares back at me before withdrawing her face and disappearing in the crowd of students and teachers. I rush down the hallway fighting through the crowd. I round the corner and fail to find her in the sea of people. She's gone. I place a hand onto my head and try to gather my thoughts. I feel disoriented and fatigued that quick. I run a hand across my face and find myself recovering from autopilot, sitting alone at a lunch table. I watch as everyone enters the cafeteria. I'll wait for Bianca to show herself. If she decides to.

The cafeteria begins to fill and my patience is wearing thin. She probably won't show her face. She knows that I saw her and that guilty gesture of trying to escape only tells me she does know something whether it's about Mike or something else. Maybe I should go out and look for her. Question her on her whereabouts and Mike's as well. To me, Bianca is the primary suspect.

I start to rise from my seat to go look for her, but then my train of thought is interrupted. Essence walks into the cafeteria and locks eyes with me. Her red hair and beautiful eyes paralyze me. Evasive action? Nope, too late.

"Hey, Evan," she smiles walking past. "Keeping the new look I see."

I need a defibrillator.

"Uhhh...Hi...Essence. Th-Thanks," I respond as my voice cracks. I sit down ashamed.

I watch her until she sits at a table with a group of people. She catches my glance and smiles. I fail to hide my blush. Maybe she got over what happened between us. Why would she smile at me? I then feel a presence. Someone is watching me. It is as heavy and uncomfortable as a stare. My hands aren't the only hands that rest on the lunch table. I look in the corner of my eyes and there sits Bianca. Smiling and silent. I stare at her unsure of what to say or maybe I have too much to say that if I speak it would all come out like gibberish. She holds a grin in the corner of her lips as though she has nothing to hide, but earlier today, her expression was the complete opposite.

"Hi, Bianca."

She continues smiling, then blinks.

"Hello, Evan."

Silence again. Okay, this is awkward. But how do I start? Maybe something like, *'do you have Mike hostage. I'm willing to negotiate.'* Nope. That's too assumptive and I have not a buck in my pocket to bet I am correct. How about, *'Do you know where Mike is? Where have you been?'* I think that will work just perfect.

"How are you, Evan?"

Wouldn't you like to know?

"I'm...alright. Just have a lot on my mind."

"Like what?"

Like you don't possibly know already. Mhm, suspect indeed.

"Well..." I look over at Essence. "There's this girl I really like."

Ugh! Why'd I share that?

"Mmmm," Bianca follows my eyes. "She's very beautiful, Evan. Just like mom."

I frown with confusion.

"Nice new look by the way. Black hair. Pale skin. Just like dad."

I quirk my head to the side.

"Guess I wouldn't know," I reply.

She chuckles a bit and leans forward, escaping my comfort space, and stares into my face. I shy my head a bit to lengthen the distance.

"What are you doing?" I ask.

Her hands rise to my face and holds me by my cheeks. *Is she trying to kiss me?*

"Um, Bianca?"

She withdraws her hands quickly and looks away embarrassed.

"I'm sorry. You're everything I remember."

"Excuse me?"

She sits quiet and her eyes begin to gloss.

"What do you mean?" I ask.

Her teary eyes look into mine, but I don't see Bianca.

"Beebee?" I whisper to myself. She doesn't budge. She sits in her white dress, her blushed face quivering in sadness. A shiver runs up my spine. Goosebumps cover my arms and my hair stands. When I blink, BeeBee is gone. Bianca looks down into her lap and I gulp.

"Mike is fine, Evan."

She wipes her face and rises to her feet. My mind shatters into a million pieces as I watch her exit the cafeteria.

"Mike is fine," I repeat to myself.

CHAPTER ELEVEN: A LASTING IMPRESSION

As school came to a close I had not seen Bianca since lunch, but *'Mike is fine.'* As strange as it may sound, I believe her. But I want to know more. I need to know more. Where is Mike hiding and why. Why hasn't he contacted me? If anyone, why hasn't he contacted his family? It just doesn't make sense nor sound like him.

As I get into the car at the end of the school day. The sky begins to rumble as expected. Never unexpected around this time of year. I must agree with my mom that today does make a great day to write. I feel I have been slacking, but with everything that has been going on, it has been the last thing on my mind. I pull my notebook from my book bag and begin to jot down my recollection of avoiding Essence, speaking with Mrs. Druin at Mike's house, and about Bianca being in school telling me that, *'Mike is fine.'*

The students pile out of the doors of the school and in that crowd, Essence stands on the sidewalk with her belongings. I close my notebook and I watch her wait as school buses pull away from the front of the school to start their routes around Oneida County. Why is someone so beautiful waiting at all? Essence should have people bending over backwards to make sure she is all set. She should be catered to.

Essence turns her head back and forth, looking for her ride I suspect. I find myself doing the same only to see that the school grounds are becoming empty from students and staff members. The rain starts to pound on the roads and roof of the car. Essence takes her bag and holds it above her head for shelter. I start the car, pull out of the front parking lot, and pull up in front of her. Perhaps it was confidence. Maybe instinct. She peers at the tinted windows cautiously and I stare at her perfect face. If only she knew she is staring back at mine.

Her eyes. I would love to stare into those without having to refrain from a blushing embarrassment. I roll the window down to end her agony of curiosity. She relaxes and forms a smile that shows her perfect top row of white teeth.

"Evan?"

"Would you like a ride?" I ask.

"Umm..." she looks back and forth for one last time. "Sure. That'd be great actually. My phone died."

"Let me get the door for you."

She smiles and I get out of the car. The rain feels great. The first ounce of comfort I've felt all day. It wets my face and hair and I gasp in relaxation. I open the passenger door.

"Thank you," she smiles.

She stands facing me for a moment. Not budging to get in. *Is she blushing?* I smile back and lick my lips from the rain. She then nods and gets into the car. I close her door and get back into the driver's seat. She sits down and places her bag on the floor, slings the seat belt over her shoulder, and snaps it in place.

"Thanks, Evan. It's really starting to pour now," she says wiping some of the rain from her arms and clothes. I begin to drive up the road.

"Don't like the rain?" I respond.

"I like it. Just not when it's trying to drown me," she chuckles.

"Understandable," I smile. "What sucks is I don't know how to swim."

She laughs and heaven sings.

"You don't?"

"Nope. I just sink," I say smiling and looking over to her. She joins in the laughter. She's drenched in water, but still looks as beautiful dry.

"So," I say. "Where to?"

"I live near the parkway. You know how to get there?"

"Sure do. In the summer, I always go to the fair on the parkway."

"Really? I haven't been since I was a little girl. My father would take me on the merry-go-round until I either fell asleep or cried." She giggles. "Where do you live?" she asks.

"Very close to the rainforest."

"Rainforest?"

I laugh.

"Well, I call it a rainforest. It's really on the edge of the Mohawk River."

"Oh yeah that's right, you were supposed to show me remember?" she reminds.

"Ah, I haven't forgotten."

I blush. I continue to drive, but then silence floods the car. I peer over at her as she looks out the window watching the rain. She is so gorgeous. Keeping my eyes on the road is a difficult task, but her safety is beyond measure. I must focus.

"If it wasn't raining so much I would show you," I finally say.

"I'm not scared of the rain," she responds quickly.

"So, are you saying you would like to go?"

"So, are you saying you would like to show me?" she smiles.

I smirk at her sense of humor.

"If it's not conflicting with any plans you have, I would love to show you."

"I don't have anything planned at all."

"Well okay...um...let's go," I shrug with a smile.

"You won't kidnap me right?" she laughs.

Crap. She's onto me. As much as I would love to, I wouldn't.

"No, of course not," I laugh. "I wouldn't do anything that would put you in any harm or make you feel uncomfortable."

"That's quite a promise there, Evan."

I look over at her and she smiles.

"I like it."

"You can count on it too."

She turns her face away as she smiles pressing her lips tightly together. *What? Did I just make Essence blush? No. No way. That's impossible.*

"You know what would make me even more comfortable?" she asks.

"What's that? I'll do anything?"

I hope I don't sound so easily submissive.

"If you met my father. At least so he doesn't question me about who I associate with."

I nod my head in agreement.

"Not a problem at all. Completely understandable."

"Okay," she smiles then grips the forearm of my jacket. My heart skips then leaps into my throat. I grip both on my hands on the steering wheel to keep us from crashing like my train of thought.

We soon pull into her driveway and head up the steps to her white house. She knocks on the door. I shiver.

"Cold?" She asks.

"More like nervous," I say fidgeting in place.

A few moments later, the door opens. A tall man with freckles, glasses, short red hair, and a fairly young face, smiles.

"Hello, dear," he says to Essence then hugging her.

"Hi, dad," she responds hugging him back. When they let go, he looks at me a bit confused.

"And who might you be?" he asks with a welcoming smile.

"Hi, umm," I respond. I pull my hand from my pocket to shake his hand. He accepts and squeezes a bit. I continue to shake his hand unable to let go. He chuckles a bit and nods waiting for me to speak.

"Dad, this is Evan. Evan Macrae."

Good save, Essence, I think to myself.

"He's a great friend of mine. Gave me a ride home from school."

I smile.

"Pleased to meet you, sir."

"You too, and please, call me Tom," he says. "Sir, or Mr. LaRoux makes me feel older."

"Sorry," I say. "Pleased to meet you, Tom."

"Much better," he laughs.

"Evan saved me from the rain," Essence adds smiling.

"Is that so?!" He exclaims, but then his face turns into disappointment. "Aw shucks, dear, I'm sorry I had completely lost track of time. I was working on a few things and --"

"It's okay dad," she says. "I know how focused you are when you're writing. Evan is a writer too."

I look over at Essence shocked. She turns to me with a huge smile and winks. I sink into my chest.

"Really?" He says. "What do you like to write?"

"Um," I say.

"I know, I know. I get this question a lot too which is always difficult to answer without cringing."

I chuckle and try to think.

"I guess anything that comes to mind."

"Best answer ever," he says with a point. "OH! Would you kids like to come inside instead of us being out here in the rain?" He steps to the side.

"Oh, no dad. Actually, I was wondering if I can take a ride with him to his house. He was going to show me around the forest."

"In the rain? You could sick."

"We'll take that chance."

"You never fail to surprise me," he smiles. "That will be just fine. Be home for dinner. And keep her safe," he says turning to me.

"I will sir-- I mean, Tom."

He nods and smiles. We shake hands again.

"See you soon," he kisses Essence's cheek. "Be safe."

"I will," she says as we head back down the steps. "Bye dad," she calls. "Thank you!"

He leans in the doorway holding a big white smile. I see where Essence gets hers. I open the door for her to get in.

"It'll be hard getting used to such chivalry," she smiles as she gets inside.

"You have no other choice," I say. She wipes her face before smiling back into mine. I return the gesture, close her door, and hop back in the driver's seat. I start the car and begin to pull out from their driveway. Tom stands in the doorway and waves us goodbye before going back inside. I then get us on the road to head for the Mohawk River Valley.

"Well, that wasn't so bad now was it?" she asks.

"Not at all," I say looking over. "He was very welcoming."

"He's always to himself, just like me," she says.

"We all have that in common."

There goes that silence again -- and my thoughts. Mike bounces off every wall inside my brain. What does Bianca know? I marked it down as my next mission: Find Bianca's house. Would that make me a stalker? Someone crazy? Or does the safety of my best friend prove how sane

I really am? You protect the people you care about no matter the cost. I'll find Mike even if it leads me to my grave.

"It's so sad about what's going on with Mike. I'm sure his family is very concerned," Essence says breaking the silence.

My hands clench around the steering wheel and I flinch.

"Yes. It is very sad. His family is worried sick."

"I know he's your best friend, Evan," she places a hand onto my knee. "I'm sorry."

Her touch doesn't allow me to move. It was comforting, so I do not want to. Even though Bianca had told me Mike is fine, I can't fathom what else is going on with him.

"Thank you, Essence. Just wish I could do something about it. Mike's not just my best friend. He's my only friend."

"I'm your friend too now, Evan. Making you possibly my only friend as well. I'll help you find him. We'll get Mike back."

I nod and can't help but believe her.

"Now, there's a smile."

"You make it easy to," I say looking at her.

She caresses the side of my face. I love how she expresses herself not only with words, but with touch.

"No more sad faces," she says smiling back at me. I nod.

"I like the sound of that."

Silence falls upon us once again, but not an awkward silence. A warm one. I continue down the road. We should be close to my house soon enough.

"Do you like being to yourself all the time?" I ask. "I mean, it's surprising you don't have many friends. I took you for someone who would have plenty."

She turns to the window and exhales.

"I'm sorry. Did I say something wrong?"

She shakes her head and looks down at a black rose bracelet around her wrist. She looks back out the window and draws circles over the black rose with her thumb.

"No. You're okay, Evan," she responds. She falls silent for a few moments.

"I use to have a friend—a best friend."

149

"What happened? Did you two get into a fight?"

She shakes her head.

"She—um," she clears her throat before answering. "She passed away. Cancer."

I gasp and look over at her regretting that I asked.

"I'm so sorry, Essence I--"

"Didn't know," she nods. "It's okay, Evan." She looks back at me and tries to smile.

"Her name was Claire. Claire Bonnet. At the time, my father and I lived in Geneseo. Claire was – beautiful. She had long blonde hair, always wore bright colored clothes, and loved flowers. Roses. Black ones."

She looks down at her bracelet and my eyes follow.

"She fought for years. Before then, she seemed so happy, you just couldn't tell that something was wrong. I didn't find out until I overheard my dad speaking to her father over the phone. I was devastated. She had been hiding it from me."

"She didn't want you to worry."

She nods.

"Yeah. I tell myself that too. I just – I just thought she could tell me anything." She clears her throat.

"So one day, when my dad and I was visiting her in the hospital, she told me to remove the bracelet from her wrist. And so I did. Then she said, 'put it around your wrist.' And I looked at her and shook my head and asked her, ' why do you want me to put on your bracelet?' And she said, 'because I want you to remember me when I go. I want you to have it.'"

Essence gulps and her eyes begin to gloss. I slow down the car and begin to pull over. I stop the car and put it in park keeping the car running. The rain continues to pour.

"I told her, 'No. You're going to get through this. You're strong. You're beautiful. You're going to fall in love and have a big family with a handsome husband.' She just looked at me and started shaking her head and I can see—I can see tears rolling down the sides of her face."

"Essence if you don't want to--"

"She said, 'no. I'm tired. I'm so tired. Keep the bracelet and promise me, promise me you will never forget about me.' I looked at her and said, 'Claire, you have to keep fighting' and she said, 'promise me, Essence.' And so I did and put her bracelet around my wrist."

Tears begin to flow from her eyes. I reach across and bring her to my chest and hold her.

"I found out later that day she had passed on," she sniffles. "Since then, my father and I have moved from place to place. Buffalo. Syracuse. Just us. My mother passed having me. The only kinds of memories I can create come from photo albums. It's always been just me and my dad."

"I had no idea, I mean I have always noticed you were to yourself and looked happy that way too. Never would have thought all of this happened."

"Yeah. Guess I'm just so used to losing people in my life it makes it difficult to make friends. No one could ever replace Claire. To this day, I have not taken off my bracelet.

We stare into each other eyes and warmth fills her face. I brush some of her red hair from her face and wander into her pupils. She breathes slowly and closes her eyes as I caress her face. She opens her eyes and looks at my lips. I look at hers and for a moment, I feel my heartbeat. I gulp and look at her pink lips then back into her eyes. I begin to slowly lean closer. She exhales and lowers her head.

"I'm sorry," she says. "It's not that I don't like you, it's just--"

"Too soon," I say nodding. "I understand."

She nods.

"Yeah."

"Hey," I lift her face by her chin. She looks into my eyes.

"No sad faces remember?" I say shaking my head with a smile.

She nods and exhales deeply.

"Right," she says in a whisper. "No sad faces."

CHAPTER TWELVE: SHARING

We pull into my driveway and I park the car. I hop out and open Essence's door. I could never get use to the smile she gives. Never in a million years or any of my dreams would I have thought she'd look my way. Never would I have thought being around her would feel so natural, so beautiful, so – mind-numbing. Who would have thought someone so perfect could have gone through what she has? She's lost her mother, her best friend, and only has her father to care for her. I now understand why she she's been to herself: She's afraid of losing people... And I'm afraid of losing her – if I have her.

We walk along the side of my house, heading to the back where the trees of the Mohawk River Valley stand. The wood and grass is damp, the clouds are gray, and the smell of rain fills the air. The leaves from the trees above sway in the gentle breeze and green furs of moss cover the rocks around us. I look over at Essence and see her smile, her face gazing up. For that, I am proud of myself. Making her smile again.

"This is home?" she says as we walk along a trail.

"Yes. Just my mother and I."

"Must be nice. To live so close to nature."

"I couldn't be more thankful," I say. "When I wake up, it's one of the first things I see. This rainforest."

I step over a small creek and hold out my hand. She smiles and takes it.

"It speaks to me," I say as she steps over to join me.

"Howso?"

"Well, it's hard to explain."

"I'm listening," she says as we continue.

"When I see the rainforest from my window, or even walk along these trails, I feel so free. Free from anxieties, stress—spilling paint," She laughs.

"But it just, makes me feel like I need to be here. When I'm not happy, I come here and almost immediately, I'm happy again."

I stop walking.

"Makes me feel like I actually belong somewhere. I never feel alone out here."

She stops and stares at me. I look into the trees above and inhale the air.

"Out here, *this* is really home."

She smiles and joins my side and looks up as well. Around us, small drops of rain smack onto the leaves.

"Ready?" I say.

"Where are we going?"

"Up."

I approach my tree, then hold out my hand.

"You make it difficult to say no."

My heart stops, and probably literally.

"I do?"

She giggles, doesn't accept my hand, but instead, hugs me. I smile and wrap my arms around her. When she lets go, I cry inside, but knowing we will be spending time together, is enough to make me smile again.

"Okay, you'll have to tell me what I'm doing or I might fall."

"Don't worry. I said I'd protect you and get you home safe."

"You promised actually," she laughs.

"Right, I promised," I smile.

I help her up, each prong that's embedded into the tree, pointing as I guide her. When we get to the vast trunk, I grab hold of her hand.

"Careful," I say. "It might be a little damp from the rain."

"Well aren't you quite a risk taker."

I smile.

"Wouldn't you like to know."

"I would actually."

I rub my palms against the sides of my pants, and take a deep breath as I try to hold back my smile.

We get to the tree's torso where my umbrella is propped open above my duffle bag, which sits on a blanket.

"I'm letting go," I say, as much as I don't want to. "Will you be okay for second?"

She smiles.

"I'll be okay," she says. "I'm not going anywhere, Evan."

I nod and smile. *I sure hope not.*

I fix the umbrella and tap my hands along the blanket to feel for any wet spots. None.

"Sit with me?" I ask, as I take a seat against the tree.

Essence sits across from me, under the umbrella. She takes a deep breath, as she looks around the forest.

"Wow, I wish I had this in my backyard. Would never get old to me."

"I love it here," I say. "This is where I do all of my thinking, writing, contemplating."

Dreaming about you.

"I'm jealous."

"I have my good days and bad days up here."

"How could you possibly have a bad day after coming up here with all of this," she says, outstretching her hands and looking amongst the trees.

I shrug.

"Well, I haven't been feeling quite myself lately."

She crosses her legs.

"What do you mean?"

I think for a while, something I spend much of my time doing up here.

"I just—feel as though something's missing or, wrong."

A wrinkle forms between her eyebrows as she tilts her head.

"Why?"

"I don't know. It's like I live here, but I feel like I belong somewhere else."

"Like would you feel better in a different city?" she asks.

"Not exactly. I love Utica. These trees, the weather, the people. That pine and mint smell."

"I thought I was the only one," she says.

"It's great here. It's more so, as though I'm still figuring myself out. Like who I am and what makes me, *ME.* You know?"

"I understand," she responds. "Aren't we all asking ourselves the same questions? Who we are and where we belong? I think one of the biggest mysteries in life lies within ourselves. What makes us, *us?* Our family? Friends? Experiences?"

"Exactly," I agree. "But-- there's something else too. About me. Something's different."

"In a bad way?"

I think for a moment and nod.

"Yeah. In a bad way."

"Should I worry?"

I shake my head.

"Does your mom know you've been feeling this way?" she asks.

"I haven't said anything about it. She tends to worry a lot."

"And your dad?"

"I don't know him nor remember much about him. Left when I was a child. Wish I could say I knew what he looked like, but we don't have any photos of him at all."

"I'm sorry to hear that, Evan."

I shake my head.

"Don't be."

I wouldn't be who I am today, but who am I? My father's son? A little fish in the big sea?

"If you are unsure of who you are," she says. "Think about the things you enjoy doing. What makes you happy? Why do they make you happy? And why do you continue to do them?"

"I like to write," I say.

Essence nods and smiles.

"Keep going. I'm listening."

"I like riding my bike to school. I like to read. Draw. Paint."

"And have yet to fail at that."

I scrunch my face, trying to keep myself from blushing. *Fail.* She giggles. I didn't think I was that well of an artist, but if it makes a difference in someone's life, that's an achievement. I always believed there was nothing about me that would interest anyone, especially a girl like Essence.

"Thank you," I say. "I didn't think you--"

"Noticed?"

There I go blushing again. She chuckles. I'm starting to think she gets a bit of a kick out of that.

"Nope. Not the slightest."

"I've paid attention more than you'd believe, Evan."

I turn my face away. *Why is she doing this me.*

"Your dreams," she says. I almost forgot she read them.

"Some of your dreams are beautiful and others, sad."

I flinch and play with my thumbs in my lap.

"Yeah. I have nightmares a lot. I don't understand most of them."

"The one about the little girl, Beebee, you dream about her often."

"Lately I've dreamed about her a lot."

"And what about the boy?"

"Him? Yes. I dream about him a lot too."

I like this. Having Essence here. Her company was needed, especially with Mike missing. I have someone I can talk to. Someone to help me cope. I'm still waiting for her to come out and say she isn't from here. Earth. I wish she'd just spill the beans already. *Gosh, if she only knew how I felt about her,* but I mustn't tell.

"I read it," she says.

My stomach twists into knots. *Dare I ask?*

"Read what?"

"What you wrote about me."

My heart flatlines. I wish there was a shovel here so I can dig my grave. No tombstone needed. I press my back deep into the tree's bark.

"I know that's why you took the book as you did."

She looks up at me and I avert my eyes.

"I'm sorry, Evan. I don't mean to make you uncomfortable."

Did I push her away writing about her? No. That wouldn't make any sense. If I had pushed her away, she wouldn't be here with me. She could have said no, but she didn't. In fact, she insisted. She turns her face away and rubs her hand up and down her arm. *Change the subject, Evan. Change the subject.*

"Essence."

"Yes?"

"When I was visiting Mike's grandmother the other day, I saw this building on the cliffs. I seen it before. I know I did. I'm just – curious about what's there."

"Shall we go sometime?"

"Yeah. I mean, my mother always makes deliveries by the cliffs. I'm just curious if that's where she goes. I would hate to ask her myself since I already egg her on about a van full of blood packets."

She smiles, uncrosses her legs, and sits next to me. She rests her head on my shoulder, and my heart jumps into my throat. Her scent is addictive and unreal, like the exotic white blossoms of a magnolia tree. She makes herself comfortable against me and closes her eyes. I put my arm around her, making my chest her pillow.

I then think about what Mike said. About Essence having mutual feelings for me. I want her to want me back. I would do anything. I mean, look at her. Her beautiful eyes. Pink lips. Rose red hair. Stunning face. Where are her flaws?

~

"I really had a great time, Evan," she says as we stand on her front porch.

"I did too," I smile.

"Can we go there again soon? Together? Just us?"

Together. Just us. I love the sound of that.

"Anytime you'd like."

She hugs me and I wrap my arms around her.

"Thanks for saving me from the rain."

"I'd do it again."

She lets go and I wish she hadn't.

"Sleep well tonight. I'll see you in school."

"You too, Essence."

She gives me one last smile before stepping inside and closing the door. I walk back to the car and take a deep breath. She's left her scent with me. I reverse onto the street, shift the gear into drive, but keep my foot on the break. I look out the passenger window at her house, a curtain in the upstairs window opens, and there she is, smiling at me, as I smile at her.

R.J. Rogue

CHAPTER THIRTEEN: SWEET DREAMS

I feel around the darkness, but nothing meets my touch. Dead space. As I walk, the ground pulls and sinks beneath me like quicksand. There's no escape.

"Evan," a voice whispers.

I turn to face my company, only to find myself alone in the middle of the forest. The clouds are black. The wind is strong, and also frigid.

"Evan," I hear the voice again, dragging onto my name.

"Who's there!" I call out, but no response.

The sky roars and lightning flashes before my eyes. I fall into the mud, and rain begins to fall. The voice returns, repeating my name as I then run beneath the trees of the howling forest. I dodge a few giants of bark, and there he stands, the stranger I seen just over a week ago, watching me with his red eyes, which hide behind black hair over a leather jacket.

When lightning flashes again, he's gone. I turn to run, but slip and fall into the wet, sticky terrain. I turn over onto my back and he stands above me, breathing as loud and heavy as a horse. Resting above his thumb is the mark; the one with the 'M' and strange symbol.

"We're watching you!" he points and growls in many indistinct voices.

"Go away!" I yell.

"Evan, I'm here."

"Mom?" I turn around and find myself standing on the cliffs. Here again, just as I was before, but where are the doors? The forest is across the small field; dark, mysterious, and monstrous. I look behind me, and there she stands in a white gown on the edge of the cliff.

"Essence?" I say. "What are you doing here?"

She doesn't reply. She stands as still as stone as the wind blows the end of her gown against her curves, the frosted grass between her toes and against her ankles. She takes a step back, my heart lunges forward.

"Essence? Essence wait!"

She allows herself to fall from the cliff, her arms out, lips smiling, eyes closed. I dash to the edge, throw my hands in front of me, and dive into the stormy sky after her.

The view is endless. No ground nor water. Just Essence, falling through the sky, her body forming a white cross. The rain joins us as we plummet. I straighten my body, and bullet towards her. As I close in, I outstretch my hand and prepare to grab her.

"Essence!" I try to yell, but can barely breath from the suffocating air.

She holds her outstretched position as we rip through a ceiling of rain clouds. The water is below, waiting to swallow us. *Almost there. Almost there. If I can just...*

"Got you!"

I pull her into my arms, and turn our bodies in the air to suppress the impact that awaits us.

"Don't worry," I say clenching my eyes shut. "You will be okay."

As the wind fills my ears, my arms hug my shoulders. I open my eyes and she's gone, but I didn't let go. Where is she? I look over my shoulder and brace for impact. I connect with the water, which felt like cement, and begin sink. *I had her. I had her in my grasp and lost her. Now, I have to save myself.*

I kick my legs and wave my arms to swim to the surface, unsure if I am getting closer, or swimming deeper. The water is dark and feels like ice against every inch of my skin. My chest tightens and I force my mouth to remain shut as water begs to enter and consume me from within. I kick and swim and kick and swim, but light is absent. *I must be swimming deeper. I have to find my way out.*

Something grabs hold of my ankle. I kick and try to wiggle free, but it's no use. My lungs feel as compact as hardened play dough. I reach below and feel around my ankle. Seaweed. I untangle the knots, and when I'm free, I throw my arms, one over the other, praying I am close to the surface. *I don't know how much longer I can hold my breath. I am going to drown. Or worse, I am going to die.*

I hang onto hope, then it shows itself in the form of light. *I am close. I am close to the surface.* I continue to swim, and soon, I emerge, taking every gasp of air as I can. Mouthfuls. Inhaling, reaching the pits of my stomach.

Evanescence

Exhaling, letting out the fear that I was sure was going to consume me.

I swim to the shore which felt like seconds to reach, but I know it should have been hours. I crawl onto the beach, hands and knees imprinting into the sand before my body gives and hugs its moisture. I roll onto my back, breathing, resting, aching. *I made it.* The sky falls onto me, my clothes stick to me, and my mind cries to me.

"Evan."

I rise to a sit and across the horizon is a mansion, sitting on the cliffs, but how? I shake my head, telling myself it isn't possible. I just left the cliffs and there was nothing, but I also believed Essence was there, and she was not.

I crawl to the water until it is elbow deep. I cup my hands together and throw it onto my face. I gather more and wash across my cheeks and through my hair. When the water settles, I stare at my reflection, and it begins to change.

A red glow fills my eyes. My skin goes pale, practically clear and my reflection becomes a frowning stranger. He smiles, and a monstrous overbite grows from beneath his, my, lips. I splash the water and back away, keeping my eyes on the ripples, waiting for him to emerge. Nothing.

"Evan."

The voice wasn't that of a whisper, but it was familiar. Cedric stands above me, his eyes glowing red, one of them peeking through his hair.

"You better watch your back, Evan." His overbite is as monstrous as his voice.

Lightning flashes and Cedric's nose is an inch from mine.

"Wake up!" he yells.

~

I fall off my bed and the morning sun is there to catch me. *I hate the sun.*

"Evan!" My mother calls from downstairs. "Wake up my little, vampire!"

I groan.

"Vampires don't sleep!" I call back.

"HA! Who told you that?"

I shrug.

"Move quickly dear! Don't be late for school!"

"I won't be!"

"I love you!"

"I love you too!"

The front door closes and I take a deep breath, resting on my bedroom floor.

"So much for sweet dreams."

CHAPTER FOURTEEN: REBORN

I'm dying. At least, that's what it feels like. The nightmare was daunting. Those glowing, red eyes. Essence jumping from the cliff, myself failing to catch her. Cedric was there as well, but his eyes were red, his skin was pale, and his overbite was monstrous. *Why was he in my nightmare?* Then there was me. Just like *them. A vampire. Why? What are my nightmares trying to tell me?*

There's not much more I feel I can take. These mood swings. Mike's disappearance. My feelings for Essence. And Bianca -- her comment about Mike sounds to me like she knows of his whereabouts. *Mike is fine. Mike is fine,* she says.

I also fail to forget my conversation with Essence about my father. Such a coward for leaving my mother and I. Why'd he leave? Were we not good enough for him? Were we not the perfect family? Didn't he want me? Didn't he care about me? About mom? Was it something I did or something mother might have said? ... Was it our fault?

Evanescence

Stop. Don't do this to yourself, Evan. Not again. No. Not again. You've been through enough already. I have to keep the promise I made to myself not to have such thoughts. It was his decision to leave. His lost. Not mine. I'm sure since he's been gone he's thankful for not having any responsibility of a child. But I'm not going to worry about that. I turned out just fine. *Didn't I?*

Luckily, spending time with Essence wasn't a dream. It was real. It was and she wants to do it again sometime soon. I can't help but find a smile. She makes me giddy, but if I were to say such a thing to Mike, if Mike was here, he'd laugh. He'd probably say something like, *'Jeez, Ev. You worship the ground she walks on!'* What can I say? She's a goddess. Hopefully, someday, mine.

I have to be careful not to push or scare her away. But I do worry though. I know how strong my feelings are, and with Essence knowing as well, it makes me vulnerable to getting hurt. Before, I had believed I can be anything she had wanted me to be whether it was an associate, friend, or, as I dream, her lover. But now, being anything besides those is unacceptable.

I park my bike into the rack outside of school. Students hop off of the buses and walk into school, none of which are Mike. I follow the crowd inside, gather my books for class, and close my locker door. My heart leaps into my throat.

"Hi, Evan," Essence smiles hugging her books to her chest.

"Hi," I say wide eyed.

"Sorry I frightened you," she says.

"No, no, it's okay, um. Just a bit exhausted. Still waking up really."

"Didn't get any sleep last night?"

HA! No. At least not any adequate sleep.

"Not as well as I would have liked," I respond. "I had another nightmare."

"What happened in this one?" she asks.

The bell rings. *Oh, come on.*

"Well," she chuckles, "Looks like you'll have to tell me about it later."

"Guess so," I exhale deeply.

Evanescence

Essence leaves me at my locker love drunk. I can't believe she came to my locker and initiated a conversation with me. Milestone achieved. Another accomplishment I can write in the books. She's everything a man would --

"Hey..." Cedric wrecks my train of thought as he props himself against his locker. I look over at him. "You dropped your jaw, loverboy." He doesn't smile, smirk, nor laugh. He holds his books in his hand. My heart sinks into my gut.

His hand. What is that on his hand?

Below the knuckle of his thumb I notice a black marking. Similar to the one I had seen in my nightmare, but the letter is a 'V' and the symbol is different.

I open my notebook to the page in which I drew the first symbol, the one with the 'M', and begin to draw the one on Cedric's hand right next to it. Similar, but different. Before, I would have said, I've never seen the symbols before, but now, they are familiar. *I know I have, and what do they mean?* I'm starting to believe my nightmares are much more than just nightmares. They're more like memories. They are trying to tell me something, but what? I look up and Cedric is gone. He's not down any end of the halls neither.

Before I know it, I'm walking into Painting class, the final period of the day, and take a seat next to Essence. Ms. Brooks begins class by giving us a new assignment which is to paint something that we feel best represents who we are. *Great. It's my lucky day.*

"Want to tell me about your nightmare?" Essence asks.

Just when I was trying to forget.

"I don't know where to begin."

"The same way you would begin any story. From the beginning," a smile forms in the corner of her lips.

"Well, I was in the rainforest again. I--"

"Yes," she says.

"I ran into the same guy as before. Not much was different about him. It was pretty dark, but his eyes glowed red. He had that mark on his hand. And then--"

I pause. The thought of telling Essence she was in the dream was not an option. I couldn't tell her about such a suicide attempt she made, even though realistically speaking, it wasn't her. I'd just rather she not know that I dream about her.

"And then what, Evan?" she asks.

"And then I was falling from that cliff I was telling you about. I fell into the water and something grabbed me by the ankle and tried to pull me deeper. When I managed to break free, I was on the beach looking at the cliff like from afar. The building was there. The mansion. When I turned around--"

I pause again. *I saw Cedric.* Does she need to know that as well? She nods for me to continue and I exhale deeply.

"When I turn around, there's another stranger. Pale. Red eyes. Fangs. Just like the man from the forest."

Her eyebrows worry with a frown, and a faint crease forms between them.

"Did he say anything to you? Either one of them."

"Yes," I nod. "Actually they said the same thing that man told me a few days ago, 'We're watching you.'"

"And the other guy?"

"His words," I say, really referring to Cedric. "Were bold. He told me to watch my back."

Essence shakes her head.

"Wonder why."

"Your guess is as good as mine," I agree. "And the worst part -- I saw myself. Just like them." I shake my head. "I'm starting to believe my nightmares are trying to tell me something."

"What do you think that something is?"

I shrug.

"I don't know."

"By the way you explain them and with what's been actually going on, it is quite a coincidence, don't you think?"

"Yeah. I don't think these are random at all," I respond staring off into space. "I'm thinking some of what happened in my nightmares, happened to me before and I'm just having a hard time remembering when and who those people are."

I nod to myself.

"I know them. I know I do."

A silence grows between us.

"So, um, you have any ideas on what you're going to paint, Michelangelo?" she smiles and I return to earth.

"Not quite. How am I supposed to paint something that describes or represents who I am as a person, if I'm already having such a hard time figuring it out?"

"That's part of art, Evan," she smiles weakly. "People in general are a work of art. We're just, works in progress that's all."

"Perhaps you're right."

"Here, let me help." She scoots her chair closer, and my leg begins to tap on the metal of my stool. *Will I ever get use to her?*

"Maybe you should close your eyes," she says.

I smirk.

"What?"

"Go ahead. Close them."

I listen and stare at the back of my eyelids.

"Okay, now take a deep breath and just listen to my voice."

"You're the artist now," I say laughing.

"Listen…" she says laughing with me.

"Okay, okay."

I listen.

"Just listen to yourself breath."

Kind of difficult with some of the chatter going on around us. Still no ideas.

"How do you feel?" she asks.

"Confused. Hopeless....Angry."

"Heh, I guess that's a starts," she says. "Okay, now let's free your emotions. They are a part of you, but don't allow them to dictate who you are. You are much more than what you feel."

My mind explores its trenches. I feel weightless and free. My hand finds the handle to my paintbrush, dips the end into the paint, and begins to dance on the paper.

"You can open your eyes, Evan, so you can see." she says, but her voice is low and faint, almost distorted. I want to open my eyes, but I can't. Instead, I continue, going from paper to paint. Paper to paint. Paper to paint. My hand begins to move faster, but I am not in control.

"Evan, how are you doi--"

My palms began to sweat and tremble. My chest runs cold and tight. I feel a great weight upon me, a depression. Then sorrow. Then frustration. Then anger. Then, something unexplainable.

"Do you hear that," I whisper.

"Here what?" Essence says gently.

I look around, and I stand in the forest, the trees above me. The wind blows, and though no one is there, I hear footsteps along the leaves. Whoever it is, is getting closer.

"Evan?" I hear Essence say.

"They're here," I whisper. "They know I'm here."

My hand stops and drops the paintbrush.

"Evan?"

I try to relax, and open my eyes. Essence cups a hand to her mouth and gasps.

"What?"

"Your eyes," she says. "Your eyes are r--" She looks over at the easel.

"How did you do that?" she asks in a gasping whisper.

I face the easel and my stomach balls into knots. It's the marking I had seen on the stranger's hand, the one from the forest, the mark that I have yet to understand its meaning. I examine the careful strokes and expertise in my use of the red and black paint. The marking covers the entire paper.

"That's impossible," I say with disbelief.

How is this possible? How did I do that?

"Evan, you look -- pale," Essence says as she peers into my face and arms.

I look into the palms of my hands and watch as my skin continues to pale. My veins turn purple, then invisible. I ball my hands into fists. Essence grabs hold of them, then withdraws and winces.

"You're freezing," she says.

"What's happening to me?"

"Evan, are you okay?"

My heart begins to race, and I can hear myself breathe. My teeth ache and I smell something metallic, but – it makes me – hungry.

"I have to go."

I rise out my chair and head for the door.

"Evan wait!" Essence calls out to me, but I do not stop.

"Evan?" Ms. Brooks says as I exit the classroom. I head down the hallway moving as quickly as possible flipping my hands from palms up to palms down, waiting for them to return to my normal blood-filled complexion. An agonizing pain rocks my head into oblivion. *What is this? It—hurts!*

I hear a crunch and crack, and hold my head by the temples. I squeeze my eyes shut and try to fight it. *Ow! Just—stop already. Please.*

I drop to my knees, still clasping my hands to the sides of my head which feels as though it is on fire. *What's happening to me?*

I crawl across the floor, breathing through my teeth, trying to fight off the headache and burning sensation. I stumble as I stand to my feet, and balance my weight by using the lockers I pass. The crunch and pain returns. I grab handfuls of my hair, wanting to pull out each strand, but lose my balance, fall into a locker, and leave my body's imprint into its door, creating my fossil.

The final school bell rings, and the pain calms a bit, yet I still feel it inside of me. *I'm angry. Why do I feel so – angry? Calm down, Evan. Just, calm down.* As I turn the dial on my lock, the numbers begin to blend and overlap each other. I look down the hall and everything does the same, blend and overlap creating two of everything. As people fill the hall, I squint to focus, but fail to see clearly. Their voices are loud, that metallic, copper smell is potent, and my anger continues to build. I stumble into a student.

"Whoa, buddy!" He says as he breaks free from catching me.

I stumble into another.

"What's wrong with you?!"

"S-sorry," I say, struggling to breathe.

I bump into a locker and try to keep my balance. I ricochet off and into something large.

"Hey watch it!"

The student pushes me back. I know his voice. It's the voice of the guy who bullies Cedric, but not anymore ever since Cedric gave him a massive nosebleed. My guess says his friends are with him.

"What's with that heavy breathing?"

He begins to mock and his laughter hurts my ears. I cover my ears, but it doesn't help. *Shut - up. Not—today.*

"Stop—talking so loud," I mumble through clenched teeth. I turn to my locker and rest my forehead against it.

"I can't hear you, Macrae! What was that?!"

I punch my locker and it dents. His laughing stops and the students around us fall silent.

"Thank you..." The pain begins to go away as I exhale and take long breaths.

He scoffs.

"Ohh, I'm really scared! *BANG!*" he yells into my ear.

I wish he'd leave. I wish he'd leave now. He taps my shoulder firmly with his index finger.

"Hey! I'm talking to you, Macrae!"

Mistake.

One second I am facing my locker, and the next, my hand grabs hold of his neck. The gasps that fill the air, fuel my fire. The boy stares into my eyes, frightened, weak, none of which phases me the slightest to let him go. His friends back away. I lift him off the ground.

"I told you to leave me alone," I say.

I squeeze his neck, and can't help, but smile. He let's out a cry as I watch his face turn into a beet. *That smell. It's – strong.* My mouth waters, my teeth prick my tongue.

"He's choking!" Someone exclaims.

"Somebody help him!" Someone else yells.

The anger slips from my grip, my hair stands to points, and I look amongst the crowd. Each face I see averts and leans away. *Essence.* She stares, worried, yet shocked. *Bianca* stands next to *Cedric.* Her expression is unreadable, but Cedric grins and crosses his arms as though he wants me to keep going.

I let go of the boy and he falls to the floor, coughing and comforting his neck with his hands. The students begin to whisper amongst themselves. I stare at the boy. *I did this. His suffrage, fear, pain, was by my hands. It's not like me. But who am I? This just--isn't right. I can't. I have to go.* I look into my palms and flip them over. Above my thumb's knuckle is the dark birthmark, 'M' that I had seen on the stranger in the forest and just moments ago, my painting easel. I place my hand on my chest, nothing. I cannot find my heartbeat.

No. No. What is this?!

I walk towards the crowd and everyone moves away hurriedly. Essence calls out to me, but my walk turns into a sprint. *I have to get out of here. I have to go. NOW!*

"Can't always run from your problems, Evan!" Cedric calls after me.

~

I push the exit doors open and they slam against the wall. I run across the parking lot and keep my pace so no one will follow. The mark is still there, bold and black. I stop and look at my reflection on a car window. My skin is pale, my eyes are almost black filled with a faint red in my pupils, and my teeth are beginning to form an overbite. *I can't be seen like this. What's happening to me?*

Thunder roars and rain begins to fall. I look above at the clouds that tumble atop each other as lighting rips across the sky, flashing the city into a blinding white. Before me are trees, at the back of the parking lot. I begin to run, not once looking back.

Everything whips past me as though I were a bullet shot from the barrel of a gun. I zigzag between the trees, jumping and running, until I trip over one of the fallen giants and become airborne. I maneuver my body as I descend, and instead of plowing into the ground, I plant my feet beneath me, and take off running again, as fast as a bullet. It felt natural, simple, and instinct. I plant my foot onto the bark of a tree, kick off to the next tree, and climb. When I reach the top, my breathing is steady. Not a single breath lost. I scan across the treetops and the gray forecast that hangs above the Mohawk River in the distance. I glance at my hand and the mark is still there. It has yet to disappear. *This is unreal. None of this makes any sense. What does this mean?*

"Evan?!" I hear Essence call.

I put my back against the tree hiding myself. I peer over a few branches and soon she stops running and looks around in the rain.

"Evan?! Where are you?!" she calls before running off again. I rest my head against the wet bark and close my eyes. Visions flash before me. *My dreams. All of them. Beebee, that family, the little boy pushing me off of the cliffs, their inhumane appearance. The stranger. The nightmare I had last night. The markings. Bianca. Cedric. All* seem relevant to each other. Somehow, connected.

And now me. Just as I was in my dreams. A monster. A -- vampire. *No.* That possibility is ridiculous. There's no such thing. Even if there is, I was never bitten by anything of the sort. But what about this mark. They all had it. I look at my hand and run my thumb across it. *Why is it there? Why do I have it too?*

I then hear water crashing against rock. I move to the top of the tree and overlook the rest of the forest once more. Across the water, I see it. I see it and a thought crosses my mind. There's no fighting this feeling. *I can't—hold it—any longer.*

I leap into the raining sky from treetop to treetop. I get to the peak of one final tree, step harsh into its wood, and leap above the ceiling of the forest. I outstretch my hands and look below. There's the trees, then sand, then water. I straighten my body into a dive, and when I'm under, I swim to the surface. The mansion is a distance away, but I feel myself drawn to it. It calls me. It's like I have to go there and do something. I don't know what, but I must go.

Those miles of water felt like seconds to swim. I'm at the base of the cliff, treading water, looking above at the terrain that almost goes into the clouds. I examine the rocky wall before me, I place my hand against it, and squeeze. The dirt is thick enough to climb without sinking. After I take my first step out of the water and onto the side of the cliff, I glance over my shoulder, and the water is far below, my breathing is heavy.

I place a hand over the top of the cliff and with all that's left of my strength, pull myself over and roll onto my back. I lay what felt like hours and days, but the sky had not change from dark to light, just gray, just rain, just me.

Alone. I lift my head and my heart begins to race. *Just like my dream.*

The vast red doors from my dreams, but a distance across the grass, housed within a large cream mansion of large stained glass windows, pillars and balconies, and atop the mansion is a church bell tower that begins to ring. The sound echoes across the sky. *I'm here.* I say to myself, catching my breath, trying to keep myself from fainting.

I look into the palms of my hands. My complexion returns and the mark is gone. I carefully run my tongue across my teeth and do not feel the monstrous overbite, instead, fatigue begins to take over my body, my vision begins to give.

The red doors open and a pale white figure steps out. I rub my eyes, hoping to clear the disorientation, but it only gets worse as my head begins to feel heavy. I plop onto my back facing the rain and soon, my head is lifted by cold hands and placed onto a lap.

"Evan?" says a voice in a whisper. I try my hardest again to focus on his face, but fail. I look around him, and there stands a group of pale people. One of them kneels before me, next to the man. A woman.

"It's him," she says.

"Yes. It is him, my dear, Valencia," says the man. "We have been waiting a long time for you, Evan. Please, do rest."

Failing to fight the exhaustion, I close my eyes, and the world becomes silent.

CHAPTER FIFTEEN: REUNION

I wake to a mural of angels and prophets covering the ceiling. Such displays of art only exist inside of chapels and sanctuaries. I try to remember what happened before I lost consciousness, but nothing rings a bell. The covers and pillows around me are red. The head board is made up of gold carvings of the sun, more angels, people with halos, and animals such as calves and sheep.

The red ocean sized bed in which I lay, sits above a polished, cream marble floor that reflects the ceiling. Long red curtains hang from the ceiling to the floor, paintings cover each wall, and large golden chandeliers hang above. To my left rests a piano in front of tall glass doors which expose an outside balcony. To my right is a desk, easel, violin, and a bin full of piled composition notebooks. There are large bushes on each side of the bedroom door. They are green and the room is fresh of mint.

I wish this was my room.

I rise to my feet and find my shoes bedside. I step into them and open the glass doors of the balcony. Rain continues to fall, wind continues to blow, and water continues to crash at the bottom of the cliff. Visions of the forest flash before me. The running, the leaping into the water, climbing the cliff, and being found by a group of strangers. I turn back to face the glass doors with a fear settling within my skin.

Oh no. Did I really come here?

I walk back into the mansion, open the bedroom door, and place my back against the wall. Music fills my ears and confusion plagues my mind. *This is the same tune that was playing in my dream. And these walls. Cream with a red border along the bottoms. Red carpeting.*

I follow the music, rounding every corner I reach. And soon, another, vision flashes before me. *Wait.* I stop and watch as Beebee runs down the hall. Her giggles echo against the walls. She turns the corner and disappears. *This is it. This is like my dream.* I round the next corner and stop. A cold air escapes the room, I hug my arms and walk in. I remember this. This is the room. The one where Beebee was...

I look up, and there sits the same chandelier. I walk over to the balcony, and open the glass doors. I step out and to the ledge and run my hands across the cement where I was pushed. *Is this really happening? Or is this just another nightmare?*

I jog back inside and down the hallways in which I came, passing the room I awakened. When I reach the end of the hallway, there is a golden railed staircase, a fountain of cherubs on the level below standing beneath a golden chandelier, red carpeting, murals along the walls, and those vast red doors from my nightmare.

The music is much louder now. Closer. Then, voices. I look to the other end of this second floor and a chill runs down my spine. From what I last remember, that's where they were. All of them. The vampires. My legs disobey, something they have grown quite fond of doing. I peek my head around the corner and wish I had not been so curious.

He *is* real. He's pale, has glowing red eyes, and a monstrous overbite. He stands at the head of the table, but I wouldn't dare see to whom he speaks. He looks over at me, my heart flatlines, but I can feel my legs beneath me, about to run for the doors.

According to my nightmares, this doesn't end well for me.

~

"Evan?" he says. I turn away and sprint for the staircase.

"Evan!" he yells after me.

I skip steps down the golden rail staircase, practically falling, and throw myself through the red doors. The sky is gray, and the wind whispers lightly. I look around for a path to run, but fail to find an escape. *Why did I come here? Why did I have to be so curious? What possibly was I expecting to find?*

I run to the edge of the cliff. If I take a leap, maybe I'll survive. Maybe. The water and rock far are far below…my stomach clenches and balls into a knot.

"Please," I hear a voice call through the wind.

I turn to face the man from my dream. He stands taller than myself in his black tuxedo.

"Who are you?! You tell me!" I yell.

He raises his hands as he steps forward.

"I'm--"

"Don't come any closer just stay away from me!" I command. He nods and keeps his distance.

The red doors open behind him. A pale woman steps out, dressed in all black, with a hat on her head. Her hair is short and barely touches her collarbones. The man looks over his shoulder and holds out his hand for her to come. She walks across the grass under the rain and wind, her eyes staying attached to mine until she joins the man at the hip.

"Valencia," says the man in the tuxedo.

"Shhh," she says holding a hand up to him, keeping her eyes on me. She steps away from him and closer to me. She brings her hands up to my cheeks, but doesn't touch. I refrain from moving. Her eyes are beautiful, soft, and familiar.

"You came back," she says.

"Who are you? What is this place?" I ask.

The man nods.

"Evan, I-."

"How do you know my name?" I ask.

He looks at Valencia then turns back to me.

"We gave it to you."

"I am Kaius Macrae," he says placing his hand on his chest. "This is Valencia, my wife." He rests his hands on her shoulders and she smiles.

"I've missed you, Evan."

I shake my head.

"Wait," I say. I begin to shiver. "What did you just say your name was?"

They stare at me.

"Answer me, please."

"Kaius."

"Kaius?"

"Yes, Kaius Macrae."

I shake my head.

"No, that doesn't make any sense, um."

I shake my head again and turn away.

"Kaius Macrae is my father."

"Yes," he responds. "I am."

I turn back to face him and stare deep into his red eyes.

"I don't believe you."

He outstretches his hand.

"It is the truth."

"My mother is--"

"Sarah Foster?" He asks.

"Yes," I nod.

"What about her?" He asks, motioning his hands to Valencia.

"What about her?"

"You don't see anything, Evan?"

I look at Valencia and she looks into my eyes. My hair stands, and I must admit, *there is something oddly familiar about her.*

"What do you mean you named me?" I ask.

They stand quiet and then look at each other. Kaius looks down at his feet and exhales before bringing his eyes back up to mine.

"You're our son, Evan. I am your father. Valencia is your mother."

I shake my head with disbelief.

"No, I am not. You are my father's imposter and my mother is--"

The red doors open again. We turn to face the stranger that had chased me in the forest and in my nightmares. I take a couple steps forward pointing a firm finger at him.

"And you stay away from me!"

"Evan, I mean no harm to you," he says raising his hands unarmed. "If anything we have been waiting for you. Watching you."

A vision flashes before me: falling from the tree, breaking my wrist, the stranger popping it back into place and saying, 'we're watching you.'

Goosebumps populate my skin. I take a step back.

"Be quiet." I tell them.

"But it is the truth," the stranger says.

"Believe us, son," Valencia says.

"BE QUIET!"

"Son," Kaius says taking a step towards me. I take step back.

"You're fine where you stand," I tell him. "And my name is Evan."

"Yes."

I gulp and take a deep breath.

"Tell me what's happening to me."

"You don't remember anything?"

"Valencia," Kaius says to her. "For him, it has been quite a while, and he was very young."

"I know, but I just thought he'd remember something, I just --- I don't know," she shrugs.

They continue to speak amongst themselves. My patience is thin.

"HEY! I'm standing right here!"

A pain hits my forehead. Another vision. *She holds me under my arms. I'm young. A small child. She kisses my* cheeks as she swings me in circles, laughing and smiling. It's Valencia. It's her.

"No! I don't know you!" I say. "You're not my mother."

The stranger begins to walk closer and I take a step back. He slows his pace when my eyes leech onto him.

"Evan. My name is Abel. We're not going to hurt you. Just give us a chance to explain everything."

"How can I be so sure about any of you? You chased me--attacked me!"

"I didn't attack you, Evan. I would never hurt you," he says.

"Evan," Kaius interrupts. "What you are going through is quite extraordinary, but we can help you."

"You don't even know me? What possibly could you know about me?" I ask pacing back and forth.

He looks at Valencia, and then at Abel before returning to me.

"Everything."

The doors open again. *What? What are they doing here?!*

Bianca and Cedric step out from the mansion and stand at the entrance. She smiles and Cedric props himself against the door crossing his arms in front of his chest. *What are they doing here?*

"Bianca," I say.

"Evan... Brother," she says.

My eyes race for answers.

"Can you--tell me who you are again?" I ask Kaius, keeping my eyes on Bianca.

"We're your family, Evan. Your real family."

A part of me--a huge part of me--believes him. Another part of me, is in denial. I fight my tears, and sniffle. I then begin to shake my head.

"I am your father," he continues. "Valencia, your mother. Abel, uncle. Cedric, your cousin. Bianca, your sister."

"I-- don't believe you. How is that possible? I live with my mother who--"

The doors open again and I shatter into fragments. I take a step back and fall to the ground.

"Mother?....Mike...?"

"Everything will be okay, Evan," she says. "Listen to your father--and your mother."

CHAPTER SIXTEEN: THE TRUTH

Mike doesn't budge nor speak, but something is different about him. His skin, pale. His eyes, blood red. His mouth, fangs. His entire person--.

Dead.

He joins Bianca's side. Cedric scoffs and keeps his eye locked onto me through his hair -- the same way he always does. I look amongst them all. Now is the time that I wake up in my bed. My mother is downstairs in her work clothes making breakfast, and sure enough, I may be late for school.

"Evan, listen to me," Kaius says as steps forward. I want to back away, but the edge is behind me. He places his cold hands onto my shoulders, "Your dreams are not dreams. They are your memories of your childhood trying to show you who you really are. Your step-mother, Sarah, has told me all about them. About the ones you see. About the little girl, Beebee or should I say, Bianca, your sister. And the boy, Cedric. Your cousin. Those dreams or, nightmares, are colliding with each other mixing memory with fear, showing you who you are and where you belong."

"But I still don't know who I am I - I've always felt—different from everyone else," I tell them. My eyes continue to search for answers, yet they have already provided them. *Why have I yet to accept this? Is it denial?*

"And that's why we are here," he assures. "We've been watching you for quite some time, Evan."

And there I was, back in the forest, face to face with Abel. 'We're watching you,' he had told me. Then back at school, seeing Bianca, smiling and waving to me on occasion. Wanting to speak, but didn't. Then Cedric. Bumping into me and watching me in the hallway. 'Watch your back, Evan, nobody's going to do it for you' he once told me.

"At school," he continues. "Outside of school, and even the place you call home. We've been watching."

I look over at my stepmother, then return my attention to Kaius.

"We never forgot about you," he says. "We wanted to wait until it was the right time."

"But I still don't understand. If this is all true, why did you send me away in the first place?" I ask. My eyes begin to tear. "Didn't you want me? Hmm? Was there something wrong with me? Did I do something to you? Was I not good enough?"

"No, no, no," Kaius says. "Not at all, Evan."

"It wasn't like any of that?" Valencia adds.

"Then what was it?" I ask as my heart pounds against my chest. "What was so – unfit for you that you couldn't take care of me yourselves? Lying to me all this time?"

"She hasn't told you, has she Evan? She hasn't told you what you *really* are?" Bianca says.

"What is she talking about?" Fearing I already know the answer. Maybe to hear it out loud would give the confirmation I need.

"You are not what you think you are," Kaius says.

I flinch. *He said, "what" and not, "who."*

"*What* am I?"

"You are like us, excluding Sarah," he responds. "You are not human."

209

I press my eyes shut and take a deep breath.

"You are a vampire. A late-bloomer."

I trail my eyes away to the edge of the cliff. *Vampire. Why is there a part of me that believes such a thing? Because I don't know myself?* Drops of rain begins to fall. I look up to the sky and shake my head.

"There's no such thing."

"There is too such a thing otherwise we would not be standing before you," he says.

"Well if there is such a thing, I was never bitten. I don't drink bl--"

"That's because you don't have to be. You were birthed, yes, a natural birth, but not by a human. Rather, a vampire," he says holding his arm out to Valencia.

"How can I be birthed by something that is dead? Something that doesn't have a heartbeat?"

"A beating heart is just a reminder that you are among the living. And here --" Kaius holds his arm out to Valencia. "-- your real mother stands before you. Without a beating heart, yet she can love and loves you. Is that not enough to convince you, Evan?"

"I just--don't see how that is possible," I respond.

Kaius shrugs. "Nature and evolution does not discriminate. Not even for our kind apparently."

He steps forward, closer to me.

"You still possess the essence of your human soul, which hides what you truly are. A vampire. It's like – a mask. It is what kept us protected all these centuries. This skin. It's just a mimic of what society accepts without fear, without doubt or confusion. Their eyes see human, but we are beasts. For our species, for those who have a natural birth by a vampire, the change is like -- what puberty is to humans. But normally, it comes much, much sooner. For you Evan, your transformation hid. Became so comfortable with your human body that it coiled itself around your human soul, but in exchange, it is killing it, and killing you. Slowly, but surely, you will turn into what you are destined to become and what your body is trying to tell you what you are-- A vampire."

I bring my hands to my head and close my eyes to shelter my sanity.

211

"Believe them," I hear my step-mother say. She steps forward. "Remember the accident, Evan?" She asks.

"Yes," I respond. "How could I forget?"

"There are some—discrepancies with that story."

"What kind of discrepancies?"

"I was driving along the road. The snow was thick, and no matter how slow I drove, it was difficult to see. I hit a patch of black ice, drove through the guardrail, and rolled down the hill towards the Mohawk River. When I woke, the van was upside down and I was trapped in my seat belt, gasoline was spilling and sparking around me. That night, Kaius and Valencia found me. They were hunting and smelled all the blood. Not mine, but the blood packets that had burst open. I was trying to free myself from the seatbelt, and that's when I see them, standing in front of the van, in the snow, watching me. I knew something was different about them because of their eyes. No one's eyes glows like that. Kaius came to my door, and Valencia ripped the windshield from the frame. She reaches in and pulled my seat belt out of its spring. Just ripped it, like it was tissue. I wanted to be scared, but I wasn't. That was when Kaius ripped the door and tossed it into the river. He pulled me out and they took me away from van, just before it went up into flames. They saved my life--"

"Since then, I felt I owed them. At first, it was difficult for them to stand too close. They were out to feed after all. I found a way to show them my appreciation. Instead of them having to run out and hunt, I would bring them a bin of blood packets to feed their family, and that's when they told me about you - "the late bloomer." The young vampire who has yet become a vampire. I took you into my home since they felt it was only right for a human to raise a human. Something they were unsure of how to do or at least, forgot over the centuries. Eventually, they made it their practice not to feed. I feed them, tell them about you, then I come home."

Everyone stands silent and watch me.

"I - can't believe this is real."

"Don't be afraid," Valencia, my real mother says.

"Evan, you're changing and it shall continue," Kaius says. "Look at your hands."

I look at the back of my palms. They are pale again. My fingernails are sharp to a point. My jaw aches. I run my tongue across my top row of teeth and feel two fangs that are a bit larger than the other hundreds in my mouth.

"I can only imagine how much of your strength has increased. Emotions as well? Perhaps. Anger?" he asks.

The bully struggles to breath within my grip. His face losing oxygen and life. I remember how strange and addictive it felt. It should not have been to my liking, yet it was.

"And your appetite," Kaius continues. "Soon that shall take a bit of a curve as well."

I remain silent touching my teeth with my fingertips. Bianca and Mike show a smile, but Cedric remains as still as a statue. Sarah watches with a tint of betrayal on her face and Abel stands content.

"Some time soon, you will die, and when you do, you will be reborn, your transformation, complete."

Kaius lifts his hand and everyone else, except Cedric and Sarah, does the same. They show the mark that I had seen on Abel's before and the one I painted on my easel back in school. I look down at my hand and below my thumb's knuckle is the same mark.

"You see, Evan?" says Kaius. "Your mark."

He takes my right hand into his.

"--The 'M' stands for our clan; The Macrae Clan. And the symbol represents who we are…Who you are. You are Passionate. You are Loving. You are Merciful. You are Evan Macrae, *my son*, of the Macrae Clan."

He lets go and I run my thumb across the mark. I drop to my knees. My lips began to form the words I thought would never escape.

"I believe you…"

Relief leaves their lips as Kaius and Valencia wrap their arms around me. I then picture Cedric's mark. *If he is family, why is his mark different?*

"And Cedric's?" I ask.

Cedric rolls his eyes.

"Cedric is of the Verin Clan," my father says. "When his father, my brother, the Dracula perished--"

"Don't speak of him," Cedric commands as he takes a step forward.

Kaius looks over to Cedric who then relaxes back against the red doors.

"When my brother," Kaius continues, "Your grandfather, *disappeared,* as Cedric would like to believe, we took Cedric into our home. I became the Dracula, by default. Cedric not ready for such a burden."

Cedric scoffs.

"I feel his pain," I say.

"Finally someone relates to me. My father would still be here if you--"

"Enough. Now is not the time, Cedric." Kaius tells him. He turns back to me.

"I'm so sorry, son" he says. "We had to send you away. Hoping you would one day return on your own. It would have been dangerous keeping you. I've tried so hard to bring it out of you, but nothing worked. You were still -- human. Sarah has been a great friend to our family. She practically feeds us all here allowing us to eat without having to leech around anymore. You are the first to live this long with a human soul. It gave us a new outlook on your--- their, species. So we curved our thirst for your sake, in which Sarah provides by her work. Everything was convenient, Evan. We sent you to live with her, to raise you, being able to provide for your human needs. But as I have said, we have always been here, Evan. Watching you. Waiting for you to come back to us--and you have."

"I just -- can't believe how all of this happened."

"Well, believe it," Cedric replies. "Live with it. Hopefully now you can watch yourself."

"Cedric," Bianca nudges him.

"No, I'm tired of watching some human, as though I'm his baby-sitter. For years, everything. All of this. For him. What about my father? He is the Dracula. How dare you all to believe he is dead."

"Cedric," Kaius says. "I watched your father—"

"My father what?" Cedric says as his eyes become as fierce as his anger. "Die?"

Kaius doesn't finish. Cedric nods his head.

"And what about my brother and sister, Mathis and Agatha? Where are they? Oh! That's right! No one seems to care!"

"Cedric, that's enough," Kaius tells him.

"He's nothing but filth," he continues, taking a few steps forward. "A weak...Tender...Puny...Meat-sack."

"At least I have a friend. Can't say much for you."

Red bleeds around his pupils and his mouth rises above his fangs with a hiss. I flinch and regret antagonizing him.

"Cedric!" Abel yells.

Cedric lowers his body and places a hand on the ground. He lunges towards me with one arm dragging behind him. With a swing of his hand, it connects with my face. I plow to the ground and catch myself before falling from the cliff. My blood boils and a hiss leaves my throat. Everyone takes a step back and awaits my next move, but the look on their faces immediately brings tears to mine.

"I didn't ask for this," I say shaking my head. "Any of this."

I turn to the Mohawk River Valley.

"Evan wait!" Kaius calls out to me.

I jump off the cliff and plummet to the water. When I break through its surface, I stay under and begin to swim as hard and as fast as I can. *I have to get away from here.* There's only one place I can go. My tree.

CHAPTER SEVENTEEN: EVANESCENCE

I drag my body across the sand panting and paining one breath after another. The rain pouring over me is soothing, but not enough to sloth away the betrayal and deception I received. *Why not tell me sooner? Before it was this late? I always, ALWAYS, questioned who I am and where do I come from! Always have! Now look at me!*

I let go of my weight and allow my body to fall onto the damp sand. The ocean of forest green trees are waiting for me as the wind whispers between their bodies. The pine and mint smell mixes with the rain and wet bark. I look to the Mohawk River in which I swam. With each rumble of thunder and flash of lighting, I crawl away and closer to the grass of the rainforest. Warmth filled my eyes which only confirmed that it is not the rain, rather, my tears. I place my hand against my chest. No heartbeat. Nothing. My arms shake as I hold my weight in a crawl.

"I'm a monster," I sob. *"I'm a monster. That's what I am. That's who I am. I can't do this."*

Evanescence

I run into the rainforest, the trees whipping past me in a blur. I step onto a fallen brown giant, leap into the air, then leaping out from the treetops, and have a scenic view of Utica. When gravity returns, I descend into the rainforest, step onto a trunk, and take a leap to the next tree. Then to the next. And then, another.

My tears of sadness become tears of anger. My hands clench into fists as I begin to move faster and jump higher. When I reach another tree, it cracks when I kick off. I then sit beneath the stationed umbrella and hold my head with my hands, listening as the rain falls and my head voice cry.

~

I don't want to always have this urge to kill someone. There are people that I love that are human. I would never want to hurt them. I can't do it! I don't want to live in the shadows having to hide what I am. I want to be me! Not the vampire me, but the human me!

And Mike. *He's one of them too! How could he do this? How could he not tell me?* And Bianca. *Bianca is my sister, Beebee, and Cedric, my cousin.* And my mother -- my step-mother. *How could Sarah keep this from me for so long?* This human life, slipping between my fingertips. *How could she do this to me?!*

I elbow the tree and it splits. I gasp, then run my fingers across the torn bark of my tree. Now it's hurt because of me. I *feel* human. It's all I know. My eyes lay upon the mark on my hand. *But I'm not human.*

I'm not human. I have a soul, but it's dying. The essence of my life is fading away, my body changing into this beast that has leeched itself to my soul. What's my life going to be like now? Will I be living with them? In a mansion? Drinking blood?

BLOOD.

No. I can't do it and I won't do it. My mouth begins to water. Yet, the thought of it, of blood, isn't quite as disturbing as I want it to be. I lick my lips and my jaw trembles. I slouch my arms over my knees and rest my head onto my forearms. I hold my eyes shut and listen to the thunder and rain. So much has happened these past few weeks, and now, in finally finding out who I am, I have been told two things: *I am a vampire and I have to die.*

Feet squishes into the mud from a distance. I listen and the sound is near. That scent. Very familiar and addicting. I turn my body away to hide.

"Evan!" Essence calls out for me.

I look around the tree's bark and her eyes lay upon me.

"Evan," she calls again, but softer.

I sit in the shadow without responding.

"Could you come down from there?" She asks holding a hand above her eyebrows to block the rain.

"...No," I respond.

"Why not?"

"Because if I'd--you'll never want to see or speak to me again. You'll be afraid of me."

"That will never happen. I can never be afraid of you I -- I actually feel something for you. I like you."

My heart beats, almost literally.

"You shouldn't. I'm not -- what you think I am?"

"Then, who are you?" She asks.

I shake my head.

"Not *who*. *What*."

She stands silent in the rain.

"Then why don't you come down from there and we can talk about it? Please?"

If I come down from here, that will be the end of me. If I stay up here, maybe she will just run off and be upset with me. Maybe that will only be temporary.

"Evan, please," she says again.

I wish she'd stop saying that. I adjust my sitting position and my body loses strength and balance. I slip out of the tree.

"Evan careful!" Essence calls.

I fall facedown onto the ground. No physical damage done or pain inflicted. But my spirit...My spirit is crushed. Essence grabs hold of my arm to help, but I withdraw my arm, and hold out my hand to keep her away.

"No. Stay there."

I kneel on the soft grass and sit on my heels. I keep my eyes and mouth shut.

"Evan?"

Essence takes a step towards me. "What's wrong?"

Everything.

"Evan talk to me."

Essence tries to look into my face, but I withdraw.

I smell her blood and hear her heart race, yet she continues taking steps towards me.

"I'm not -- human."

I slouch my head. She pulls me into her lap and I wrap my arms around the backs of her thighs, hugging her. She runs her hands through my hair. I exhale deeply.

"What do you mean you're not human, Evan?"

"You won't believe me if I told you. You won't believe your eyes," I murmur.

"I'd believe anything you show and tell me. I will never judge you."

I fight to not look up. I am unsure of how she would react seeing for herself. Her hands began to caress atop and behind my head, then down to my cheeks. She begins lift my face up to her. I resist, at first, but then give into her alluring, addictive scent, and touch. I close my mouth and kept my eyes shut.

"Evan."

I could never resist her voice saying my name. I slightly release my jaw exposing the monstrous overbite. I open my eyes and allow her to see the red embedded into my pale face. Essence takes a step back gasping and cupping her hands to her mouth. Her scent becomes stronger. *Fear. She is afraid of me as I expected.* Petrified rather. I hear her heart race and can smell the blood rushing through her veins. I fight to not think about a taste. *This is exactly what I would have to fight every day.*

"Evan," she says through her hands.

I gulp and drop my head back to the ground.

"I'm a vampire," I tell her trying to fight the anger building within.

"But vampires --"

I nod.

"Aren't real. Well, they are...I've been lied to. This whole time. My entire life just...One big lie."

"Evan I..."

My hands ball into fists.

*"A LIE! HOW COULD THEY DO THIS TO ME?!
HOW?! WHY!"*

Essence gasps and backs away, but then grabs hold
of my face with her hands and pulls me back into her lap.

"NO! STOP!" I grab hold of the sides of her thighs
with my hands, she winces, fights back to hug me, and when
her hold breaks, she grabs me again.

"ESSENCE! STOP! LET ME GO!" I yell at her trying
not to cry. She grabs my face and forces me to look up at
her. I bite down, pressing my two rows and teeth together,
trying to fight my anger. *It's—slipping.*

"Evan," she says softly.

I look into her eyes and submit. She looks at my
lips. I look at hers. She closes her eyes, presses her lips
against mine, and our lips press and fold against each other
with fragility and passion. I weaken beneath her as my body
begins to slouch, but she holds my face firmer than before,
and continues to kiss me, as my lips become weak, and we
breathe between each smack from our lips. I gulp, and can't
keep going, but she slowly, caressingly, continues. She

stops for a moment, kisses my bottom lip, places her forehead against mine, and doesn't let go of my face for even a second. I try to catch my breath.

"I'm here for you, Evan. I'm here for you."

My teeth no longer ache or feel like knives hanging from my gums. I look into my hands and my complexion returns. I fail to hold my weight up any longer against her lap and fall forward. She falls back into the mud, catches me, and wraps her arms and legs around me.

"I can hear your heart beating," I whisper.

She catches her breath as she runs her hand through my hair, beneath the falling sky of the forest.

"I can feel yours," she says. I squeeze my hand between us, and it's there. My heartbeat.

"Everything is going to be okay, Evan," she says. "Everything is going to be okay."

CHAPTER EIGHTEEN: LOST AND FOUND

I've never slept so well in both my human and vampire life. No nightmares. No tossing and turning in my sleep. No waking up in a pool of sweat. Just peace and quiet. There's no use denying *what* I am. I can only hope that with time, I can accept it. To be able to live my life. It's just a matter of what's expected of me. What's a vampire's daily life? What are their routines? What do they do to have fun?

"Good morning, Evan," mom says as I take a seat at the kitchen island.

"Good morning."

"I made you breakfast. A veggie wrap, orange juice, and toast."

"Thanks. Maybe blood would have been a better."

She exhales and her face hugs the floor.

"I'm just kidding."

She exhales relief placing a hand on her chest as she chuckles. It's short-lived.

"Evan, I can't explain how sorry I am for all of this."

I begin to fork at my plate hoping this conversation will end as quick as it begun. I can't say that I blame any of them. I did learn more about myself and my past but still, of anything in the world, I would have never guessed vampires exist let alone I be one.

"I'll be fine."

"Well, I know this is hard for you and I would never mean to hurt you. Please understand that we --"

"Did it for my protection and to be safe," I nod. "I know and really, it's okay. I'll be fine."

She tries to find a smile.

"Okay. I just want you to know that this doesn't change anything between us. I have and will always love you. You're still my son. Nothing will ever change that."

I would hope not.

"I know, Mom," I say.

"I don't want you to still feel obligated to call me that neither. If it makes you more comfortable, you can call me, Sarah. I'll understand."

I shake my head.

"No. I like calling you mom. I can't just be who I am because of this mark," I say looking down at my hand. "I believe a part of who I am has to be because of you also. And Mike."

She smiles and a tear forms in the corner of her eyes. She pulls me into her arms and hugs tight.

"I love you, son."

"I love you too, mom."

She lets go and I wish she hadn't.

"Oh, and Mom?"

"Yes sweetie?" She stops before leaving the kitchen.

"I have questions. I want to go back and speak with them more, but I just don't want to go alone."

"I'll go with you," she smiles.

"Can Essence come as well?"

"Essence?" she says walking back into the kitchen with a smirk.

I blush.

"The girl from school you've had that crush on?" she asks smiling.

I chuckle yet sink into the stool a bit.

"Ahhh, gotten closer I see?"

I nod and smile.

"We're close...and she knows."

"About --"

"Yup," I nod my head. "She knows what I am."

"And she accepts it?"

"Well, yeah," I say trying to believe it myself. "Yeah, she does."

"I like her already," she smiles and kisses my forehead.

"I'll let Kaius know to expect us."

"Okay. Thanks, Mom."

"You're welcome," she smiles and walks away. "Oh and Evan?" She calls coming back.

"Yes?"

"You're a *who*. Not a *what*. Okay?"

I laugh.

"Okay."

She rubs my cheek and heads upstairs. I text Essence about coming with us and smile at her acceptance. Apart from all the questions I have for my family, I most importantly need to talk to Mike. We have yet to have an actual conversation since his disappearance over a week ago. His family is worried about him and why hasn't my best friend stayed in touch? Guess, I can actually answer that last part myself. Even so, I want to hear how'd this happen with him. I was born this way – different. Mike was human all the way down to each cell in his body.

I sit in the back of the car watching the wet forest, houses, and small businesses, pass on by. My mother loves to drive while listening to my writing playlist of peaceful and relaxing music. It goes very well with the weather and can reduce stress.

"Just to let you know I have to leave out of town for a few days," she says.

I squint.

"Such a late notice I know," she continues, "but if I land this, well it will be good for us both. Would mean a better position within the business and more food for you and your family."

"Sounds good I guess," I say looking out the window.

"What's wrong, Evan?"

Drinking blood. Something you're all going to have to force down my throat.

"I just hope I don't go through this change while you are gone."

She sits quiet a moment.

"I hope not either. I'm sorry. I wouldn't, but your father insisted that I go while they help you prepare."

Kaius stepping in as a father figure already? Not use to that.

"Well, you did say it was for the family," I say. "Since it's for the best, I hope you do get the job."

"Thanks for understanding. Try not to change before I'm back. Wouldn't want you to forget who I am?"

"How could I forget who you are?" I chuckle.

She doesn't respond. Her eyes blink slowly in the rearview mirror as she eyes the road.

"So, your birthday is in a few weeks."

It is. Completely forgot.

"Yes."

"What would you like as a gift?"

My heart can stop beating at any moment so there's only one possible thing I want, but is not promised.

"To live."

"You'll be able to forever once you die."

"But when I wake I won't be human."

She nods slowly and exhales gently.

"Right. You won't be."

She looks at me in the rear view mirror. I turn my face away and look into the clouds above. Soon, we are parking in front of Essence's house. Giving her directions helped weed out our talking about my death.

"Don't forget to be a gentleman," she says as I take a step out of the vehicle.

"I know, mom."

As I walk up the front steps, Essence steps out of her house and smiles that perfect smile before hugging me. Her father stands in the doorway.

"Hello, Evan."

"Hi, Mr. LaRoux...I mean, Tom." I say with a smile.

"Here to steal my daughter again?" He says laughing.

"Just for a bit if you don't mind."

"With how she's been all prancy and smiley around the house, by all means have her."

"Would love to!" We laugh. I look over at Essence and she's as red as a beet. I smile inside. I caught her blushing.

My mother honks the horn and waves.

"Hello!" Mr. LaRoux call to her.

"Hello! We'll keep her safe!"

"Please do!" He calls back.

"You two have fun," he says.

"Thanks dad," Essence kisses his beard. He nods a farewell to me.

"Evan."

I nod back and chuckle.

"Mr. LaRoux."

He heads back into the house and closes the door.

"Hi, Essence. Thanks for coming. I couldn't do this without you."

"I told you, I'm here for you." She smiles and kisses my cheek before making her way to the car. I open her door and she hops in. I then get in from the other side and my mother reverses out of Essence's driveway.

"Nice to meet you, Essence," my mom says as we pull away from the house.

"Nice to meet you too, Ms. Foster."

"Evan was just telling me about you and please, just call me Sarah."

"Oh, was he?" she asks looking over at me and smiles.

I avert my eyes and look out the window shaking my head with a blush.

"Sure was."

"Is it supposed to rain again, today?" I ask.

"We're supposed to be having a storm coming in," my mom says. "Hope it doesn't get too bad out."

Mission accomplished. Subject changed.

"I hope not either. My father is supposed to go on a camping trip over in the Valley. I can try to convince him otherwise, but I doubt he'll listen."

"That's men for ya."

They laugh and I roll my eyes.

"So, how'd you two love birds get so acquainted?"

"Well," I say, "we're in the same painting class at school."

"Evan, rescued me from the rain."

"Oh, did he?" My mother smiles through the rearview mirror.

Gee, thanks, Essence.

"Sure did. He's been nothing, but a gentleman. I learned of how great of an artist he is. All of his work in painting class surpasses anything I've ever seen."

That's a bit far from truth, but I'll accept the compliment.

"I also learned he is a passionate writer."

My cheeks burn from smiling as I scratch the back of my head.

"He sure is," my mother looks at me in the rear-view mirror. "He writes every day."

"He's even shown me where he does his writing," Essence adds.

"Ah, the big ol' tree he used to always climb as a child."

I did?

"Yes," Essence responds to her. "I've read a bit from his notebook and --"

"Really?" My mom asks in disbelief. "I've wondered myself what is written in that notebook of his."

"Thoughts, dreams," Essence answers. "Like one big diary."

I wish Essence would stop snitching, yet, a part of me likes hearing how she feels about me.

"Is there anything in there about me?"

"Okay, let's not talk about that right now," I say and Essence begins to laugh.

"Anyway, Essence you do know why we are going up to the cliffs, right?"

Ugh. Let's not talk about that either.

"Yes," Essence nods. "Evan told me all about it yesterday. Well -- shown me really."

"You're not afraid are you?"

"Not as I would have expected to be. I mean -- he won't hurt me."

"Not intentionally."

239

WHOA. Stop right there. Too much information.

"We almost there?" I ask now sitting up and gripping the headrest of the passenger chair.

"Yup, almost there. Just up this trail."

We parked outside in the grass in front of the cream stained glass windowed mansion. Walking around to the back is impossible, and to see it, you would need a boat and even then, the cliff would be high above you.

"Sarah," my father bows standing in between the now open red doors with Valencia my mother.

"Always welcome," she says bowing her head a respectful gesture.

"Hello, Kaius. Valencia," Sarah responds with a smile.

"Is this...Essence, Evan?" my mother asks as they gaze at her.

"Yes, Essence LaRoux," I respond. "Essence this is my mother, Valencia, and my father, Kaius."

"Hello, Mr. and Mrs. Macrae," Essence smiles.

"She's beautiful," Valencia compliments.

"Undoubtedly," Kaius agrees.

"Thank you," Essence smiles. "It's nice to meet you."

"We're happy to have you join us this afternoon," my father says. "Please, do come in. Lunch is prepared."

I flinch. I hope they remembered that some of us here are human – or still human, a vegetarian at that. We follow them inside and the doors close behind us. The aroma that fills the air smells of freshly baked bread, butter, and something sweet.

"Smells amazing in here," Essence says.

"Yes, very," Sarah agrees.

"What is it?" I ask now wanting the surprise to be spoiled.

"Come and see. Everyone is in the dining room waiting," Kaius responds.

Everyone. I would have smiled, but my attention redirects to the questions I have. They lead us up the golden railed staircase. As everyone continues to walk to the dining room, my eyes lay upon a beautiful painting. It's the entire family and – myself? I had not noticed the last time I was here. I was too busy finding my way around and running.

"Evan?" my mother, Valencia, calls.

They stand in the doorway of the dining room waiting, but I continue to stare at the painting.

"Beautiful isn't it?" father says joining me.

"Yes," I reply. "Who painted it? I don't see a signature."

He stares at the painting and I find him smiling with no response. He looks at me and his head nudges forward slightly.

"I did," I say softly.

"You were always so talented, Evan. It was the last painting you made before--"

"I was sent away," I finish. He flinches and redirects his attention back to the painting nodding.

"Your anger is very much expected. I don't blame you, son."

"I'm not angry, just afraid."

"Shall we eat and talk about it?"

"Yes."

Without another word, we meet in the dining room where Abel, Bianca, Mike, and even Cedric, sit. The table is covered with a white sheet, and there's baked potatoes, mixed vegetables, biscuits, a huge bowl of minestrone soup, and chocolate cupcakes and cookies. For a species that drinks blood, they sure remember how to cook and bake human food.

"Hope this would suffice," Kaius says as he and Valencia take a seat at the table.

"Hello, Evan," Abel says as he stands to his feet. "And who might this be?" he asks turning to Essence.

"Essence, meet my uncle, Abel. You know as much about him as I do," I joke.

He chuckles and pats me a welcoming pat on the back.

"He most certainly gets his wit and humor from me I can tell you that much!" he boasts. "It's great to meet you, Essence. I hope you're hungry. I prepared majority of what you see," he says with a whisper.

"I'm starving actually," she chuckles.

"Same here," I agree

"Splendid! Dig right in!" he pats both of our shoulders and takes a seat.

"Wow, your family is very welcoming," she says.

"Just don't get too close. They bite," I chuckle and she joins.

"You really do have your uncle's wit.

"Evan!"

By the tone and loudness of such a voice, one name comes to mind. Mike. He and Bianca rise from their chairs and meet us in the doorway. Mike then gives a strong pat on my shoulder. I wince.

"Nice to see you buddy," he laughs.

"Yes, just remember I'm not as strong as you," I remind rubbing where he hit.

"Not yet at least," Bianca corrects smiling. "Anyways. Hi, brother."

Her hug is tight and strong. She must have forgotten that I'm not as strong as her either -- 'not yet at least.'

"Nice to see you too, Bianca," I struggle to get out after getting beat up by them both.

"Not surprised to finally see you next to Evan," Bianca says smiling at Essence.

"In the flesh," Essence, smiles. "And blood.

"Nice to see you," Bianca hugs her.

"It's great to see you and Ev together. No more of him drooling over you," Mike laughs.

I nudge his arm with an elbow. Essence giggles. I look over at Cedric who has not moved an inch since we arrived. His hands are clasped together, elbows on the table, and hair covering one of his dark eyes.

"Ahem!" Kaius grabs our attention, "The food's getting cold," he smiles.

We all take a seat and I reach for a piece of fruit.

"Uh, uh, uh, not so fast," mother says. "Prayer."

She holds out her hands. Kaius grabs hold and we do the same with one another.

"Vampires pray?" I ask.

"Yes," father answers. "Doesn't hurt."

I nod and hold a hand out to Cedric. He sits still with his hands in his lap.

"Cedric," mother says.

Cedric grabs hold of my hand with a cold, tight grip. It hurts, but I try to ignore it. I look over at him. He looks at me. A smile spreads across his lips behind his hair, then his face become serious and annoyed again.

"Go ahead dear," mother says to father. We close our eyes and bow our heads.

"Today, Lord, we give thanks for this wonderful meal we have prepared for our guests. May this food give the nutrients they need to stay strong and healthy. We say prayers over Essence and thank you for bringing her here. For Sarah. She has been such a great friend to this family, we couldn't ask for anyone better. And prayers for Evan,"

I flinch.

"--for guiding him home. Bringing him back to us. His family. Filling the gap that has been awaiting him. May his destiny rest in your hands and may we guide him selflessly. Amen."

"Amen," everyone says.

"After the three of you eat," father says, "we shall show Evan how to be vampire."

"Ah, yes! Can't wait for that, brother," Abel exclaims.

"You think you'll be able to handle it?"

I look up to Bianca after taking a bite of cantaloupe and see everyone awaiting a response. Essence slips her hand into mine. I look over and smile at her.

"I think he'll be able to manage. I believe in him."

I blush.

My father throws his arms to the ceiling.

"A woman with faith in a man! Splendid!"

"It's good to see that Evan has taken a great liking into you," mother says. "Sarah informed us of it."

I grimace at my step-mother.

"Throw me under the bus why don't you," Sarah jokes.

"That'd be too easy," mother responds laughing.

"Eventually, it will be for Evan too," Mike adds.

"Why yes, I'm rather thrilled to begin his training. As his father, I'll train him well."

Cedric readjusts himself in the chair and coughs, but it sounded fake. He looks over at me and smirks, then rolls his eyes.

"Now, before we get into greater detail about training," Abel says, "care to share a little about yourself, Essence?"

Essence clears her throat from chewing.

"Well...umm, my story is...um. I'm originally from Rochester, NY, but... "

"Ah, Flower City," Abel interrupts. "Home of the annual Lilac festivals."

"Let her finish, brother," father says.

"Well, I moved to Utica with my parents and haven't visit Rochester since. A vacation or two here and there, high school is a bit of a drag. I guess if what you're asking for is some excitement, being here and meeting all of you has been the most excitement I've had so far, I mean, I've had my fair share of heartbreaks."

She begins to toy at her bracelet. I grip her hand and she looks over at me and smiles. She holds my hand with both of hers.

"I use to live in Rochester," father adds. "Well, before then, it wasn't called Rochester. Nor a city actually. It was um, dirt."

"Not that much of a difference to what it is now," Cedric says. Essence flinches, and father looks at mother and shakes his head.

"And what is it that you like to do?" mother asks.

"I like to read, go hiking, biking, swimming, but I do LOVE to play the violin."

"Now that sounds marvelous," Abel says. "We'd like to see you play sometime. Evan's birthday is coming up in a few weeks. Why not then? Yes?"

"Great! I'd love to."

"Teach me," Bianca says.

"Of course."

"Maybe, I'd like to learn too," Mike adds.

Bianca exchanges a smirk.

"So, you can compete with me I'm assuming?"

"Always am," he laughs.

We finish our meals and push our plates away.

"How was it, son?" mother asks.

"It was very good. Thank you."

"So," father clasps his hands together. "Are you ready to learn more about being a vampire?"

"I'm ready," I nod sounding much more excited than anticipated.

Cedric rises from his chair and walks out of the dining room without a word.

"Why does he hate me so much?" I ask.

"Ohh, he doesn't hate you, Evan," mother assures. "He's just having a rough time -- misses his father."

"Part of the most reckless of all vampire clans if you ask me," Abel comments.

Father clears his throat and Abel listens.

"You see, Cedric's father, the Dracula at the time was destroyed in a war between vampire versus vampire. Of course, Cedric believes his father is still alive. Claims that he can still *feel* him breathing somewhere and claims to have had a dream that he's locked someplace dark. But the war raged, between the vampires and --"

"Over what?" Essence asks.

"The humans," mother answers.

"Humans? Why?" I ask.

"Ages ago," Kaius says, "Father Verin, well, my brother, Lucid, became very -- power hungry. I couldn't understand what more power could he possibly want over the vampires. To play God, perhaps? So, he spilled human blood maliciously bringing risk to the exposure of our kind believing only one species shall exist – vampire. Many clans joined together to overthrow him. Not exactly smart to wage war against the Dracula – your own species for that matter. Despite my difference and beliefs, I sided with him, not against him."

"You lost?" I ask.

"Yes. There had been many fatalities human and vampire alike. Full cities and civilizations destroyed over those many years. In the final war, over twenty years ago outside of Paris, we were outnumbered and there were massive amounts of betrayal. They took something delicate from Lucid. The source that separates his strength and power, as a Dracula, from any other vampire."

"What's that?" Essence asks.

"The Viscus Charm. A necklace worn by the Dracula containing a small vile of the ashes of Viscus Maudere, the first Dracula, or 'god' to some vampires."

"What does it do?" I ask.

"The charm works as an enforcer. It really has a mind of its own or more accurately, it carries the spirit of Viscus Maudere himself. He created this charm and vile, if he were to ever be destroyed, he will live forever in spirit amongst his kind. When it's time for a new vampire to rule as the Dracula, the charm would make its way. It would coil itself around the neck of the new, righteous owner, unlocking the true power of the vampire beast--a piece of Viscus becomes you."

"How'd they get it from Lucid?" I ask.

Mother places her hand into father's.

"While I was fighting amongst many, my brother Lucid, allowed his strength to become his weakness. He got lost in his madness, it made him careless. While he was fighting, they overwhelmed him. I tried my best to help, but the crowd was too thick. One mistake in turning his back, a vampire removed Lucid's head from his shoulders, thus the charm was freed."

"I'm so sorry," Essence apologizes.

Father nods.

"So we lost the war. The vampire ran off with the charm hoping to put it to better use. They tried to negotiate with him in the past, warning him of a revolt if he does not contain himself for the sake of our species. At the time, I knew they weren't wrong, but he was my brother. When they killed him, his wife, built a vengeance and disappeared for a few years. But when she returned, she laid waste to many vampires and became even more destructive than Lucid himself. She tried to locate the charm and was completely outnumbered. I then found her in the streets of Paris, dying. She had been attacked. It was then she told me of her son."

"Cedric," I answer.

"Yes," Kaius continues. "But not only that, she told me she had succeeded and reclaimed the charm. After telling them the charm had been destroyed, it devastated the vampire species. They vowed not to ever fight amongst their own kind for destroying a divine relic of Viscus – a representation of who we are and where we came from. We then took Cedric and our family away from Paris and came here to live a new life, but of course, the charm wasn't actually destroyed."

"Where is it?" Essence asks.

Father reaches into the neck of his collar. A diamond shaped necklace with a vile of ash is protected by golden swirls like thorns from a rose wrapping its body.

"Where it is safe. I knew that lying would make our kind see the error of our ways and selfishness. I knew it would create peace among us if it was believed to be destroyed. Before her last breath, Scarlet's spoken will was for me to have and protect it and to take care of Cedric, but I can never be the true Dracula apart from not having any people to govern besides our clan…family."

"Why is that?" I ask.

"The charm hasn't chosen anyone since Lucid's death. It hasn't glowed even faintly. Cedric believes by default, he should have the charm because it's technically, still his father's until it chooses, but he needs to understand that he must be chosen and the responsibility that comes with it. Besides, I'm afraid if Lucid were alive, or even where Cedric's mind is now, the charm would be misused. He curses me for the death of his father during war and not helping his mother thereafter, but had I known of her intentions, I would have been by her side. Instead, she wanted me to protect Cedric."

"That's not your fault I'm sure you tried your best," Essence says.

"Yes, but it was not enough," father shakes his head. "Please do understand, Cedric is a good kid. He's just been through a lot and has so much on his mind."

Everyone sits quiet.

"Sooo, uhh, great story, yeah?" Mike says trying to ease the mood. But I have more questions.

"Tell me about my childhood," I say.

"Mike, let's let them speak," Bianca says rising to her feet.

"You can stay if you'd like. I don't mind," I tell them.

"I'd rather not, Evan, sorry," Bianca says. "We'll see you in a bit."

She smiles, but it wasn't convincing at all. Mike shrugs and follows her out of the dining room.

"Your childhood, yes," father begins. "To begin, you've always took a great liking to art and nature--"

As I know.

"--you loved to climb trees, you'd climb practically as high as they would go with no fear of a fall. Sometimes, we'd have to go out and find you. You were fearless, Evan. You've always had those random outbursts of vampire, but never fully completed transformation at your early years unlike your sister and cousin."

"Do you remember the day I did that painting? I don't remember it at all," I say.

"Not too long before you were sent to live with Sarah. You were starting to feel and act out of place. You'd shut down, but I blame myself for your hard days."

"What do you mean?" I ask. Father pauses and thinks to himself.

"Your father--we all--had tried our best to get you more acclimated with the family. You were still—human longer than expected. We did not understand at the time, but were aware of the dangers that can occur with having a human child live with vampires. We alone were a threat to your life..."

"What'd you try to do? What dangers?" I ask.

"We've tested your strength, speed -- and appetite," father says. "Each test failed. We didn't understand why you couldn't be vampire *all* the time."

"My appetite?" I ask. "What'd you do?"

"We...We tried to..."

"We tried to feed you blood, Evan," mother finishes for father.

"But you rejected each time," Kaius adds. "We figured, well maybe if he drank blood, it would force you to change. But you wouldn't even eat meat. And so, it came to pass that it'd be best you grew up someplace more suitable to your needs. We had done all we could for you, Evan. It was a danger keeping you here."

I can remember what Bianca had told me from my nightmares. *'But you have to eat or everyone will be sad again.' That dream. That was when I was sent away.*

"Evan, if it means anything," mother says, "we didn't want you to go. We loved you and only wanted what was best for you."

Essence rubs her hand across my back.

"I was blessed having you," Sarah says.

"What happens next? What am I to do? What's to come of this?"

"You are to do as you please," Abel says. "May I? Brother?" He asks.

Father nods his head. Abel brushes some of his long black hair back away from his face.

"If you wish to live here with us, you can. This has always been your home. And if you so wish to continue to live with Sarah, you may do so as well, but --"

Of course there's a 'but.'

"You will still become what you are destined to be – a vampire. And you will not be able to change that. It *will not* be easy, you *will* make mistakes, and you *will* lose yourself from time to time at least until your body and mind fully adjusts to the change."

"How will it happen?" I ask.

"It will hurt. It will be painful. You will die."

Father clears his throat.

"Details," Abel continues. "Your teeth will develop, giving you a teething sensation. They will be as sharp as a swords end, and they will mature, but with time, you'll learn to hide the bite."

"What else?"

"Your eyes will change. A blood red around the pupils, but soon, you will learn to hide their color as well. They develop as the teeth do -- and nails for that matter."

"And I will look dead?"

"Of course. Permanently. Your human soul is dying now as we speak. That's why you have those outbursts of anger, strength, speed, and agility. Think of the vampire gene as a caged animal. Your cage is cracked open, and you're fighting to get out from the tease of being free. Eventually, that cage will break, and you will be freed. The animal is your vampire. The cage is your human soul. That will be when your human soul dies. That will be when you die, and your heart will never beat again."

Everyone sits quiet.

"As I thought... I have to die."

That I knew.

"Yes," Abel confirms, "And not only that but you will also forget about--"

"That is enough, Abel," father interrupts.

"No tell me? Forget about what?" I ask.

Sarah exhales and turns away.

"It is not important right now," father says. "One step at a time."

Not important? I'm here for answers. I want all of my questions answered. The more I know what to expect, the better I can prepare.

"Leave your trust in us, Evan," father says. "When you change, we ask that you stay here a while, like Mike, so you won't be a danger to Sarah, your school, and most importantly, yourself."

"And we will be with you each step of the way, Evan," mother says. "Don't be afraid."

"You are not alone in this," Sarah adds.

I nod and understand much more about myself and my family than I had before. I believe it. It's just hard to grasp that I have to die and that it can happen at any moment. I rise from the table and feel the heaviness from their eyes watching me.

"Can I -- go for a walk?" I ask.

"Take as much time as you need, son," father says. "We'll be right here when you are ready to begin training."

I head for the hallway.

"And Evan?" mother calls after me.

I stop and turn to face her.

"Yes?"

She rises from her chair and meets me in the doorway before speaking quietly.

"There's someone you should really talk to who really took a beating when we sent you away."

"Who?"

Her lips press together.

Bianca.

CHAPTER NINETEEN: BIANCA

It is my destiny. To become a part of this unknown world that has always coexisted with my human life, but in shadows. I will be reborn after I die, only this time I will know who I am and I will know where I come from. Would that constitute as a loss or a gain? To live your life, not knowing who you are, or to die young, and find out sooner? Unfortunately, it wasn't my choice to make. It is the happening.

My mother, my real mother Valencia, insists that I speak to Bianca. But what do I say? I have always known something was troubling her. The way she looked at me or didn't look. She had been watching me. Trying to see if I had become what everyone has been waiting for, but apparently, she was the most anxious.

A few turns down the hallways have led me to that vast room with the piano stationed in the center, just as I dreamed before. Each step I take echoes on the marble floor. I examine the dusty black and white piano keys and position my hands above them. I begin to play a song by my favorite band, *Evanescence* called *My Immortal*. Before I reached the bridge of the song, a hand rests onto my shoulder.

"You play the piano with great sadness, Evan."

Bianca removes her grip and heads to the balcony of the room opening its glass doors. I follow and meet her next the ledge that overlooks the horizon -- the best view from the mansion I have yet to see. The openness, small ruffles of wind, soft waves smoothly shaping the sandbars, and marshmallow clouds above the Mohawk River Valley.

"You were always such a great artist and musician," she says. "Haven't lost an ounce of talent."

"I just create what I see and play what I feel."

She chuckles.

"I understand. You have many more gifts."

"I guess I wouldn't know. I'm just afraid of what's next," I say. "Whatever is expected of me."

"Don't be afraid. We're all here for you."

I couldn't help but picture my memory of leaving Beebee, Bianca, when I was younger.

"You mean just how I was there for you?" I say shaking my head.

"That wasn't your fault, Evan. I had missed you, but I was strictly told to only watch you."

"And not speak to me," I add.

"No," she corrects. "That was my choice. I knew if I spoke to you, I probably would have scared you away."

"You wouldn't have."

"Oh, I would have. Off impulse. I'm pretty sure I'd come to you saying I'm your sister, Cedric is your cousin, and that you will die and become a vampire."

Okay. She's right. I would not have believed her and would have thought she was insane. Then, I'd tell Mike he should probably consider a new potential girlfriend.

"Yeah, guess you're right."

"I told myself to be patient. To wait for the day, you would change. Or come looking for us. Or simply remember me."

"But I didn't."

"Yes," she looks at me. "You did. It took a while but you did and everyday, I struggled not to talk to you. I wanted you to remember us. To remember me."

"I'm sorry, Bianca."

"Our parents told me and Cedric to be careful not to expose who we were and not to speak of our kind or family to you because they knew it would be best you learn on your own."

Her face blushes with sadness.

"When we were younger, do you remember how close we were?"

"Yes," I say. "I do now."

"We would always play together, and chase each other up and down the stairs, and I would even sometimes hide from you until you'd find me."

"Now that I definitely remember," I smirk.

She finds a smile and chuckles a bit. It fades.

"Since you've been gone, I've done nothing but long for you to come home and be with us again. Sometimes more than our parents. I guess you can say."

"And why's that?"

It takes her a moment to respond.

"We were born a pair, Evan."

"A pair? What, like twins?"

"Yes, yet we do not physically resemble what stands for being "twins" by human definition. We share a special bond and are most susceptible to mortal partnerships because twins are of the human nature, not vampire. Making it easier for vampires like us to have a natural liking and attraction to humans."

"I see."

"Other vampires see us as abominations. Being able to mix our genes with humans has a much greater chance than those who are lucky, like our mother who is child bearing. They are envious of child bearers and birthed vampires because we still and will always have a small piece of what others lose at an early age and will never have again."

"And what's that?"

"A soul."

I look out to the ocean and nod.

"So, are you saying this is why I love Essence? Just because I am birthed and because I -- we -- are a pair?"

"No. Maybe that first attraction for her, yes, but love? No. Love has no rules nor discriminates. You love Essence, because you love, Essence."

That's good to know.

"As our father said, over the centuries, vampires have evolved. Some women have that child-bearing blessing. Most do not, so they bite their way into creating members of their own family. So, few are naturally born, but very few are born as pairs -- like us. Being naturally birthed is as close as it gets to having a soul and reaping the benefits of both human and vampire. Those who are born naturally have the gift of offspring. We start off as human, eventually dying rather young, and become vampires -- 'with a soul' as some would say."

"But I didn't."

"Correct. You didn't which is a first, but you are getting closer to becoming one fully."

Soon I will be like everyone else.

"Our parents believe the fragility of our bond is because of our pairing."

"I'm assuming our bond would be much closer right now if I had not forgotten everything."

"Perhaps. Pairs have a strong mental connection. When your changes began, I was first to know. That's when Uncle Abel came to you. To see for himself, hoping my judgment was factual. I knew it was happening. I felt it."

"Really?"

"Yes," she responds, "But your body is pushing hard for you to change. Either way, you're still my brother and you're not alone in this. I'm always here for you."

"Because we are a pair, huh?"

"No," she responds. "Because I actually care about you."

She smiles and we hug. She exhales deeply.

"Mike is fine."

I chuckle.

"The last time I heard that I had no clue where he was."

"If you climb up you'll find him on the bell," she says.

"Climb?"

She looks up and my eyes follows hers. A pale figure sits on the lip of the large, copper bell.

"You can do it. That's how you got up here to the mansion before. Just have to tap into it. It's already in you, Evan."

I stare at the cream stoned wall and look up to the bell again.

"I don't know how."

"Just try," she says. "Give it an honest go."

I brush my palms against my pants and take a deep breath. I approach the wall and grip on a few rocks while stepping onto a couple others. I struggle to reach for another rock above me, but stand on the tips of my toes and grab hold of it. With all of my strength, I pull my weight off of the rocks beneath my feet and catch another rock with my other hand only to find my feet dangle. I am stuck.

"Uh, I don't think this is right," I tell Bianca helplessly.

She laughs.

"Come down, Evan."

I let go of the rocks and catch myself on the ground. I turn to her dusting off my palms.

"Okay, face the wall."

"Are you sure this --"

"Face the wall, Evan."

I exhale and listen. She chuckles.

"Okay, now close your eyes."

I obey and listen to her voice. I remember when Essence had told me to close my eyes in painting class. She had me focus on what I was feeling most and it became my guide. It felt like an adrenaline rush, but soon turned into much more than that.

"Now, dig deep into your deepest emotion and grab hold of it."

Fear.

"When you are ready, I want you to place your hands on the rocks and climb."

Okay. What am I afraid of? I have a list. Losing Essence. Losing her love. The future. Above all, becoming a vampire. Ah, and, myself. Me. That is what I am afraid of. I am afraid of myself. I am afraid of being a monster, unable to control myself. A terror in the dark. A beast that feeds on blood. So that alone is my biggest fear, myself.

I open my eyes and gripped in my hands are rock. Beneath my feet, rock as well. The air around me feels different. Much windier. The water crashing against rock sounds much further away, rather, below. I look to my left and there are clouds. I look below myself and can barely see Bianca. I look above, and the lip of the bell is just a few feet away. *I climbed?*

I grab hold of the lip with one hand and pulled myself up. I crawl to the top, a flat surface on the bell, and there he stands.

"Evan," he says.

"...Mike."

R.J. Rogue

CHAPTER TWENTY: MIKE

We stand atop the bell tower and keep our distances. Mike's appearance bothers me, but the secrecy he held with my recently discovered family bothers me much more. His eyes are soft, but dark. His skin a frost white beneath the black jacket he wears. His nails are sharp, and his overbite is hidden.

"You look dead," I say.

"Yeah. That's kind of what happens given the circumstances," he laughs half-heartedly.

"You know your family is looking for you. Worried about you..."

Obviously right?

"...why would you do this to them? To yourself?" I ask.

"It's complicated."

"Do explain." I shrug and place my hands into my pockets.

He studies me for a bit before walking to the curve of bell. He slides to a sit on the lip of the bell which overlooks Utica and the green Mohawk River Valley. I slide to a sit next to him and look amongst the clouds and light that stretch across the sky, above the water.

"You know," he says. "I haven't quite been in contact with my parents besides their last visit which was almost a year ago."

"Why not?"

"They want me to move in with them. We'd argue about it on the phone, but I'd always tell them no."

"I wouldn't be surprised if your parents are on a plane now, coming here."

"I've spoken to them."

"You have?" I ask.

"I told them I needed time to myself and that I'll be back soon. My mother and father said they'd come up. I convinced them it'd be best if they didn't."

"And they listened?"

"Not so easily, but yes."

I shrug.

"So, what's the real reason you left? I mean, you allowed us all to worry about you, but you were fine."

He scoffs.

"Mike, your grandmother cares about you. Why would you so suddenly decide to do something like this. Make them, *us,* worry?"

"And what, you think that was easy? That simple? My family has given me such a hard time these past few months I felt alone and wanted to be alone."

"So, that's what you based your decision on, Mike?"

"No."

"Then what was it?"

He sits quiet and stares at the horizon. I try to exhale the tension that builds in my head. It doesn't work.

"The last I heard, my parents want to move across seas. My grandmother wants to go. I don't want to."

"But why not? You'll be together," I say. "You can start fresh and get to know your parents much more. I thought you wanted that above anything?"

"I know. I can still see them this way as well but it's not just the moving as to why I decided to do this to myself."

"What is it?"

"Fear..."

"Fear of what?"

"Death."

"Death? Mike. Death? Are you serious right now? Something that you can't run from? You're human. It's inevitable."

"Well, at least not anymore that is," he reminds.

"So, that's it? You don't want to move and be with your family and you're afraid to age and die just as any human should."

"I'M NOT HUMAN!"

I shake my head.

"You're an insult to yourself," I tell him.

"If you see it that way then so be it. I like it here. I love Utica and I feel like I belong here. It's home and no place replaces home."

I can relate to that to an extent.

276

"You belong with your family."

"Then, why do you keep rejecting yours?" He points.

"I don't," I say.

"Not anymore at least," he adds. "I will still be able to see mine anytime, Evan, and probably more now."

"So, why haven't you seen your grandmother?"

"My thirst is still too great. So I'm here working on it with Bianca's help. Sarah's as well obviously."

"You seem to be doing just fine around me."

"That's because you're one of us."

"--not yet," I correct.

"You smell like it to me..."

I shake my head.

"I can see my grandmother tomorrow hopefully," he says. "And stay with her until she leaves in a few weeks."

"And then what?"

"I'll just tell her I'm staying here."

"Oh good luck with that Mike."

"It'd be difficult for them to even notice a change in my age."

"In other words you get to watch them all age and die."

He frowns and turns to me.

"Now that's just heartless," he says.

"Yours isn't beating anymore remember?"

He scoffs.

"And you'll experience the same with your stepmother, Sarah, and Essence for that matter."

I flinch. *Touché'*.

"At least in their eyes, I'm not some vampire watching them all age and die as you say. I'm still their son and grandson."

He rises to his feet.

"Mike wait," I say getting up. "I'm sorry."

He looks over his shoulder at me.

"I didn't mean it like that."

I really didn't. I've been so stressed out about what's going on, I should have been more understanding and heard him out. He is my best friend. My only friend for that matter. I've already got a taste of what life is like without him.

He faces me.

"Believe me. I was very careful about my decision, Evan, but understand that even if I wanted to go, it would be difficult to leave now."

"Why is that?" I ask.

"Bianca."

"You love her."

"Yes."

"When did you know this for yourself."

He moves the collar of his jacket away from his neck.

"She bit you."

"I told her to."

"Wait, how'd you know that she was a vampire?"

He puts his hands into his jacket.

"The morning of the day I left, my grandmother sided with my parents about moving. I argued with my grandmother while I was getting ready for school. When school ended, Bianca had told me to meet her by the football field, skip last period to spend more time together and so I did. Sure enough there she stood on the field, waiting for me. She didn't say much. Just asked if I trusted her. Of course, at the time, I didn't know what she was going to show me. So we walked through the forest, alone, and when she told me her feelings about me and asked how I felt about her..."

He shrugs.

"I told her I felt the same. I told her I've always had eyes for her. And then she told me about you."

"Me?"

He nods.

"Yeah. About how she cares for you, the family, everything. How she's afraid you may never recognize her or 'come home.' At first it was just all too weird and a bit much. I wasn't quite following. She was afraid that you'd never remember or ever come home. That you would remain human for the rest of your life. That your vampire self will never come out and you would forget your family existed."

"Wow," I shake my head. "I had already forgotten they existed."

"But you came back," he reminds. "I told her about my family, about moving, about dying. She said she could make it possible that I live forever, but that would mean I need to turn away from a few things in my human life. It sounded funny like some old scary story, talking about immortality. But she told me it was real. I could never die and I could be with her, offering me the two things I wanted. The rain fell, her eyes changed color, and she was different. She told me what she was, not to be afraid, and asked if this was what I wanted for myself. That there will be no turning back. That it would be difficult. I told her it was what I wanted, and then, she bit me."

I devour his story.

"I died that night, Evan. When you are bitten, that person, or vampire, becomes your life and for vampires like Bianca, you become theirs as well."

Now I understand. As much as I didn't while he was gone, now I understand. It's not just about his family, but about himself. About where he wants to be and feels he needs to be. About who he is and what he believes in. I'm his best friend. He needs me now.

"Does it hurt…to die?" I ask.

"In becoming a vampire? Yes. The pain was excruciating. It will hurt. I can't sugarcoat this one for you, buddy."

I smirk.

"Guess I have something to look forward to."

"Ohh yeahh," he says laughing.

"But I'm glad you're back, Mike. I really am."

We shake hands firmly before he pulls me into a hug.

"Glad to be back, brother."

He lets go and smirks. He looks over the ledge and then back to me.

"They're waiting for you. I'll see you below."

He flips off the bell and heads down below. I smile and shake my head

Showoff.

When you become a vampire, you lose your life, but I guess, you keep your personality.

CHAPTER TWENTY-ONE: AWAKENING

We stand in the small field that rests before the cliff. Everyone, excluding Cedric, awaits nearby as father and I are face to face.

"Okay, Evan," he says. "We're going to start with the basics and then things will get a little tricky."

"Okay," I respond.

He nods to Mike, who then runs inside, then returns with a wall of red brick above his head. He places the wall behind my father, gives me a smirk, then rejoins the rest of the family on the side. Mike might have always been that strong. I don't think that was the vampire in him.

"Now, Evan, what I want you to do is put me through this brick wall," my father says. "Simple."

I examine the brick wall behind him.

"You want me to put you through that brick?" I ask for confirmation.

He smiles and nods.

"That is correct. Good luck."

He stands with his cane beneath both of his hands. *He's not going to brace himself?*

"Well, alright," I shrug.

"Whenever you are ready," he says.

I position my feet firm into the ground and focus on the best possible way to push him. *Not the shoulders.* I shake my head. *Not the stomach; too soft.* A direct force to the midsection will be best. *The sternum.* I shift my weight back, then throw my arms and palms to his chest. He doesn't budge. Not an inch. Mike chuckles, but Bianca nudges him to stay silent.

"Care to try again?" he smiles.

"Uhhh, yes."

He motions his hand for me to try again. *More force, Evan. It was weak. He didn't even budge. Okay. Here we go.*

I try again. Nothing. I back off.

"I don't understand," I say.

"Because you aren't fully vampire, you can't assume that everything you do will be vampire."

I was doing just fine a minute ago climbing the mansion and jumping from the bell. Had I known an off-

period can occur at any time, I'm pretty sure I would not have taken neither of those life threatening risks. I'd be spaghetti or a smashed watermelon.

"Your body is still adjusting, but I shall teach you how to trick it with your mind."

"I kind of taught him," Bianca says.

Father smiles and slightly bows.

"Well, thank you, dear."

He turns back to me and clears his throat.

"This time Evan, I want you to focus more, but not on putting me through this brick wall. Focus on a time when you felt endangered. Now, careful I tell you," he lifts a finger. "Anger is inevitable; however, do not allow anger to provoke careless action. Allow the essence of your soul to find peace within yourself. Only then will you know how to bring out the better, stronger, you."

"But what if I can't and won't learn how to do any of this?"

"You can do it, Evan," Essence says. Everyone looks over at her and smiles. "I believe in you."

"I'll try," I say returning a smile.

I nod and position myself for another try. *I remember when I first ran into uncle Abel. He had frightened me. Moving about from tree to tree. I remember breaking my wrist, running through the rain and how cold it was. Then knocked unconscious from smacking into a tree.*

My fingers begin to tingle and I feel strong. The mint smell of the rainforest fills my nostrils and water continues to crash against the rocks at the bottom of the cliff. *I can do this,* I tell myself. My father smiles as I shift of my weight back, and focus on his midsection.

I pushed him and I pushed hard. The blow echoes in my ears as I watch his body leave the ground beneath him, his arms and legs throw forward, and his torso cave in. When his body connects with the wall behind him, it cracks as loud as thunder. I had imagined it to be painful, however, father has yet stopped smiling.

The wall bursts into pieces and he tumbles and plows across the ground, then, gracefully, catches his weight on his feet, his staff, beneath his hands once again as though nothing happened at all. *It worked. I brought the vampire out of me.* Everyone claps and cheers, except Cedric of course.

"Bravo, Evan!" my father, Kaius, exclaims as he claps then outstretches his arms. "Now, how did that feel?"

I smile much greater than anticipated.

"It felt similar to when I was angry at the bully in school yet different. Even different from when Bianca had helped me tap into myself when I climbed the mansion. Similar, but different." I respond.

"Different than before, yes," he agrees. "That is because, instead of anger, or any emotion that stems from it, we used a substitute. Self- awareness; acceptance. Recognizing that we have to address the issue before us and instead of running from our problem, fix it. We can choose to act, just as you did, or do nothing, and be consumed by fate. Do you want everything in your life in the hands of fate? Or would you rather have more control over your life?"

"More control," I answer.

"I thought so," he says nodding.

He dusts himself off and clears his throat.

"Now," he says. "Are you ready to continue?"

287

"I am."

"Splendid!"

Father flicks his wrist, and like magic, an apple appears in his hand. He holds it up for all to see.

"Now, we are going to test your sense of sight," he says. "This here, is an apple."

As I can see.

Mike snickers and Bianca nudges him again. I'm pretty sure he was thinking the same thing I was, so I smile inside.

"Okay," I listen on trying not to think of eating it.

"I am going to drop this apple and I want you to get it," he says.

"That won't be too hard," I respond.

"You got this, Ev!" Mike calls still laughing a bit. Bianca hits him again, but he ignores. "You got this."

"Come," father says walking me to the cliff. He places his hand on my back and leads me to the edge. We overlook The Mohawk River Valley. It is beautiful as always. Trees encompass the perimeter of the large ocean of water, the gray clouds are calm, and birds flutter from across the river and throughout the valley.

"You see the water below?"

I look down at the water crashing against the wall of the cliff.

"Yes."

"Good. Now find the apple."

He lets go of the apple and it falls through the sky until it disappears from view.

"How am I supposed to--?"

Father shoves me over the edge and I flip and plummet through the sky. *Okay, you can do this!* However, such confidence has not stopped me from yelling, and partially, suffocating on the rush of air. I readjust myself to the fall, straight as a pencil, and take the deepest breath I can. *Okay, here we go.*

I throw my arms above my head and water engulfs my surroundings. The water is freezing, my ears are plugged, and my body sways like a falling feather, as I sink. I hold my breath, kick the water beneath me, and swim to the surface. I can barely see my father on the cliff, and the rest of the family joins him looking down at me. I wipe the water from my face and inhale as much oxygen as I can. I dive below and sound muffles. *How can I find an apple in this water that is so dark? This is impossible.*

I continue to swim, arms thrusting and legs kicking as I head for the bottom. The temperature of the water feels as though it is dropping by the second. My face is numb, I think my ears are bleeding by now, but I must continue. I can't give up.

Where are you? I think to myself. *Oh no.* My chest tightens and my muscles begin to submit. *I need air.* I can't be anywhere close to the bottom of the river which is where I suspect the apple to be by now. *I have to go back up.*

I adjust my swim back towards the surface. I have to hurry. I reach frantically through the water kicking harder, trying to hold my breath as best and as long as I can. Water fills my nostrils, my eyes begin to burn, and the cold is unbearable. Before my lungs burst, I emerge from the surface. I throw my head back, coughing and gasping for air. The worst is over. I cough up what is left of the water and look to the top of the cliff.

"I can't find it!" I yell, exposing my failure.

Someone jumps from the cliff. The body dives into the water like a bullet, but smooth and fluid. A few moments go by and Bianca springs from the surface like a dolphin. She swims towards me.

"Looking for this?" she says as she smiles and holds up the apple. "I'll lead you back up, Evan. We can try again."

When Bianca and I get back up to the cliff, everyone awaits with towels. I hug my goosebump-covered skin and my clothes are wet and heavy.

"Evan, come," Kaius calls holding a hand out to me.

"I'm freezing," I say. "I can't do it."

"You must remember what I told you before. You know you can withstand the cold if you really wanted to, Evan and barely have to hold your breath."

Bianca nods and lightly shoves me to try again.

"Alright," I say, trying to keep my teeth from chattering. Bianca hands Kaius the apple then joins the others on the side.

"Let's try this again only this time, we'll take the advice I've given, hmm?"

291

I don't want to, but I have to. I have to learn how to be what I am. I can't give up. No matter how hard it is. I come from an amazing history. *This is in my blood. I am meant for this.* If I want to make everyone proud, I'm going to have to try harder no matter how many times I may fail. That's how lessons are learned, and greatness is born.

"I'm ready," I say.

He smiles.

"Now," he says holding the apple up to me. "This time, Evan, this is not an apple. This is something much more important to you. This is something you cherish with your life. Save it. There is no other option."

I nod my head.

"Got it."

My father holds the apple over the edge of the cliff. He nods, then lets go of the apple. Without hesitation, I immediately jump after the apple and watch as it spins and descends through the air. I hold a hand in front of me, ready to grab it when I catch up. And then I see her. The apple of my eye. Essence. Just as she was in my dream.

Evanescence

Adrenaline fills my body and boils my blood. Essence is in trouble and I must save her. Thunder rumbles and rain begins to pour. My heart tries to creep into my throat, but I ignore the doubt that tries to distract me. As we plummet through the raining sky to the ocean below, I extend my arm and hand to Essence. She is unconscious, but I will catch her. I will save her.

Essence breaks through the surface of the water, and I am right behind her. As I continue to dive to the bottom, she is gone. I kick and swim, deeper and deeper, ignoring the cold, ignoring the need for air, and ignoring the will to live.

The apple is gone. Images of Essence trying to breathe begin to plague inside of my mind. *I have to find her. I have to find her or she will die.*

I swim as fast as a bullet, and there she lays, on the ocean floor, still and cold. My heart pounds against my chest as I swim to her and bring her into my arms. I sit on the river's floor, close my eyes, and kiss her forehead. I throw her over my shoulders holding her legs and squat to gather strength. With one push off the floor of the river, we rocket to surface. The water flies behind us like a speedboat and the light from the surface begins to shine around us. *Just a bit further. Just a bit further,* I tell myself.

With a few more kicks, I emerge from the surface holding the apple high above me.

"YES!"

I saved Essence, the apple. I succeeded.

I splash the water with my hand and look up the cliff. They watch from above, as I swim to the rocks, and stuff the apple into my pocket which forms a huge ball, and begin to climb, one hand after another, one step after another. My hand reaches over the top and my family was there to congratulate and pull me up.

"Jeez, you're freezing!" Sarah says as she hugs me. "Great job! I'm proud of you."

"Thank you," I smile and wipe the water from my face.

"Son, you have made me proud," my mother says bowing her head.

"Ev, man, that was awesome!" Mike says handing me a towel. "I think you were faster than me! I knew you could do it!"

"Uh huh, sure you did," Bianca says shaking her head. "Great job brother."

"Great job indeed, Evan!" Abel agrees.

My father joins us and places his hands on my shoulders.

"A job well done. You'll make quite the vampire, Evan."

"Thanks," I smile.

I try to bite the apple, but unable to puncture its surface. It pops open and inside is a weight.

My father laughs.

"That was to keep it from floating, Evan."

"Oh," I chuckle. "Right. Of course."

"Are you ready for your next lesson?"

"I'm sure I can manage."

"Great. We're going to test your climbing and agility. You've done this one quite a few times, but I'm going to make it a bit more of a challenge."

"I'm ready for it."

He looks up to the mansion and we all follow his eyes.

"I want you to grab that pole and bring it to me."

I stare at the silver pole that stands above the bell. I think the best way to do it is the way in which I am used to. I will climb the pillar walls, make it window to window, grab hold of the lip of the bell, and pull myself over. The pole will be right there in front of me. Not too difficult actually.

"--Without touching the bell."

I turn to him with raised eyebrows.

"Wi--without touching the bell?"

"Go on. Try," he says inching me over to the mansion with a hand.

I stand at the bottom of the mansion and look up. Much taller than when I first climbed because Bianca and I were up a floor already, which made it a bit easier. I can't stop now. I believe in myself and must continue.

I exhale deeply and brush my palms against my pants. Either they are still damp from the water and drizzle of rain, or it's sweat. I place my hands and feet on a few rocks and try to climb. After a few feet, I lose grip and slide back down to the ground. I look over my shoulder at my family who watches quietly. My father holds his grin and I decide to try again.

I have to discipline myself. My father will not always be there at times like this to coach me along the way. I have to get this down on my own. I close my eyes, take a deep breath, tune out my surroundings, and focus on breathing. Maybe if I approached my situations while in a brief meditative state, I can focus more.

My best friend Mike, I was starting to think was either lost or dead. I had forced myself to believe otherwise. That he was alive and well. His family. All of them were afraid. I was afraid. I can't imagine a world without my best friend, and for weeks, I was forced to experience what that would feel like. *Unbearable.*

I open my eyes and grab onto the rocky walls of the mansion. My feet leave the ground and soon, I am coasting up the mansion wall, grabbing one window, climbing to the next, then grabbing hold of another. A sound from below catches my attention. I look over my shoulder. The ground is far below, but just beneath me--.

"Mike? What are you doing?" I call down to him.

"Kaius upped the standards a bit," he responds climbing the mansion. "Since you're making it look too easy," Mike continues to climb and grunts a bit. "You have to get the pole before I do."

"But I never beat you at anything?" I say.

"HAHAHA!" He laughs hysterically, and his voice gets high pitched. "I knowww!"

Mike is crazy. Apart from trying not to laugh, I try to move faster. He's gaining on me. Mike has always been much more athletic than I am. I can't let him win. I have to not only prove to myself that I can do this, but also prove to myself that I can beat Mike sometimes as well. Here is my chance.

CHAPTER TWENTY-TWO: SECRETS

The wind gusts against us, but we manage to stay against the mansion's walls. I take a brief moment to look back. *Where is he?* Mike. I search for him, but nothing.

"Better hurry, Evan," I hear him say.

He climbs up one of the pillars of the mansion's corners. The bell is centered in the middle of the mansion.

The bell hangs by metal prongs that come from the four pillar-towers of the mansion. I leap for a pillar and almost lose my grip. My body suspends from the wall by one hand and my feet kick to find balance. *Don't fall. Don't fall. Don't fall.* I regain control, hug the pillar, and climb to its top. Mike stands above his pillar and sizes up the bell, the pole standing, centered above it.

I struggle to stand to my feet, but manage, and look across at Mike. He grins and I know he is about to jump for the pole.

"Sorry, Ev. I'm taking this one."

Mike leaps from his pillar. I turn back to the pole, but Essence is there holding her arms out to me. *No, Mike. I am.*

I take a leap of faith, rising above the lip of the bell. Mike extends his hand to grab the pole, still holding onto his confident grin. I extend my arm for it the pole, but my heart sinks. *He's going to make it before I do.*

Mike grabs the pole, but then we collide in the air. The pole fumbles, and we fall into the sky, plummeting after it. It flips and descends to the water below. I adjust my body into a dive. Mike trails behind me.

"It's mine, Evan!" he yells.

"Not this time, Mike!" I yell back to him.

"We'll see about that!"

I extend an arm out for the pole. It continues to cartwheel in the air. Mike hovers above my back, slowly taking the lead. He extends his arm above mine as he then passes in front of me. *No! No! I can't let him win. I can't always fall short of Mike all the time. I was born a vampire. He was bitten. I am supposed to win!*

Mike falls closer to the pole and his body falls in front of me. *I have to do something. Think!* I grab hold of his ankle, pull as hard as I can, and flip above him, taking the lead

"Evan!" he yells. I place my foot on his shoulder, kick for a boost, and straighten my body into a dive.

Got it!

We fall into the river. I keep my grip on the pole. I swim to the surface and look around.

"Mike?" I call out. Nothing.

"Mike!" I call again.

He bursts from the surface of the water.

"You still have to give it to Kaius!"

I jump out of my skin and begin to swim for the cliff. Mike is on my heels.

"Give it, Evan!"

"Come get it!"

I grab hold of the cliff, place the pole into my pants belt holder, and begin to climb as fast as I can. Mike follows behind monstrously, anxiously trying to grab hold of my ankle, yet missing. He reaches and reaches and almost grabs hold. I leap for another grip on the cliff hoping that would grow the distance between us. I slip from the cliff, the pole drops from my hip, but I manage to catch it by its end.

Uh oh!

Mike leaps towards me, with his arms out and wide open. I quickly climb out of the way, avoiding the tackle. The edge of the cliff is just above, but Mike is nowhere in sight again. Perhaps he called it quits? I reach for the top of the cliff and grip it with one hand. I look back. Then reach over with my other and begin to pull myself up.

"Evan!" I hear him yell. Mike is in the air with his arms spread once again for a tackle. I pull with all my force and roll over the edge of the cliff. Mike grabs hold of the edge, tries to find his grip to keep himself from falling.

"Ev," he says. "Could use a hand here."

"Oh?" I say. "You look like you're doing just fine."

"Oh, come on," he says. He holds a hand out. "I'm your best friend."

I sigh and walk over. He smiles, and keeps his hand up to me. I smile back, but not for reasons he believes. I crouch down to him and kiss the pole.

"I win." I say.

Mike drops his forehead to the ground. He then looks up and glares at me through his eyebrows.

"That's cold-blooded, man," he says.

I shrug and stand to my feet.

"We're vampires, remember?"

Mike nods with a smirk, loses his grip and falls to the water below.

Mission Accomplished.

My family begins to clap.

"Impressive! Very entertaining," father exclaims. "It was—theatrical!"

"You deserved it brother," says Bianca.

"You're not upset I let him fall?" I ask.

Bianca looks over the edge of the cliff, then shakes her head.

"Nope. He'll be fine with his little alone time before he gets back up here."

"You're doing better than Mike," says my mother. "You're a natural."

I shake my head smiling.

"I just--."

Essence kisses my cheek.

"Great job, Evan. I knew you could do it."

I blush.

"Think he'll be okay?" Sarah asks.

"Mike is fine," says Bianca

"What'd you like me to do next?" I ask earnestly. "Hopefully, it will be on land this time. The water is getting a bit old."

"That was my final test," he responds. "I would teach you how to hunt, but that would be unnecessary.

I feel slightly disappointed.

"...Oh."

Mike makes it back up the cliff.

"Ah, yes, there he is!" my father says. "In one piece."

Mike manages a smile. He is soaked to the bone, but apparently not cold.

"You won, Ev," he says shaking my hand. "You finally beat me."

I return a smile.

"Well, you didn't exactly make it easy."

"I figured if you are as strong as they say you are, then I should expect to lose."

"You didn't just lose, Michael" Abel says.

"You got owned," Essence jokes.

We join in laughter.

"What about killing? Defending himself. Fighting." a voice calls.

Cedric.

"You gonna' teach him that?" he asks as his eyes sting mine.

"No, Evan wouldn't have to kill anyone," father responds. "He has no enemies. Besides, we don't want to force his transformation. We want it to come naturally. The correct way. That incident in school should have been a reminder to you, if Evan gets overwhelmed, emotionally, it can trigger his transformation."

"You never know who's an enemy nowadays. It's unpredictable. He wouldn't be ready, so why not force his change now, by teaching him, while we are all here together, which would promise safety? Why leave him vulnerable?"

"Because he's is not ready and apparently his body isn't either. When it is ready, he will change. Until then we will continue to watch over him."

"Watch over him? I'm sick and tired of babysitting!"

"I didn't ask you to," I say.

"It is for the best son," father says to me.

"Besides," Cedric continues. "When the time comes, we'll see how strong he can fight the thirst. Won't be able to be around her for a bit. Not without wanting to kill her."

"Cedric!" Valencia calls. "You'll frighten her."

Essence clasps her hand into mind, intertwining our fingers. It hurts.

"I'm just being honest," Cedric says. "She has a right to know what to expect right, just as Evan must as well."

"Yes, but you don't have to be so rude about it," Bianca says as Mike places hands on her shoulders to keep her back.

"She's right, Cedric," Abel agrees. "There's a way to explaining things just as there's a time and a place for it."

"So, why not now? While we're all here?!" he yells back.

"Because now is not the time. As the Dracula, I will--
"

"You are not the Dracula," Cedric says pronouncing each word harshly. "And I think it's a perfect time. Essence." He turns to face her. "The smell of you, will be irresistible. He'll want to kill you, feed on you, rip you apart."

"Cedric," father calls. Essence tightens her grip.

"All he'll be able to eat or drink," Cedric ignores, "Are the humans. Like you. Your friends. Your family. Maybe the family dog if he isn't full by then."

"CEDRIC," father calls again. He continues to ignore.

"Tell him, Mike," he says. We all turn to him. "Why don't you and Bianca tell Evan how we had to keep chasing you down because you couldn't resist the scent of your grandmother."

I think about the time I felt the same towards Sarah when she was asleep on the couch. I cringe and shake my head. Mike's face hugs the ground.

"I'm sorry," he murmurs to himself.

"Due to evolution," Cedric continues, "we're able to go into sunlight, but, that doesn't weaken the beast. Nope.

Not anymore. Unfortunately, the thirst becomes this unavoidable frenzy because as the sun shines across the sky of this oh so beautiful world, it heats the blood of the humans. The scent of them fills the air like barbeque in the summer."

He nods.

"Lucky for you we stay on this cliff and drink watered down blood packets just so we won't rip you precious humans apart...Like we couldn't if it were a rainy day or any other. You're far luckier than other places that are infested with our species."

"Cedric!" father calls with the base of his voice.

Cedric looks over at father then turns back to Essence.

Everyone remains silent, Cedric smiles, then shrugs.

"As I said. You sure you don't want to teach him everything? Kaius? Er, I'm sorry, uncle? Like what *really* happens when he dies?" he says. Father turns his head away.

"*What really happens?* What is he talking about?" I ask.

Everyone shies away a bit and doesn't respond.

"I am a vampire right?"

"Yes, of course you are," my father answers.

"Then what is he talking about?"

"You see what you've done, Cedric!" Bianca yells. Mike pulls her back again. Cedric smirks and leans against the red doors of the mansion.

"He has a right to know," he responds, crossing his arms.

"Yes, and we would have told him when it was the right time," my mother says.

"Now, we don't have much of a choice do we?" Abel jumps in.

"I guess not," Sarah says.

"Wait, wait, what is everyone talking about?" I ask again.

"Well, it would have been better to tell him a bit later," my father says.

"But then again if he would have changed..." says my mother.

"Then we would not have been able to tell him at all," Bianca finishes.

"HEY!" I yell. "I'm standing right here."

They stand quiet and listen.

"What is it that you have to tell me?"

My mother turns to father and nods. He steps forward.

"Evan, when you die," he says carefully. "Everything you have known or experienced in your human life will be forgotten like...an amnesia."

"What? Why? I don't want that," I tell them. "I'd like to keep my memories, thanks."

"I'm afraid it's not in our control," he says. "It's like, some sort of defense mechanism we have yet to understand. It normally isn't such a big deal because usually, the awakening happens at a very young age, but for you, it would be more drastic seeing how you are indeed sixteen years old...Sixteen years to be deleted."

My heart leaps into my throat and goosebumps populates my arms. Sixteen years of my life will be deleted from memory.

"No," I say. "Not again. I've already forgotten once...That can't be right. Mike remembers everything."

"Sweetie," my mother says placing her hands on my cheeks to hold my face. "Mike was bitten. It is different for him and other humans that are bitten."

"Then if that's the case, since I'm still human, bite me now," I look to them. "Bite me before I change so I won't forget."

"I'm afraid it doesn't work that way, nephew," Abel interrupts.

"Because you are born to be a vampire, you already have vampire blood," my father says. "It is mixed with your human blood. Biting you will do nothing."

My head hangs to the floor.

"But...That's not fair," I say.

"You want to know the worse part, Evan," Cedric says. "You'll forget everyone."

Everyone.

"Everyone like Sarah," he says with a smirk.

I look over at my step-mother who refrains from looking at me.

"You'll even forget the one person you care about and love," he continues.

No. I place my arms around Essence and squeeze. He nods.

"Yes, your curly red-head, Essence LaRoux."

Not only will I become a vampire, but I will forget my human life. My memories. Memories that make me, ME. I will forget sixteen years of my life. I will forget Sarah. Worst of all, I will forget Essence.

"All that would be remembered," my father says, "is the vampire within you. Everything human, will be forgotten. You will remember us, your family, including Mike because of what he is now. You will also remember your history and your training. Maybe not the happenings of it, but you will know what you have learned today. It will be like second nature to you. As easy as breathing."

"Evan," Essence says to me silently. "What does that mean about us?"

I shake my head.

"Don't listen to them," I tell her.

"Kaius," Sarah says. "You mind if I..."

"Sure, go on ahead, Sarah."

She nods.

"Evan," she approaches me. "I knew this day would come. I've waited for it. I knew one day you would also forget about me. About everything we've been through."

"Why didn't you tell me?" I ask.

"I didn't want to distract you. It was not the time. So, I made you keep a diary and write."

It makes sense.

"So, that's why you were so firm with me writing every day? So, when I do forget, it would help me remember?"

"Yes," she answers, "and no."

"And no?"

"When you forget, it will be as though it never happened. There's no guarantee you will even believe what you've written. You can read it all you want, but you won't remember. You won't even have those feelings you had when you wrote those recollections. It will just be words on paper, but for me, I will still have you in my heart as though you passed on, yet I know when I visit, you'll be right here."

Essence coils herself around my arm and places her forehead against it.

"Everything. Everything will be gone. My school. You. Essence and the feelings that come with it."

"I'm sorry, Evan," Sarah says, "we tried our best."

I nod

"Is there anything else I need to know? Please, tell me now."

"Ah yes," Cedric interferes. "Not to spoil the moment."

"Haven't you done enough?" Mike says.

"Not quite," he responds. "I'm doing more for him than all of you. I'm actually helping him prepare aren't I? Aren't I Evan?!"

"What more could you possibly want him to know?" Bianca asks.

"Just one last thing that I believe to be important," he says. "How to fight."

My father shakes his head.

"I have made my decision and it is final. No more of this, Cedric," he commands. "I will not teach him to fight."

Cedric shook his head.

He laughs.

"Then allow me," he says as he walks up to me.

My eyes lock into his which glow red.

"Cedric no!" my father yells.

He strikes my face and Essence falls to the side. The blow is the most painful thing I have ever felt in my life. I feel bones in my face shift and a flash of white light blinds me. I tumble to the edge of the cliff and lay still, fighting the blow.

I clench my fists, full of grass, and get on my hands and knees.

"Cedric," I say as he stands above me.

A cold sensation spreads across my body; freezing. I look into my palms, then flip them over. Pale, and my mark appears, but it glows of red and orange. My mouth aches and pains and my tongue cuts across them.

Am I changing?

Each breath is as loud as a gavel slam. I stand to my feet, and Cedric begins to back away, but his face held fear. Everyone does the same.

"His eyes, his mark," mother says.

They all turn to father as he grips onto his necklace. One by one, they take a knee and bow their heads, placing a fist against their cold, still heart, their clans marks exposed. Sarah, Essence, and Cedric remain standing. My father hisses at them and they stand to their feet. Not one of them look me in the face. He then turns to me and stares with a worry across his face. Cedric heads back into the mansion, keeping his eyes upon me until the doors close. I fall, but catch myself on the ground.

"I'm alright," I say, though no one had asked. "I thought I was changing." Essence joins my side and helps me to my feet.

"That will be all for today. Everyone inside," he commands as he studies me. By everyone, I had assumed he doesn't mean myself, Essence, and Sarah. Without a word they listen. Bianca looks back at me, but I can't read her expression. Mike is also unreadable.

"Come back soon, Evan" my father says. He then heads back into the mansion and closes the big red doors. No goodbye. No good job. Just leaves.

"Are you okay, Evan? Let me see," Essence says as she examines my face moving it here and there.

"We must go now," Sarah says.

"What's the problem?" I ask.

"Nothing. It's just time to leave."

Why is everyone acting so strange? Essence puts her hand into mine and we head back to the car.

~

The car ride back is quiet. I can't help but think about the tests and more importantly, what Cedric had said about me forgetting everything. Just when I thought things couldn't get any worse. I was starting to look forward to becoming a vampire because I learned about who I am and where I came from. I would never reject that, but now, things have changed and I have no choice, but to keep moving forward. The two things I have to look forward to: dying, and forgetting who Sarah and Essence are.

Essence stares out of the window. She hasn't said a word since we got in the car. Sarah is focused on the road and has not said a word neither. *What's going through her head? Why is everyone making me feel as though I had done something wrong? I just did what I was asked and it was Cedric who started all of this. Not the other way around.* We pull into Essence's driveway.

"Goodnight, Essence," Sarah says to her.

"Goodnight, Ms. Foster."

We step out of the car and head up her front steps.

"I'm sorry about today," I tell her. Her face hugs the floor. She shakes her head then looks into my eyes.

"It's not your fault. We went for answers and we got them."

"Yeah," I nod. "Not the answers I expected."

She cups her hand to my cheek. I place my hand above hers and press it more firmly against my cheek.

"You look so sad."

"I have a reason to be," I respond almost choking.

"I'm here for you, Evan," she says.

"Until I forget who you are."

She stands silent for a moment.

"No. Even then, I'll still be there."

I kiss her forehead, then we wrap our arms around each other listening to the rain.

"I'll see you tomorrow?"

"Yes," I smile. "We'll make it special."

"Special?"

"Yes," I respond. "Special."

She hugs me one last time before letting go. She places her hands on the doorknob and stops.

"Goodnight, Evan."

"Goodnight, Essence."

CHAPTER TWENTY-THREE: BONDING

This morning was the first time in a while that I received a text from Mike. He went home to his grandmother, who missed him, but apparently the happiness was short lived when he broke the news that he wasn't moving and staying in Utica. I can only imagine what his parents are going to say, especially his mother, when he lays it on them.

The best talks I've had with my family were with Mike and Bianca, and I can honestly say they look great together. At least now I understand why Bianca always acted a certain way around me. Now my family awaits my transformation, but I wish it could be postponed. I can't say I wouldn't want any of this to happen to me, because I have to accept who I am and not who I had originally believed I was. It's only right.

"Go again, Evan you're really getting the hang of this!" Essence exclaims.

"Alright, here I go!"

I shift into position, crouching down to the ground in a track stance. I close my eyes, take a deep breath, and start to run as fast as a bullet out of a gun. A tree approaches. I leap up half of its body and climb, then leap to the next and climb, then repeat once more onto another tree. When I get to the very top, I press my foot onto a branch and become suspended in the air with my arms outstretched as I back flip. I toss my head back and Essence gazes into my eyes. I smirk and tuck into a ball for a finish. When my feet plant on the ground, I bow. She claps.

"You make it look so – easy. I feel like I can do it, but I know I can't."

"Yeah? Guess I'm loving it a bit too much myself," I smile. "It is getting easier."

But then that can also mean I'm getting closer to dying. Forgetting. I walk over and stand before her as she sits on a rock. She has on denim shorts and a fitted t-shirt covering her model shaped body. Never seen this much of her flawless skin before. My shirt, shoes, and socks are somewhere around, but my shorts are comfortable.

"So that's what's under your shirt," she says grinning and hugging herself.

I look down at my body and blush.

"You like?"

"I love."

"My love," I say pressing my lips against hers. She holds my face and our lips dance beneath the trees.

Her surprise.

"Let me show you something," I say taking her hand to follow me. She grabs her violin.

"Where are we going?" She asks.

"You'll see."

I walk her down a path and to the sands of the beach. I watch as a smile spreads across her lips.

Out of sand and wood, I made a circular pit. Five steps down and into the sand, is a table for two with two chairs. Hand-picked blue and lavender flowers are around the perimeter and in between each vase of flowers are small white candles pressed into the sand. Each candle sits inside a glass bulb. The sun's departure is near. Timing was never more perfect and on my side.

"Evan, this is beautiful!" She exclaims, turning to me. "I don't know what to say, honestly." She then jumps into my arms.

I catch and hug her.

"Let's enjoy it," I say.

I lead her down the steps and into the pit. The flowers and candles are at shoulder level, and on the table is a picnic basket. I cover the table with a cloth and then remove the loaded turkey sandwiches, I prepared for her and her can of soda. I then remove my veggie burger that's wrapped in aluminum foil to keep its warmth, a big bag of chips to share, soda, and a huge bowl of fruit I got from the market. Inside, I leave the necklace I made for her.

"Wow," she says. "You never fail to surprise me."

"I try my best with you," I say.

She reaches across the table and rubs my cheek.

"You're doing more than anyone else has."

I smile and brushes some of her red hair from her face.

"Looks like sundown is near. Shall we light the candles?" She asks.

I pat the outside of my pants' pockets and that was the one thing I forgot to bring. A lighter.

"May have to do it the caveman way."

I search the ground for sticks. I have no experience with the old fashion way. I find a few in the forest. I step over the circle of candles, but my heel knocks one and it begins to roll.

"I'll get that," she says.

"No, I got it," I smile. "You stay there and enjoy your food."

"Okay," she giggles.

I step into the pit and the bulb rests at her feet. She smiles at me as I bend over and pick it up. When I do, a flame appears, the candle is lit.

"How did you--?"

I shake my head.

"I--I don't know I just...grabbed it."

"Do it again," she says staring at the candle in my hand. I grab the next candle in the circle around us. It lights as well. Essence exhales deeply with excitement and I look at her just as surprised. I place the two candles down.

"Evan, your eyes. They're...not like before. They're different."

"What do you mean?"

She stares into them.

"They're orange, a bit red. Like fire."

I reach for the third candle, but before I can touch it, the candles all light one by one. Our eyes follow each candle around their circular path.

"Am I doing this?"

Essence looks around at the candles and shakes her head.

"We both know it isn't me."

"How is it possible that I can do something and don't know I'm doing it?"

"Something to do with becoming a vampire perhaps?"

I shrug.

"Maybe. I'll find out from them."

"Come. Sit. Eat with me and be careful with those," she says eying my hands.

I smile and we begin to eat.

"They seemed afraid of you after what Cedric had done."

"Yeah, I can't imagine why."

"Your face it...It healed like instantaneously, but now that I think about it..."

She pauses as I bite into my veggie burger. I wait for her to finish, but she sits in deep thought.

"What's wrong?" I ask. She eyes the candles then looks back at me.

"When he hit you, you healed. Remarkably fast, but like it glowed. Like fire. Like how these candles lit."

"What are you saying?"

"I'm saying whatever you did yesterday, and from what I seen just now, I think they are somehow related. And from the expression on their faces, maybe it's just me but, I doubt they don't know something about this."

"If you're right, I wonder what this means. I wonder if it's something good or, bad or—I don't know."

She shrugs and shakes her head.

"I'm not sure, but if this is true, I'm willing to bet they have the answer to that."

I bite into my food and take a drink of soda. The sun departs over the horizon. Orange and red no longer bleeds across the sky. Instead, the pit shines orange and red like a campfire. The sky begins to glean of star light.

"Are you afraid? Of us?" I ask.

"Not of them personally. Maybe. It's more of the nature of what they are and what you are."

I stare at her.

"You mean who?"

She captures the offense I took.

"I'm so sorry, Evan I didn't mean it that way. I'm not used to, you know, myths being true."

"Don't worry about it," I try to laugh. "Even I'm afraid of myself, but I'm surprised you haven't run from me yet."

"Well, apparently, you'd catch me if I tried," she jokes.

"Good point. I would."

"You know, who would have thought two guys that are best friends go to my school, become vampires, and that there has been a family of them living here in Utica for years?"

"I would've never thought this was where my life was headed. I had believed high school, college, have a family, grow old, *then* die, was life."

"Are you afraid?"

"Petrified," I answer almost immediately. "But all I can do is accept myself for who I am."

"And not 'what' you are," she smiles.

"And not 'what' I am," I agree

We sit quiet and finish our meals. She looks to the water troubled.

"What's on your mind?" I ask.

She stays quiet a moment longer.

"I'm just afraid of what Cedric said. About what happens when you die."

Her face begins to blush. She licks her lips and still keeps her eyes averted from me.

"All of the memories we're making now. The talks we've had. Me. There's a strong possibility you will forget, but I won't. I'd have to live with the fact that I only lose people. I don't get to keep them."

I get up from my seat and sit next to her.

"I won't forget," I say. "I will remember you. I have my notebooks to help me."

"We don't know if that's going to work. It may all just be words to you, Evan."

"It won't be!"

She finally looks into my eyes. Tears sit on her bed of eyelashes. Her bottom lip tries to hide beneath the top.

"But how do you know? How do you know that once you die, you will wake up, read your notebooks, and believe? Even if you do believe, you won't feel those memories you wrote. It will all just be words. Words. Words. Words!"

She begins to sob.

"It won't be that way. I just know it won't."

"There's nothing you can do about it, Evan," she cries out. "At any moment, your heart will stop. You will die. When you wake, you will no longer know who I am. You will forget about this. About me. About...us."

My heart begins to pain and my throat begins to choke.

"Essence, no. I love you. When I die and wake, I will still remember you."

Her eyes shake and quiver holding tears above her beautiful eyelashes.

"I would hope so because I love you too, Evan."

We hold onto each other's eyes a while longer. I reach into the basket and pull out the chain and heart-shaped jewel with silver wings. My step-mother, Sarah, had given it to me when I was a child. It used to hold an oil inside that kept bugs from the forest away. She figured it be perfect for me since I was always in the forest, but I barely ever worn it. She understood that it looked more feminine than masculine to wear, but she never wanted it back. *Give it to one of your girlfriends*, she always joked. Of course, I've never had eyes for anyone except Essence. The story of Viscus had given me the idea.

"What are you doing, Evan?"

I place the jewel onto the chain so that it hangs.

"I'm giving you my necklace."

She smiles.

"And to make it better..."

I grab the pocket knife from the basket.

"Evan?"

I cut the tip of my index finger finger and hold it to the opening of the heart-shaped jewel.

"What are you doing?"

My blood fills inside of the jewel and I put pressure around the cut until it fills to the top. I insert the small plug to keep it safe from pouring out, wrap my index finger into a bandage, and hold the necklace up to her.

"I want you to wear it. To always have a piece of me with you."

She stares at the necklace, and to my own surprise, a golden glow begins to shine through some of the red, a small light. Essence gazes at the jewel.

"It's...It's beautiful."

She stands and I place the necklace over her head. The jewel rests perfectly atop her chest glowing against her skin.

"Don't ever feel as though you only lose people. Know that you will always have me."

CHAPTER TWENTY-FOUR: HISTORY

The weekend has come. I have spent hours sitting in this tree filling pages of this past week with school, speaking with my family and Mike, training, Cedric and I's encounter, and bonding with Essence. I have to be sure to keep a record of everything. I want to be sure I can come back and remember.

I will not forget about the talks and time I have spent with the girl I love, Essence LaRoux. I will not forget about Sarah, the one who has helped keep me safe through this transition. And I will not forget about the pain Cedric has been putting me through, making this transition much more difficult than it already is.

Before mom left out of town, she had informed me that she will be back before my birthday and hopefully, transformation, but for all we know, I can die at any moment. If that happens, she will return and find that I have become a vampire. A step-son who might not recognize her. It would be nice if I can at least say goodbye before I die. I mean, if I am to awaken as a vampire and not remember my human life, I'm practically being reborn as a new person. Everything before then wouldn't exist to me. When my heart stops beating, my soul will depart. My body left as a vessel to this monster. There must be something else I can do to remember. And so, I shall continue to write:

Fire. A 'gift,' as Essence had put it. Apart from the excitement, there is fear. Fear that I don't know how to use and control it. I wonder if the others are able to do the same, create fire, or something similar. Hopefully, they can tell me all the answers I need to know. Fire is destruction. Why would one want to possess a power that cannot be tamed?

But, when the time comes, when I die, I have to believe these words. No, YOU have to believe these words. So listen to me, Evan, writing this as a human today, reading this as a vampire, possibly tomorrow. Believe every word. Believe everything your family tells you. Believe that Sarah is your step-mother, your caretaker for sixteen years. Believe that Essence loves you, and that the human in you, loves her in return. You love her. You DO love her.

Evanescence

Sarah and Essence are not only afraid that you will forget who they are and your relationship with them, but they are more afraid that you will ignore these words or what they will tell you. They are also afraid, that upon reading these words, you will understand and accept them, but you will not have the emotion that your human self, me today, has for them. So be gentle.

These words will feel as though they belong to another being. A human. Not a vampire. But you were indeed human and you are loved... My breath has gone weak, and each second that passes, feels as though it may be my last.

I ask that you believe and still be there for them. I know, they are strangers, but do it for them. Do it for me; yourself. They were there for YOU when you needed them. They helped you with the transformation you have today. You owe it to them to TRY....So believe.

I am still a part of you. Believe that your heart use to beat which was once mine. So give it to Sarah, your step-mother, and most of all, give it to Essence, your love. Believe, Evan. JUST BELIEVE."

With truth,

Me and You to You,

Evan Macrae

P.S. - Tell her, I love her.

There. Maybe apart from reading those notebooks a personalized letter to myself will help. Does all of me transfer over as well? Will I be more or less stubborn? More or less happy? More or less caring about how they feel?

I don't know. I think my family would have an answer to that, but I haven't spoken to them in a while. I have not received a call or text; Bianca, Mike, and Cedric have not been in school; and I've had this house to myself, yet occasionally, Essence would keep me company as we sleep the day away.

Time is crucial right now, and with Sarah gone, I need my family as much as possible before I change. I feel as though it's coming. It's coming soon.

"You ready, Evan?" Essence asks.

"We're here in one piece?" I ask jokingly placing my notebook on the dashboard.

"I told you my father's truck is reliable."

We hop out of the truck and look up to the mansion's pillars. Lights shine from the windows.

"Well they're definitely home," Essence says.

"Yeah, hopefully I find what I'm looking for."

"And what's that?"

"Closure."

We walk to the red doors hand in hand and before we knock, the doors are opening.

"Evan? Essence?" my father says. "What a pleasant surprise. Come. Come in."

He outstretches his hand for us to come inside. He shuts the door and leads us up the golden railed staircase. We stop at a door in the hallway and he knocks. The door opens and it is my mother Valencia and sister Bianca.

"Ahem," my father clears his throat. "We have a couple visitors."

He opens the door wider. My mother and sister smile and rise from the bed.

"Son, how are you?" She hugs and squeezes. I'm getting use to her strength.

"I'm fine, mom, just wanted to talk to dad about a few things."

"Hi brother," Bianca welcomes hugging me. Then hugs Essence.

"Hi Essence."

"Hello," she responds to them.

"Always a blessing to have you here," my mother tells her.

"Thank you for being so welcoming."

"Evan and I will leave you two to care over Essence," my father says. "We're just going to have a little chit-chat about a few things and return."

"That's fine with us. We're doing some planning for his birthday," my mother says. Nice to see I was on their minds at least. "Care to help?"

"I'd love to," Essence responds.

"Speaking of which I love your necklace," Bianca admires. "Where'd you get it?"

"Evan gave it to me. As a gift."

My father places a hand on my back and speaks softly.

"Let's let them tend to activity," he whispers. "Come."

Essence then walks into the room being stolen by the hand by Bianca and my mother. She gives me one last smile before the door closes.

"Follow me, son."

I follow my father down a few hallways--long hallways. We soon enter into a round room in which the walls are covered with books like a library. A few paintings hang high above the bookshelves on red carpeted walls. A desk sits in the center of the room, covered in papers and a few open books. He closes the door and meets me next to the desk.

"This is all yours?" I ask gazing around. I walk to one of the shelves and run my hand along the titles.

"Well, my office, but it is open to anyone who needs a book or three."

My father pulls a pipe from the drawer and lights it. He blows the smoke into the air.

339

"Tastes disgusting," he chuckles. "But the act makes me look younger, I'd like to think. But anyway..."

He claps his hands together.

"We have a bit of some catching up to do. I'd imagine your time is almost up."

"Yes, I believe so. I mean, I can feel it." And I can feel my heart race from the thought of it happening.

"Hmm."

"Dad, I was wondering about what happened the other day. You guys were...I don't know, upset maybe. Something I did?"

He nods.

"Hmm. I'm sorry about that, Evan. Just a... misunderstanding."

"What kind of misunderstanding?"

He approaches a painting on the wall. It looks like him and my mother. They don't look a day older.

"Leonardo di ser Peiro da Vinci painted that. Of your mother and I. One of your favorites. We were lucky to meet him. Rest his soul."

He blows smoke from his pipe. I join his side and stare at the painting.

The Leonardo Da Vinci? I would have never, in any lifetime, would have guessed that.

"I met your mother ages ago, decades before he was born. 1408 to be exact. I was working hand in hand with my brother during his rule. It became a stressful time for France and Italy. Our people were growing hungry, and our officers weren't quite cooperative themselves. So they fed and indulged every chance they had. They were pigs. No amount of blood was satisfying enough. We searched for them, and killed them off, but could not find one of our officers. We chased him as he ran corner to corner of the world, dodging justice. Until one night, he came home, and fed on a humble family. Your mother's."

"A vampire that eats humans and other vampires?" I asked. "That's like..."

"No, Evan," he responds. "Remember, before, your mother was no vampire. She was a human."

R. J. Rogue

I had forgotten mother was bitten and miraculously, had been blessed, along with other female vampires over the centuries, with being able to procreate.

"I was much too in love with your mother before that night. She had not known. She was the only human I had eyes for and felt protective of. This of course, during a time I was feeding on humans. She made flowers, decorations, and jewelry for weddings. It was her passion and she was very good with it. We've came eye to eye before, but never spoke a word. I always watched her from a distance though knowing what monsters lurk in the night. And that night, when your mother found him, he had just finished with her family. I had been away on duty, trying to make sure nothing was becoming conspicuous. I heard screams in the night and immediately came. The house was to shreds. Blood was spilled. Her family was slain. Her pain had become my own."

He pauses for a moment, exhales, then takes a puff from his pipe.

"I opened a bedroom door and there she was, sitting against the wall covered in blood, her family, lifeless. But even more surprising, she, a human, managed to kill that vampire. When she seen me, she immediately jumped into my arms and cried telling me she had nothing left to live for. Later, my brother found out about the vampire and what happened. He became angered that now, our secrecy falls in the hands of a human woman who then began to lead a life of slaying vampires. He ordered for her to be found and killed, and I knew he would succeed if I chose to go through with it."

"He ordered you to do it? To kill her?"

He nods slowly.

"Yes, but because I loved her, I could not see myself doing such a thing. I found her finishing off a vampire. She knew the purpose of my visit, but I did not kill her, to say the least."

"You changed her."

"Yes. I was honest with my brother and told him the reason for my actions, and hers, expecting that he'd still have me killed and probably her. Surprisingly, he respected my feelings for her and spared her life. And so, the order was off. She was no longer a concern to my brother Lucid,

The Dracula, but she hated me. Hated me for turning her into the monster that killed her family. Many, many ages had gone by and she disappeared. That's when all the wars began when others heard of Lucid's generosity. They hated his leadership and soon, Lucid hated them and became viscous, killing masses of our own kind until armies of vampires fought and fought and fought. I was exhausted, owing my respects to my brother for sparing Valencia, but I also became sad with myself wondering if she had rather died that night. Until one night, I ran into her in Florence, feeding on a man. She saw me and immediately tried to fight through fists, nails, teeth...and tears. When she calmed, I took her home, paid my respects to her family, and showed her everything about being a vampire."

"That's when she fell in love with you?"

"Yes. We heard of the famous Leonardo Da Vinci and paid him a visit."

"Did he know what you and mother were?"

"To this day," my father says. "I honestly do not know. But, he was quite the artist. Artists have keen eyes, like an eagle, so I would not be surprised if he knew, and took our secret to his grave. And so, he painted us together, and that was the day I asked your mother to marry me. It was then we eloped. Hopping place to place for hundreds of years as the wars continued. I felt like a traitor and soon returned for my brother. That was when we fought together one last time. That was the night he was killed. Valencia and I came here, built our home, and protected ourselves from humans and other vampires. All while keeping the Viscus charm safe and has yet to shine."

He clears his throat and puts out his pipe.

"Technically, Cedric is right, the charm is still his father's until it chooses another. Until then, it is in my possession and has yet coiled itself around my neck no matter how fit for the position our family sees me."

He lifts it from the necklace it hangs upon.

"When the time comes, which I would not be surprised soon, someone or many will come looking for it. But I'll be ready."

"Dad. That's unbelievable," I say. "I can't imagine ever going through what you and mom have been through."

"A strong woman she is, Evan."

"So the wars are still...?"

"Yes, well not entirely still waging, but I presume there are vampires who believe the charm is destroyed, but others, have hope, and are in search of the Viscus Charm. Little do they know that He, Viscus, chooses you. Not the other way around."

"Has any vampires come here in the past?"

"A few, when you were a child. But they were immediately disposed of. You see, we rather not kill at all, but to protect this family, and to keep them from telling our whereabouts, and yours, we mustn't allow them to go free."

"And that's why you were watching me. In case they had found me. I would be defenseless."

"Yes, and so, you must be wondering what startled everyone the other day?"

"Yes."

"When you and Cedric..."

The door opens startling us.

"Brother, don't you knock?" he exclaims to Abel.

"Well, my apologies but I was excited to hear that nephew had come? Did you not allow him to say hello?"

"Hi uncle," I say giving a smile.

"Hello Evan," he hugs. "A pleasure it is; might I steal him for a bit?"

"Well you are interrupt--" my father says but is interrupted.

"Splendid! Please Evan, come with me. I'll have you back shortly. I promise."

"We'll finish later," my father says.

Without any word Abel leads me out of the room. My father goes behind his desk and takes a seat. We begin to head back down the long hallways leading to the front of the mansion.

"I watched you as a child," he says. "You were quite impressive in many things. But I knew, there was more to you than that. You are indeed special Evan, different from us all."

Where is he going with this? We approach the bottom of the staircase and stand next to the fountain.

"Your birthday is very soon," he reminds. "I wanted to ask if you would like to share it with us. Here. By afternoon, Sarah will be back and instead of heading up, and us coming into town, the strangers and outcasts, everyone can come here. Would also be nice for you to meet some friends of the family."

"Other vampires?" I ask.

"Ehh, no not all of them, but uh, what'd you say?"

"Sure, I would love that actually."

"Great. I thought it would be nice being that we haven't had your birthday here in quite a while."

"I can barely remember."

"Gentlemen!" yells a familiar voice. *Gee, I wonder who.* "Great to see you!" Mike calls from the second floor railing.

"Hey, Mike" I say.

"Sorry. Was napping."

"You sleep?"

"He tries to," Abel laughs. "Being the immortal that he is I would say it's rather difficult for him. He hasn't got it down just yet."

"Yeah, well, I'm getting close. I think it's all the excitement," he says.

"I concur," Abel responds.

Abel begins to head back upstairs and I follow.

"Essence, Bianca and Valencia seem to be having a good time. You hear that laughter?" he asks.

"What are they doing?" Mike asks meeting us at the top.

"Making jewelry and birthday planning," I say.

As we get closer to the room, the laughter continues. Abel knocks, and then opens the door. *Wow, he does knock before entering a room. That's a first.* The three of them sit on the bed next to a pile of albums.

"Awww look at his little bottom! He is so gorgeous," Essence laughs.

"Mom, I can't believe you kept this one!" Bianca exclaims.

"Well of course! It is too cute!"

Abel and Mike look over at me and smirk then back at them.

"Can we ask what's the laughing matter here?" Abel asks.

Bianca stands to her feet holding a naked baby photograph. *Yup, it's me.* Has to be. The embarrassment sets in as Abel and Mike join in the laughter. I blush.

"Okay get it all out," I cross my arms smiling and shaking my head. "At least now I know there are actual baby photos of me in the world."

A firm hand grips my shoulder. It hurt. It is my father.

"Dad, you scared me," I say trying to relax. His eyes are still and his expression is blank.

"Dad?" I say. The laughter dies down. He presses and leans against me almost knocking me over. Mike and Abel catch him.

"Whoa, easy does it, brother," Abel says. Mother, Bianca, and Essence rise to their feet and meets us by the door. *Something isn't right.*

"What's wrong dear?" She asks holding his face. He looks sick. I never knew he can get any paler. He looks at everyone and begins to stutter then turns to me and whispers like he's in pain.

"Cedric."

He falls to the floor.

"Kaius! Kaius!" my mother calls holding his face.

He is as stiff as a statue; his eyes are lost. Father brings his hand to his chest. Bianca, Abel, Mike, and my mother step back and hiss. A deep bite wound is pressed into his mark. My heart pounds against my chest.

What is going on?

"Where is he?!" Abel yells. "Where's Cedric?! Cedric!" Abel yells again.

"Mike, come with me. Now!"

Mike follows Abel out of the room.

"What do you think happened?!" I ask Bianca as my mother holds father in her arms.

"Cedric bit him," she says.

"How do we know it was him and not another vampire. Dad just told me that from time to time--"

"We know Cedric's bite. He bit him. He did this."

"He's already a vampire, what would Cedric biting him possibly do to make him react like this?"

"When we bite we inject a venom that paralyzes the victim," my mother says. "It's how we feed. A bite from another vampire isn't much, but on your mark, from a vampire of a different clan and bloodline, it is as lethal as a punctured artery, and tampers with your blood. The venom will be just as effective as it is on humans and animals; paralysis, sometimes, death. Most do this during war to either disable or instantly kill their opponent when removing a head becomes difficult. I could only hope Cedric wasn't actually trying to *kill* his uncle."

"But I still don't understand what father said before about Lucid," I say. "If Cedric's father is his brother, how could they be of a different clan and bloodline?"

"Kaius was adopted."

My heart sinks deeper into my gut. *Father was adopted.*

"What should we do?! Can we take him to a hospital!" Essence exclaims.

"Oh definitely not," I say. "That will expose him."

"Either way," Bianca says. "No medicine will work."

"So what can we do? We just can't leave him like this!" I say.

"There's nothing we can do," my mother responds. "Your father is going to have to fight this. I need you all to go and find Cedric."

I shake my head.

"Where is he?"

"Not sure," she responds unbuttoning father's shirt. "He hasn't been home since --"

Mother and Bianca jump back and hiss once again. Essence and I crawl away.

"What's wrong?!" I yell.

"The charm!" Bianca says. "It's gone!"

I crawl back to my father and his neck is naked. *Cedric.* I scurry to my feet and run out of the bedroom.

"Evan!" Essence calls.

I hop over the banister of the second floor and shove open the red doors. The wind fills the mansion and the chandelier rocks back and forth wildly. I step outside and into the drizzle of rain.

"Evan!" I hear a voice call from the forest through the wind. Abel and Mike emerge from the trees and run up the hill towards me.

353

"We can't find Cedric!" Abel yells to us.

What does Cedric plan to do with a charm he can't use? Essence and Bianca comes outside.

"Do you see him anywhere?" Bianca yells.

"No," Mike calls back. "He's gone!"

"Look!" Essence yells pointing up the mansion. We back away to get a better view and see a small figure standing on top of the bell tower just beneath the clouds that tumble atop each other, hiding the sun.

"It's Cedric!" Mike calls. "He's wearing the charm!"

"Oh no," Abel says. "Even worse. The charm is glowing."

CHAPTER TWENTY-FIVE: IMMORTAL

Cedric looks down upon us with piercing, red eyes. The charm around his neck glows a dim green. *Has the charm chosen him? How can someone as maniac as Cedric even be considered by Viscus to be Dracula, a leader?* Cedric is no leader. Cedric is an abomination.

"Dad had told me that the power of the Dracula can only be used by its reigning king, but since the king is dead, the power can't be used until it has chosen another," I tell Abel.

"Yes, that is true."

"Is that why the charm is lit?" I ask. "Has the charm chosen, Cedric?"

"No, it's lit green, yes, but not in respect that Cedric is chosen," Abel says. "Green was the color it emitted when Cedric's father was in power and alive. When a new Dracula is chosen, it should be a shade of red and orange, like fire."

I think about how I lit the candles that day Essence and I were at the beach.

355

"But if the charm is green, wouldn't that mean...?"

"No," Abel interrupts. "It would not mean Cedric's father is still alive. Your father watched Lucid die. The power of the Dracula is much greater than what you see now, but I believe, since Cedric is the son of the reigning, yet dead Dracula, his father, he can tap into some of that power by direct blood relation. And if this is not the case, and the charm is not lit because of Cedric's relation to his father, then my brother has some explaining to do about what *really* happened to Lucid Verin."

"This isn't good Abel. We have to do something," Mike says.

Cedric yells to the sky and we shelter ourselves. The light emits stronger, the wind becomes strong, and the water below moves like a raging river.

"Abel, we need dad!" Bianca yells through the wind.

"You saw what happened! He is in no shape to be out here! We need to talk Cedric down!"

"Talk?!" Mike says. "Look at him! Does he really look like he wants to talk?!"

Cedric stands still with his head to the sky.

"Then what do we do?" Essence asks.

"I say we fight!" Mike exclaims.

"No," Bianca shakes her head. "He's family. We just need to calm him down and see what's wrong."

Mike holds Bianca's face between his hands.

"Listen to me. Look at him," he points to the top of the mansion. "He already put Kaius out of commission. If we don't stop him now, what's to say he won't do the same or worse to us? What if he tries to kill someone? I won't let him hurt you."

My eyes look over to Essence. She stares at Cedric in fear and shelters herself with her hands. I pull her into my arms.

"I don't think you should be out here," I tell her. "You should go back inside with my mother."

"No, I'm staying with you, Evan."

"Essence please," I ask grabbing hold of her hands.

"No, Evan!" she yells withdrawing them. "I was here from the beginning and I'm here now. I'm not going anywhere! I told you that! I meant it!"

I try to battle the urge to persuade her to leave, but I can see in her eyes that she will not submit.

"Alright," I nod my head. "Just try not to get too close. I can't lose you."

She shakes her head.

"You won't."

Cedric continues to look into the sky as thunder rumbles and lighting rips through the clouds.

"Let's go," Mike says. "We can take him. He can't handle all of us."

"Wait," Abel says placing his hand in front of Mike. "It's worth a try...Cedric!" he yells cupping his hands next to his mouth.

"Cedric! Stop this!" Bianca yells.

"Do you think he can hear us?" Essence asks.

Abel nods his head.

"He can hear us, but who we see now may not just be Cedric. Just – anger. Malevolence. It's taking over."

Cedric doesn't budge. Thunder roars and lighting strikes his body, but he doesn't flinch. The power in the mansion goes off. The electricity runs across his body. He raises his arms above his head to the sky, it gathers into his hands, then he throws his arms and fists towards us.

"Look out!" Mike yells.

I dive onto Essence and the crunching explosion connects nearby, knocking the sound from my ears and blinds me like flash bang grenade. The force of the explosion throws us across the grass. When I find the strength to sit up, white and red dots blur my vision momentarily. When my sight stabilizes, we are scattered about. Bianca holds a hand to her head as she sits up. Mike is comforting her. Essence is next to me, where I want her, in my arms.

"Are you alright?" I ask her placing a hand on her shoulder.

She sits up and groans a bit, holding her head.

"I'll be okay," she responds and coughs.

I look around, and Cedric is still above.

"Uncle!" Bianca yells scrambling to her feet, now sprinting. Abel lies farther away from the rest of us on his side. We rush over to him, and smoke rises from his body and jacket. We turn him onto his back and he groans pain.

His side is exposed through his clothing showing a nasty burn.

"Abel," I say.

Mike stands to his feet and looks up.

"What is he doing?"

Bianca continues to comfort Abel.

"How is he able to do that?" He asks. "Is it the charm?"

Bianca nods.

"Partially. He's using himself as a strike zone for the lightning. When he is struck, the lightning coils around his arms and fists, then he redirects to towards us."

"I thought lightning couldn't strike in the same spot twice?" Mike says.

"You also thought vampires and Draculas didn't exist."

"What do we do?" I ask.

When I look to the sky, Cedric's arms are raised and he throws them towards us again.

"We have to--"

"Mike, look out!" I yell, holding a hand out to him. My warning is too late. I place my arms over Essence to protect her. Mike is struck, thrown towards the forest, and hits a tree. It splits and he flops to the ground.

"Mike," I whisper to myself. "Mike!"

"Mike, no!" Bianca yells going over to him.

I glance up to the sky at the bell tower. Cedric is still. His eyes and charm glow.

"We have to move him, before Cedric does it again," I say. We throw both of Abel's arms over our shoulders, but he withdraws.

"I'll be fine," he struggles to say looking at his burn. "I'm not fragile, but this sting really burns."

He chuckles and I fail to join in the humor.

"You two alright?"

"Yes," I say.

"We're fine," Essence responds.

"Okay, good. Go check on, Mike."

We run over to Mike and Bianca who holds his head in her lap. Mike groans and shows his fangs with a hiss.

"I'm going to kill him!" Mike yells trying to push himself up. "Ah!" he holds his hands at his midsection as Bianca tries to comfort him.

"Try to relax," Bianca tells him. "You're hurt. You'll make it worse."

"I'm fine," he responds through clenched fangs.

I look up to the sky and Cedric is gone. He stands on the edge of the cliff. He holds a malicious smile, exposing his top and bottom row of fangs. His eyes and the charm begin to dim. He stares as Abel joins us in helping Mike to his feet.

"Cedric," I say. "Why are you doing this?"

He lets out a chuckle then smiles menacingly. We stand at the edge of the forest. The trees are behind us.

"Why?"

"Yes. What have we done to you?" I ask.

"*They* have done nothing! It's you!" he yells. In an instant he is gone.

We look around for him, but fail. The wind picks up.

"All of this because of you!" The tree next to us begins to fall. Cedric's hands are placed against its body as he pushes with all his might.

"Move!" Abel yells. Bianca pulls Mike away to dodge the falling giant. We all dive out of the way as it slams to the ground. We lay still and await his next move.

"Where is he?!" Bianca yells.

"Over here," we hear him call from a distance.

He stands at the cliff again, his arms hanging to his sides. He breathes heavily, beneath his hair, each breath, blowing strands away from his mouth.

"You all look scared of me."

"Cedric, you have to stop this," Abel says stepping forward and out to the open. We follow closely behind. "This has gone out of hand. What would Kaius think?"

"Kaius is not my father!" he yells. Thunder above roars across the sky as the rain gets heavier. *Why is he so angry?*

"This is nonsense, Cedric!" Bianca calls.

"Cedric," Mike says stepping forward. "If it's a fight you are looking for, I'm more than willing to--"

"You should just be quiet," Cedric interrupts. "You're still as weak as the human you once were."

"And you're still as weak as you have always been."

"Enough!" he yells.

His eyes and the charm begins to glow again.

"Oh no," Bianca says.

"Abelll," Essence says. "What do we do?"

"I'm working on it."

"Now you will witness how strong I am and how weak you all are!"

He crouches low to the grass, then runs towards us. We brace ourselves, but then he's gone. We look around, but nothing.

"I can't believe he's actually doing this?" Bianca says.

I pull Essence behind me to shelter her. Mike, Abel, and Bianca stand their ground.

"Hey!" He yells.

We turn around and he's in the air, coming towards us. When he's close enough to grab, a foot connects with his face and sends him into the forest. A loud bang follows in which the trees and bushes shake.

"Mom," I exclaim as she hugs us.

"I see things have escalated a bit too much."

"He's lost his mind," Mike says.

"He needs help," Abel exclaims. "It appears the source of his tension is with, Evan. Not sure over what exactly, but he did make it known."

"And I see he isn't being cooperative," my mother says.

"Not the slightest," I respond.

"How's father?" Bianca asks.

"He will be okay. Still a bit stunned, but he will be fine."

"Do you hear that?" Essence says. We listen. "It's coming from the forest."

We look to the forest and see a large object coming towards us.

"What is that?" I ask.

"Everybody move!' Abel yells. The object escapes from the forest. We jump out of the way and it disappears over the cliff.

"What was that?!" Mike says.

Abel exhales deeply and moves his hair from his face.

"It was a tree."

"A tree?" Mike says.

"Uh huh," Abel responds.

"What kind of vampire throws trees?" Mike says perplexed and confused.

"One that is upset apparently."

Cedric steps out of the forest placing his hands onto two trees that stand on each side of him. He pushes his arms apart, and the trees begin to snap from the root, and fall against two others.

"No more of this!" he yells pointing to me.

"Cedric stop!" Abel commands.

Cedric prowls to the ground. In an instant, he runs, practically glides, across the grass, towards Essence and I.

366

"Evan!" he roars. Mother cartwheels and lands another hit. He spins sideways in the air like a wheel before she strikes his body again throwing him into a tumble across the grass. He immediately recovers and stands to his feet.

"Your mother has quite a background with killing vampires. Cedric wouldn't be a match," Abel comments.

"Cedric! You stop this nonsense now!" she yells pointing a finger to him.

"This has nothing to do with you! Any of you! This is between me and Evan!"

"What do you have against Evan?!" Bianca yells.

"Be quiet," he tells her.

"What has he ever done to you?!" Essence says.

"SHUT UP!" he yells as wind gusts around us, his hair blown above his head. He sprints towards us again.

One by one they sprint towards him. I keep Essence behind me. Abel attempts to grab hold of him and fails. He is pushed to the side and tumbles across the ground. Mike tries to charge through him. Cedric flawlessly leaps over him, plants a foot into his back and pushes with a force that knocks Mike across the grass. Bianca swings towards his face. He catches her arm, puts his back into her torso, and flings her over his body. Our final hope, my mother, goes for a grab. He ducks and wraps his arms around her waist and tries lift her from behind. She locks her ankle around his. He moves his foot, and tries again. She throws an elbow over her shoulder to hit his face. Cedric ducks, lifts her onto his shoulder, and pushes her legs up. She flips over and her falls onto her back.

"Cedric!" I yell.

He stops. My mother places a hand on his ankle. He looks down at her and kicks her ribs. She lets out a shriek.

"Mom!"

He kicks again and she rolls holding her forearms to her stomach.

"What are we going to do?!" Essence says.

I throw my hands to my head to try and think, but nothing comes to mind. Cedric kicks one last time sending mother into the air. She tumbles to Bianca. He then starts walking towards us. *Think Evan! Don't be afraid!*

"Leave him alone!" Essence yells leaving my arms.

"Essence no!" I yell losing my grip of her.

He catches her punch by the wrist and smirks. My heart falls into my stomach. Cedric kicks her at the hamstring and she drops to her knees.

"Cedric!"

He holds her head by the hair. Essence's eyes meet mine as she grips onto his hand full of her hair.

"You see? Strong," he says. He then places his hand on her throat and raises her into the air. *Why aren't you doing anything!* My heart bleeds. I try to save Essence. When Cedric is arm's reach, a devastating blow connects with my nose and I drop to my knees cuffing my face. The pain shot to the bone. He broke it. Warmth fills my hands. *Blood.*

"*Cedric. Please. Stop this.*" I beg holding my nose, looking into Essence's eyes as she struggles to breathe. He doesn't respond.

I hear his grip tighten around her neck and immediately a tear falls from my eye. *I feel weak, but...but I am not. I can't be. This is why I am here with my family. So I can become strong and accept myself. I am not weak. I can do something about this. I may not have changed yet, but I promised myself I will always protect Essence and would never let any harm come to her. But here she is. Held high above the ground, choking within Cedric's merciless grip.*

I look over at my family who are on the ground trying to help each other. *He's hurt my family and he's hurt me. Now everyone is counting on me to do something.*

"Ev-Evan," I hear Essence choke.

"Why should--?"

I ball my fist and shove it into his stomach. He chokes on his words. Essence hits the ground, gasping for air as Cedric hovers himself above his knees, wincing and grunting from the blow. I stand above him.

"You can't beat me," he says shaking his head and laughing.

He swings and the blow hits my cheek, throwing me from my feet and onto my back.

"Cedric stop this!" Abel yells running over.

"Cedric!" mother calls.

They surround him.

"You all wish to fight me?" he says. "I'm too strong. For you..." he points at Abel.

"You..." he points at Bianca.

"You... And you," he says pointing at Mike and my mother. "And I'm definitely stronger than you." He points looking over at me.

"You don't have to do this," my mother says. "We can talk about what's bothering you."

"No," he responds.

"Let us help you," Abel says.

"I don't need help!" he yells.

"What is it that you want?!" Bianca asks.

"I WANT EVAN DEAD!" he yells.

"Why?!" Mother yells.

"You see, at first, I was just upset over babysitting and may have exaggerated a bit about killing him. But then, he wouldn't just stop taking everything from me! Everything I've ever wanted!"

"What are you talking about Cedric?!" Bianca asks.

"You all saw it. You saw it! When we were teaching him! You saw his eyes! You saw the charm glow! It's choosing him! Waiting for his transformation! Just so he can take what belongs to my family!"

A shiver runs down my spine, everyone looks at each other, then at me.

"Is it true?" I ask them.

My mother nods.

"Yes, but we were unsure."

"No you weren't," Cedric says through his clenched fangs. "The moment you seen the charm glow, and the color of Evan's eyes, you all bowed."

Essence tugs my arm and I nod. That would probably explain the fire.

"He will not take what's mine," he shakes his head. "I have to get rid of him before he transforms. If he does, the charm will coil itself around his neck, while I be nothing, have nothing, and have no one!"

In an instant, he knocks Bianca to the ground. Mike angrily throws countless punches, but each of them miss as Cedric dodges effortlessly. He then plants a foot into Mike's chest. I hear a crack and Mike cries in agony.

"MIKE!" I yell.

Evanescence

My mother and Abel charge for Cedric. He waits. Mother extends her foot for a kick, but Cedric catches her ankle, swings her body like a bat, and let's go. Abel catches her and they both hit the ground. I stand in between what can be the fate of us all. Here is my chance.

I dig my feet into the ground, crouch my upper body, and sprint towards him. I hold my fist behind me gathering as much energy as I can. Cedric has yet to see me coming. *My punch is going to land and it's going to land hard.* I throw my fist through the wind and towards Cedric, but then, my confidence falls. His eyes lock into mine and a grin spreads across his lips. Before I can brace for his counter, his foot leaves the ground and connects under my jaw.

What follows is a pop in my neck that makes my body feel like pins and needles and then, nothing. I flop onto the ground and roll towards the cliffs edge.

"Evan!" I hear a scream.

I struggle to lift my head. I try to move, but I feel paralyzed. My daze sees figures approaching me. I blink and the corners of my vision are a blur and begin to fade, but I don't feel any pain. One of them holds my face close to theirs. It's Essence. I know her scent, but I cannot respond nor move.

"For years," I hear Cedric say. "I've sat back and watched how engulfed this family was with Evan. Neglecting me. At least he had Sarah, Kaius, Valencia, Mike, Bianca, and now, Essence! Now, possibly the next Dracula?! No! That's mine! It belongs to me! If my father is dead, which I highly doubt, I must avenge him as well as my brother and sister, Mathis and Agatha. Better Evan be dead too!"

"Evan," I hear a cry. "Open your eyes. Please...Wake up."

I feel myself slipping away. I feel light as a feather. Sleepy. Cold.

My mother, Valencia, holds me on her lap, singing to me.

Bianca and I chase each other down the hallways of the mansion.

My stepmother, Sarah, sits next to me on my bed, comforting me from the nightmare I was having.

Evanescence

"Everything will be okay," she says.

"We always had to watch Evan in school and wait for him to remember us! And then Kaius! Kaius becomes the Dracula by default? Stealing the throne from my father? It should be me! My reign!"

~

Mike and I are at the rec center; he saves me from the kids who try to toss me into the pool. Essence is in the hallways seventh grade year, then eighth grade, ninth, and now, tenth, but I never speak.

Abel stands above me.

"It's you. It really is you, Evan," he says.

Mike is gone. I speak with his grandmother.

"He's happy here. Isn't he, Evan?" She asks me.

My family finds me on the cliff.

"We've been watching you, Evan," my father says.

Essence finds me in the tree. She kisses me for the first time.

"I'll always be here for you," she says.

"I want what is mine! No one ever cared about my feelings! Made me feel special! I was treated as an adopted kid to everyone given the bare minimum! And Kaius! He was supposed to remain loyal my father and didn't! And I am supposed to care about all of you?!"

My family teaches me how to be a vampire.
My father shows and tells the family history.
Cedric attacks us as he stands above the bell tower.
He hurts my family. They fall across the grass, one by one.
He hurts Essence...

He...Hurts Essence.

"It's...it's happening," I hear someone say. It is my mother.

"No," cries Essence. "Please. Not right now."

My heart slows. I try to hold on, but death is strong. When it wants you, it takes you. I can't move. I can barely breathe. I am dying. I am dying and when I wake, I will no longer be a 'who,' but also a 'what.' A vampire

"Evan," Essence whispers. "I love you."

This is it. This is the moment. This is the end of me.

I love you too, Essence.

CHAPTER TWENTY-SIX: FADING FROM DECEPTION

I walk through the darkness trying to find light. There is nothing and it is cold. Beneath my feet is a moist, thick texture like mud. It reminds me of the forest when it rains, but I don't smell the rain nor do I smell the mint.

"Hello?" I call out. My voice travels onward, but no voice returns.

"Hello?" I call again. Nothing. I can tell no difference between blinking and keeping my eyes open. I begin to walk and feel through dark for anything I can touch, but nothing meets my hands. Then, the air around begins to warm and the smell of burnt wood grows stronger with each step I take. Instantly, I stand amongst a charging crowd of people yelling at the top of their lungs. Some leap into the fire lit air, some hiss as they are laying in the dirt wounded, and some are fighting others…Vampires. I look around and fire blazes everywhere around us and burns wooden buildings and houses. No one acknowledges me. It's as though I am a ghost.

"I can't hold them off much longer!" I hear a voice shout.

On a large mound of rock stands two men back to back as masses of vampires jump and fight them. They dodge and throw some vampires here and some there.

"Don't fail on me, Kaius!"

Kaius?

"Father?" I say to myself.

I begin to run through the crowd pushing vampires away to get to my father. I get tossed about as the two vampires continue to fight the hundreds; dodging, throwing, and killing. I fall to the ground and immediately scramble to my feet now closer to them both.

"Lucid! We can't take them all!" I hear my father yell.

The vampire with the heavy scar that cuts across his face from eyebrow to his chin stops fighting and turns to my father. He pushes him.

"Then go! Get out of here! I don't need you," he tells him.

"No!" my father shakes his head. "I'm not leaving you alone. You can come with me!"

"Leave!" he yells again as a heavy wind knocks my father, myself, and everyone away and across the ground. I push myself to a sit and stare at the green light that emits from Lucid's necklace. My father stares at him momentarily and Lucid looks betrayed. My father then leaps away, disappearing amongst the crowd of fighting vampires.

"Dad!" I call out.

I try to follow and look amongst the hundreds, but fail to find him. Lucid continues to fight the vampires who are beginning to close in on him. He kills and dodges and throws one after another. Fire leaves each punch he lands and death meets each vampire thrown, but the crowd is too difficult to manage and continues to grow. They manage to grab hold of him. I can try to help, but I know I would not succeed. I am no match.

The vampires try to pull him apart. It doesn't work. A vampire steps in front of him. The others bring Lucid to his knees, struggling in the process. The vampire raises his arm high above his head wielding a sharp wooden object, and with one quick swipe, Lucid's head is removed. A clean kill.

Evanescence

The crowd goes wild as the vampire holds the Viscus charm high for all to see. The green light dims within the necklace. I look around for my father, but he is nowhere to be found.

The cheering suddenly dies down and turns into a small, chatter as they look to the sky. I follow their eyes, but the sky is dark. I see nothing.

A boy and a girl land on the ground and immediately start to take out vampire after vampire. They can't be much older than myself, but they are much quicker and stronger than they look. The boy has short black hair that spikes up to white ends. Black paint runs from his bottom lip, down his chest, and disappears behind his black leather clothing. The girl has a white bob and wears black lipstick. Her neck and hands are covered in black symbols. They fight through the crowd flawlessly and some flee away. I stand not too far away from them as they look about for anyone else that wishes to fight.

"Mathis!" says the girl as she runs over to where Lucid's body and head lies.

The boy turns his attention to her and runs over.

381

"NO!" he yells. "No! No! No!"

He holds Lucid's body into his lap and puts his face into the chest. They both cry over Lucid. When the crying stops, Mathis lifts his head and anger fills his swollen eyes and fists.

"Agatha," he says through clenched teeth. "Get his head. There isn't much time."

"What do you plan on do--?"

"Now!" he shouts. She rises to her feet without another word and picks up Lucid's head. Mathis throws Lucid's body over his shoulder and they leap over the fire, escaping.

I look around and I am alone. I walk over to where Lucid had been killed. Nearby, the Viscus charm lies in the dirt, the light still dim. A woman with white hair, startles me as she brushes past and falls to her knees panting. She picks up the necklace and stares at it.

"Lucid," she whispers to herself. "I am too late." She cups the charm to her chest and bows her head. I watch as she sits still moments longer, before she lets out an angered yell.

"Vengeance. Vengeance will be mine and with my family!"

She stands to her feet and leaps away with the Viscus charm.

"Kaius!" I hear a woman cry out.

I turn to the voice and find myself standing in the night on a wet paved road, no longer the battlefield. The woman who took the necklace lies on the ground. My father rushes and tends to her. She is badly wounded.

"Scarlett! What happened?!"

"There isn't much time for me. I won't make it."

"You must stop this."

"No Kaius!" She pleads. "I fought for him," she nods. "And for my family...Mathis and Agatha."

"Where are they?"

She cries out in agony and winces at the pain. She chokes, but recovers.

"There is talk that they are now dead. I mustn't believe it, but I haven't been convinced they are alive. Please, there is a boy at my home. His name is Cedric. The last of my family and your relative. Take him Kaius. Take care of my boy."

Kaius clasps his hand around hers and nods.

"As I would my own."

"And take this." She holds out the Viscus charm. "Protect it. Keep it away until it chooses another."

Kaius hesitates, but accepts and pockets the charm.

"Go. Hurry before they find my boy. Watch over him Kaius. Love him."

"I will. I promise you." He stands to his feet. "Goodbye, Scarlett."

She smiles gently and her face goes cold. Her body begins to ash and blow in the wind. My father takes off.

A pain cuts across my head. I clasp my hands to my temples and drop to my knees. The pain digs deeper.

It's happening!

I let out a cry in agony and drop my forehead to the wet paved road. I hear a crunch in my ears as the pain intensifies inside my head. My vision begins to fade and disorientate. My eyes burn like fire, my mouth aches, and my skin begins freeze.

Evanescence

I pound my fist onto the ground hoping it would stop, but it is no use. I begin to choke as though the air is being sucked dry from my lungs. The inside of my chest becomes as cold as ice as my hands begin to shake and tingle. I look into my shaking palms, then flip them over. My family's mark appears and a final yell leaves my throat. All becomes still before the darkness consumes me.

CHAPTER TWENTY-SEVEN: DESTINY FULFILLED

The rain pours upon me. I sit up in the grass and cough. My head hurts, my mouth aches, and my body feels – different. They all kneel before me and stare. I bring my hand to my head trying to ease the pain. It doesn't work.

"What just happened?" I ask.

"Evan?" Essence says.

"Yes?"

She jumps onto me hugging tight. I wrap my arms around her. When she lets go, she kisses me, smiles, but then it fades.

"You're..."

"A vampire," my mother says.

I feel them. The fangs in my mouth. I gasp and look into my hands. Pale. My fingernails are sharp. I press my hand to my chest. No heartbeat and something tells me it will never return.

"I died."

"Yes," Abel says.

"It fits you," Bianca adds.

"Well! Lookie here!" Cedric calls. "The prodigal vampire. Tell me Evan, how does it feel?"

A sharp ache in my jaw settles in and mother tries to comfort me.

"Ah," Cedric continues. "Someone needs that first meal."

"Here Evan, drink," mother holds her wrist up to my mouth. "It's not human blood, but it will hold you for a while and make you strong enough."

"I can't," I shake my head.

"But you must," she says.

"No," Bianca says. "We're a pair. It'd be better he gets it from me." She then holds her wrist before my mouth. "Drink."

"Oh, I can't let that happen," Cedric starts for us.

"Hold him off!" Bianca tells them. Mike tries to fight and fails. He is thrown to the ground. Abel is next to join next to him, and my mother lands a few punches and kicks before she is tossed to the side as well.

"Drink, Evan! Now!" Bianca yells. I grab her wrist, bite deep, and take a gulp. Cedric knocks Bianca to the side and pushes Essence and I apart.

"Nice try!" Cedric exclaims. "You really thought I would let--"

What is this feeling? My body won't stop shaking.

"No," Cedric says. "Ugh! Nooo!"

I stand to my feet and wipe my mouth from the blood.

"Do you think you--"

I land a punch to his face, he stumbles back, then shakes his head.

"Cheap shot."

"You deserved it."

One step forward, and we're face to face. His eyes widen.

"How did you…"

I clench his shirt within my fists and toss him towards the forest. He slams into a tree and slides down its now broken, wooden body. When he hits the ground, I stand above him. Waiting for him to look me in my eyes. He can't be forgiven. He laughs, but I can tell through that laugh, he's hurting.

"Well, that was a surprise. Someone's angry."

He looks up at me, but before I can land a blow to his face, he tackles me into the ground. We tumble deeper into the forest. When I recover, I jump to a tree and begin to climb.

"Where are you going?!" he yells. He throws himself at the tree, trying to knock me down. I hold on and wrap my arms around the wood. It slowly begins to tip. I stand to my feet, run along tree, and leap to the next. Cedric runs along the falling tree, and jumps after me.

"How far will you get?!" he says.

I'm not running. I'm planning my next move.

"Come down, Evan and fight me!"

I get to the top of the tree and stand. I look above the treetops through the rain and wind. Cedric emerges from the tree's branches and leaves and tackles me into the raining air towards the mansion. My head rocks with pain and tosses back with each swing of his fist connecting to my face.

"You can't win!" he yells.

"I will," I say.

I look over my shoulder and we descend towards a window. I shift our weight, and put his back towards the mansion. Cedric looks over his shoulder as I hold him in my fists. We brace for impact.

We crash through the glass window, a ceiling, and tumble into the dining room breaking the table, chairs, and chandelier. I lay still on the floor and try to catch my breath. I don't hear Cedric, but I know he must feel worse than me.

Glass crackles nearby. *It's him.* I push myself off the floor and stand to fight. Before I can defend myself, a glass cup I smashes across my face and shatters into a thousand pieces. I shake it off, but then a fist full of knuckles meet my eyes.

"You're still weak. I'm tanning your hide, newborn," he says.

His punch hurt more than the glass. My head retracts to face him again. Before my vision can stabilize, another fist meets my face. I stumble and grab hold of the walls of the doorway behind me. When he steps forward to swing again,

Evanescence

I jump, tuck my knees to my chest, then extend my legs and feet to his chest. I fall onto the floor landing on my back, but his feet leave the floor beneath him and he is thrown into the wall, it catches him like a baseball glove. *He's stronger than I thought. I have to keep going, but I have to end this quick.*

I step out of the living room, trying to catch my breath.

"Don't turn your back on me! Is that all you got?!"

I turn to face him which might have been a mistake. He charges and gores his shoulder into my stomach sending us through the railing and down to the first floor ten feet below. We lay on the floor, coughing and stumbling to stand. He's up before I am.

"Get up," he says as he brings me to my feet. He lands a punch into my stomach and then my face. I fall to a knee holding myself up with a hand placed on the floor. When he reaches for me again, I swing once, twice, and a third time, each connecting with his face. I grab him by the neck and waist and hold him above my head. He struggles to fight my grip. I toss him up, he hits the chandelier, then slams into the marble floor.

"You're only prolonging your death cousin," he says.

I shake my head.

"I'm not the one who is going to die. It didn't have to be this way, Cedric."

"No. It did."

"I can take you."

"Looks like you're struggling to me," he says.

"Yet, you're the one on the floor."

He yells and charges at me. He throws his weight into my stomach, we break through the red doors, and tumble across the grass. He crawls on top of me.

"Evan!" I hear Essence call.

Cedric's fist rises above him as he uses his other hand to hold me by the neck. I avoid the blow and his fist sinks into the ground. He swings again. Another miss. I roll on top of him and take a swing. It lands. I take another, but he catches my wrist and flips me over his body. I stare into the falling sky, but force myself to get up.

"Evan, look out!" Essence yells.

Evanescence

I turn to face Cedric and his fists connect with my chest and send me to the edge of the cliff. I lay for a moment and look over at Bianca.

"Get the charm, Evan!" Bianca yells.

I look at Cedric's neck. The charm glows as he charges towards me. *I will.*

I brace myself to catch him, but underestimated his strength as we tumble closer to the edge of the cliff. Cedric's grip is unbreakable as he rolls onto his back holding me above him to toss me over. He smiles as I rise above him, soon to fall into the sky. My eyes lay upon the green light from the necklace. I place my hand around the charm, and when he tosses me over the cliff, it breaks from his neck.

"NO!" I hear him say as my body plummets through the sky to the water below.

I break through the surface of the water and allow myself the sink and rest. It is dark and quiet and the only visible light is that of the jewel. With this out of Cedric's possession, he has become less of a threat, but I still worry. He is strong.

I swim to the surface, using the necklace as a guide. When I reach the bottom of the cliff, I begin to climb, one hand after the other. One foot after the other.

"I don't need it to beat any of you!" I hear him yell as I pull myself over the edge.

I raise my hand into the air holding up the charm.

"This?"

"Give it back," he commands.

"I thought you said you didn't need it," I tell him.

"That's not the point. The point is it doesn't belong to you!"

"It doesn't belong to you neither. The charm hasn't chosen anybody."

"It belongs to my family! It belongs to my father!" he yells.

"Your father is dead!" I say.

"Shut up!" he yells. "No more talking! Evan, give me the charm. Final warning!"

"Or what Cedric?" Bianca says. "You'll kill us all?"

"If it comes to that, then yes. I will kill all of you. For now, I just want, Evan. So stay out of this."

"We are a family, Cedric," mother says. "And family sticks together."

"We're not a family! My family isn't here. For all we know, Kaius is the reason my father is dead!"

"You can't blame him, Cedric," Abel says. "Your father was reckless."

"My father was one of the greatest Dracula's that had ever reigned."

"No," Abel says shaking his head and stepping forward. "He wasn't. The power of Viscus doesn't make you a true Dracula. It is the choices you make with that power. Kaius was more of a Dracula than Lucid. And if anything, Kaius was more of a father to you as well."

"Enough!" Cedric hisses at Abel.

"That's it I'm taking him!" Mike says running towards him. Abel follows behind, but both he and Mike are tossed aside by Cedric. *How is he so strong?* Mother and Bianca try and fail as well. I prepare to step in, but my heart almost dies. Cedric's eyes are upon Essence.

No. Not again.

Cedric grabs Essence by the neck. She chokes my name and grasps onto his wrists. Her feet leave the ground and she kicks for freedom.

"This one is fragile. Careful, handle with care," he says.

I close my eyes and focus on breathing. I drop the charm.

Focus on a time when you felt endangered. Now, careful I tell you. Anger is inevitable; however, do not allow anger to provoke careless action. Allow the essence of your soul to find peace within yourself. Only then will you know how to bring out the better, stronger, you. "

I open my eyes. Before Cedric can land a blow, I clench his forearm in my hand. I look deep into his eyes and his laughter dies. He lets go of Essence and swings. He misses. He tries again. He misses again. I jump and watch him from above as he looks around.

"Come out you coward!" he yells.

"Up here," I say.

Cedric looks up then jumps out of the way. He angrily throws his fists, but I dodge.

"Give me the charm, Evan!"

He lifts his foot from the ground to kick my chest. Another miss, but this time, I throw my elbow to his face, and when it connects to his nose, I hear a pop. It's broken. Just as he did me. He shakes it off and waves for me to come again. As I walk to him, he tries to tackle me. *Typical.* I catch and hold him beneath me and strike my knee into his stomach. He hurls. I kick his face upwards. He falls onto his back.

"You can't beat me!" He says.

I stare at him waiting for him to get up. He yells at the top of his lungs and begins to swing wildly one fist after another. I dodge continuously without losing a single breath of air. When he throws a hook to my face, I duck and push my hands outward and into his chest just as he had done me. His feet leave the ground and tumbles towards the cliff.

"Evan," I hear Bianca call.

I will finish what Cedric started. He lifts his head and I stand above him. His next move, he will try to kick my face again. He yells his last, plants a hand on the ground, and his legs sweeps upward to the side of my face. I duck and when his body spins back to me, I begin to land countless blows to his face.

"Evan," Abel calls to me. I continue to land punches on Cedric, each making him take a step back closer to the edge.

"Evan!" Bianca calls again.

Cedric's body goes weak but I continue to punch his nose, then his cheek, then his nose again, then into his stomach. He twists his body for another attempt to kick to my face. I wait as his foot rises. I raise my forearm and stop it. He swings and I catch his fist. I punch his arm and hear a crunch. Agony leaves his lips and throat with a hiss. He drops to his knees holding his arm to his stomach.

"Ev!" Mike calls.

"Brother?!" Bianca yells.

Cedric lifts his head kneeling before me. His eyes are low and barely glow. I raise my hand above my head. He waits, breathless.

"You're not talking much anymore," I say. "Any last words?"

"I was wrong," he says trying to keep his body from falling over.

"What are you talking about?"

He smiles through the blood and pain, then licks his lips. "You're not a human at all. You're a monster." He spits to the side then begins to laugh. "Just like me, Evan."

He laughs hysterically and glares through his hair.

"You're just like me!" He yells.

My hand feels as hot as fire. He nods.

"Do it," he says as he lifts his head with pride.

"I planned to."

"EVAN!" Mother and Abel yell.

"Don't!" Bianca yells.

I swing towards his face, to remove his head, but I stop. She coils herself around me. Her head presses against my back, legs around my waist, arms locked around my torso, and her hair blows in the wind and against my face.

"Evan," Essence whispers as I hold my hand above Cedric.

"Don't. You're not a monster. You're not like him."

Her grip tightens around me. I try not to submit, but her love is compelling. I give in. Cedric falls to the ground and lays still. I turn to Essence. She is out of breath, but finds a smile as I move her hair away from her eyes.

"Thank you."

My family joins our side. My mother cups my face with her hands and hugs me.

"Evan," my mother says. "I'm so glad you're okay."

"Nephew," Abel says practically out of breath. "Are you alright?"

"Didn't expect to see that," Mike says as Bianca crutches him and holds a hand on his chest.

"Me either I guess," I say, still trying to calm down.

"Nice teeth," he smirks.

"They hurt."

"Brother," Bianca says hugging me tight. "You're...You're you."

"I am," I smile. "Oh!" I groan. My jaw aches and my body is weak. I stumble, but Essence holds me up.

"Take it easy there my immortal," Essence says. "You worry me enough."

"Hey!"

My dad crawls from the mansion and across the grass.

"Dad!"

We run over to him and he rolls onto his back, exhausted.

"Just relax," I tell him. His eyes widen.

"Well, look at you," he exclaims. "A vampire. Wow, Evan. I have been waiting for the day. How do you feel?"

I smile.

"I feel okay. Still the same, just, hungry.

He nods his head.

"Yes, yes, I see." He tries to sit up. "Where's Cedric?"

"He's--"

We look over to the cliff. My heart leaps into my throat. It is them. The two I seen in my vision before I died. The boy's hair is black, gelled to a small white-tipped mohawk. A bold black line, as wide as a finger, runs from his bottom lip, down his chin and neck, and disappears behind the zipper of his black jacket. The girl has a white bob, and wears black lipstick. Her neck and hands are covered with black symbols. They both stand on each side of Cedric, watching at us. The boy is a bear in size, like Mike, but bigger. The girl is much smaller, but her facial expression is that of strict authority. We stare back without moving an inch. The boy throws Cedric over his shoulder.

I begin to stand, but father grabs hold of my arm.

"Mathis? Agatha?" my father says.

They turn away from us and jump off the cliff.

"How can it be?" my father says. "They--I thought they were dead."

"This isn't good, Kaius," mother says.

"Oh no," Abel says as his face hugs the ground.

"That was his brother and sister, wasn't it?" I ask.

"Yes," Abel responds.

I become dizzy for a moment and my head aches. I fight and ignore it.

"You alright?" Father asks.

I nod.

"Mathis and Agatha?" Bianca says.

"If they have returned, then this is only the beginning making Cedric the least of our problems," father says.

The ache returns and I bring a hand to my head and rub against it. I shake it off.

"We have to get them," Mike says. "Stop them while we have them here."

"No. I am more worried about how they found us," father says.

"Oh, almost forgot," I reach into my pocket and pull out the charm.

He smiles and bows his head as I place the charm around his neck. We help father to his feet. The dizziness returns and I try to ignore it once more, but it intensifies. My brain feels as though it is being punctured with pins and needles. I wince.

"We should get you back inside," mother says.

I look around and the place is a wreck.

"What happened?" I ask.

My family look at each other then back to me.

"You and Cedric destroyed the house."

I think for moment, and nod.

"Sorry, must've slipped my mind."

"Are you feeling alright, Evan?" Asks the curly red head. She is beautiful. Her eyes are gentle. And her skin is flawless.

"Yes," I respond. "Thank you for asking, um."

I try to get her to say her name. She waits for me to complete my sentence. *Why not help me out here?*

I look around at everyone else. *Why is everyone staring at me like that?*

"What's wrong?" I ask.

She stares into my eyes and I stare back.

"What's my name?" She asks.

I search for a clue from everyone else, but they all await an answer.

"What is my name, Evan?"

How does she know mine?

"I don't know, but you know mine. Tell me. What is your name?"

She shakes her head and slouches to the floor. She cups her hands to her mouth, then looks at me. The corner of her eyes begin to glisten into tears.

"Did I do something wrong?" I ask looking around.

"I--I'm Essence, Evan," she says. Her name doesn't ring a bell. Everyone remains quiet. Mike looks away. Bianca's face hugs the ground.

"You—love me," she says.

"I—love you?"

"Yes," she says immediately. I look at everyone and let out a small chuckle.

"Whoa, that's uh. Pretty deep, I mean. I would know, right?" I smile. *What kind of joke is this? We have more important things to worry about like Mathis, Agatha, and Cedric. Where are they headed?*

"Is this some kind of a joke?" I ask. "We should be worrying about--"

"Why would you think it's a joke?" she asks.

"How can I love someone that I don't even know? I've never seen you a day in my life, but you say we are in love."

Her face hugs the ground. She's pained by my words, begging for the heart I don't have.

"So you were wrong. You said that you would remember."

"Remember? Remember what?"

"Take Evan inside please," my father says. I sniff the air and my stomach aches with hunger.

"That smell," I say stepping towards Essence. "It's -- it's--"

"Let's go, Evan," Mike says taking me by the arm with a strong grip. My eyes stay with hers as a tear leaves her eyelash and goes down her cheek.

"Essence," Bianca says. She whispers something to her and Essence nods her head. She turns away and before I can get another word out, they walk over to a truck that is nearby.

My mother, father, Mike, and Abel lead me inside.

"Who was that?" I ask them.

"My son," father says. "In due time."

CHAPTER TWENTY-EIGHT: THE DAY DREAMER

It is my seventeenth birthday. The past couple weeks have been difficult dealing with this...thirst. I almost went insane with hunger when my father handed me a blood packet after the fight. The smell of blood is addictive. The taste, greatly irresistible.

The first few nights were horrid. Despite how hungry I was, I had refused to eat. One by one they'd come to my room and knock, trying to offer me blood. Explaining how it is important that I try. I smelled it though. Potent. But I just couldn't see myself doing it.

The days and week that followed changed everything. The smell became much more irresistible. It was impossible to ignore. One night, Mike wasn't taking no for an answer. He told me I was the most pale of everyone. An *unhealthy* pale. I laughed at the thought of a certain tone of 'pale' being unhealthy, but I understood what he meant.

And so he burst into my room, held it to my face, and when I smacked it from his hands, the beast within me burst free from its cage. The blood pack busted open, and before I knew it, I was on the floor, licking it off of the marble. I spent hours crying in my room afterwards. Hating myself for giving in.

The very color of it is such a pleasure to the eye. I would kill for it, but I shouldn't. My family is teaching me how to control the thirst to kill for blood. I laughed when they told me I use to be a vegetarian. They even oppose killing animals. Both acts seem to be a monstrosity to them, and so, we are fed -- by a human. A woman that works for a blood donor company that's just outside of the city.

They say she is a close friend. I've seen her a few times, but only from the window. Supposedly, I known her for years. All of them to be exact. *She took care of you,* they told me. She would drive up to the mansion and hand my father a supply of blood packets. My favorite type; O negative. It's sweet.

She would do as she always does and look up to my window before she leaves. I'd wave and she'd smile. Each time, despite how addicting she smelled from where I stood, I feel protective of her.

Evanescence

And the girl. The irrevocably beautiful, big curls of red hair to the shoulder, I was once in love with. Her name; Essence LaRoux. Today, I get to meet them both, Sarah, my stepmother, and Essence, my *'love.'*

I have not been able to attend school nor do I remember much about school. Even though I've always attended, I'll feel like a new student in every classroom. As people say my name, I will not know theirs. I wonder what excuse my family gave the school as to why I was gone. When I go back, will my thirst entirely be under control with all those people crowded around me? Or will I lose it?

It didn't take much time to repair the house from the damage caused by Cedric and I and since then, there has been no sign of him. No sign of his brother, Mathis, or sister, Agatha, but something tells me I'll see them again. They will try to fight us. They will fail.

I can't remember much of how things were before I died. Each time I try, all I see is tension I had with Cedric, meeting my family, and Mike. Everything else is as choppy and random as a dream.

Mike and I sit on the lip of the bell.

"We should probably start getting ready," he says. "Some people are already here and more are coming."

He stands to his feet, and looks down at me.

"What are you thinking about, Ev?" He asks.

I shrug.

"When we die, and our soul lives on, what becomes our purpose?" I ask.

"To accept at we lived," he says.

"Then what was our purpose while we were alive?"

"To accept that we'll die."

"That's...tragic."

He laughs and pulls his hood over his head.

"What's the worry, Evan? We don't have a soul and we're already dead, remember?"

I look up to him and stand to my feet.

"You think we don't have a soul."

He places his hands on my shoulders, then laughs.

"It shouldn't matter what I believe," he says. "What matters is what you believe."

I nod and try to laugh. Mike's expression goes from seriousness to a smirk. He's is being a shrink again and knows it, but I appreciate it. I really do.

"Let's hurry, the band is already playing and we have to get out of these clothes and into something more …formal."

He jumps from the bell and makes his way to his bedroom's balcony. I jump down onto mine and head back inside my room. After I get dressed, someone knocks on the door.

"Come in," I say.

It's Bianca.

"Happy Birthday, brother," she says. She hugs tight, but it doesn't hurt.

"You look great," she says.

I look down at my black dress shoes and both of the arms of my black and white tuxedo. "Look kind of like dad," she chuckles.

"Thanks," I smile. "That's what I was hoping to achieve."

"Everyone's waiting for you downstairs."

"Yeah. I at least wanted to look at myself."

"Didn't work huh?" she laughs.

"Nope," I smile. "Guess I'm the only one left in the house who has a mirror."

"Shall we throw it away?"

"No, it's fine. I still like it," I say fixing my tie, though my reflection is absent.

"Okay, I'm ready. Walk with me?"

"Of course," she says.

As we get closer to the top of the golden railed staircase, it is quiet. I had thought I would hear people or music or Mike's voice bouncing off every corner of the mansion.

"Anyone get here yet?" I whisper.

She smiles.

"See for yourself." She motions me to keep walking. I step into the light and peer over the banister.

"Happy Birthday, Evan!" they all say as balloons rise to the ceiling and confetti bursts. Music blasts and send vibrations throughout the lobby area of the mansion. The crowd consists of my family and faces I've never seen before dressed in black dresses and tuxedos. The band plays on a stage.

"Thank you and I appreciate all of you for coming. Please enjoy the party and, um, yeah," I say trying to find the right words, but laugh.

Red and black streamers hang from the ceiling, red and black balloons and confetti cover the floor, streamers also twist and lock around the railings and pillars throughout the lobby, and a huge banner hangs from the chandelier which read, *"Happy Birthday! Welcome Home!"*

"Come join the party!" Mike calls from below, waving his hand.

I walk down the golden railed staircase and join the party. People pat my back and shake my hand.

"Happy Birthday, Evan!"

"Nice to meet you, Evan!"

"I haven't seen you since you were a baby!"

I get to the fountain where Mike and Abel wait, dressed in their tuxes, black roses beneath their collarbones. They pull me into a hug.

"Looking sharp, Ev," Mike says. "This is the first time I've ever wore a bowtie."

"Fits you well," I say.

"Nephew!" Abel exclaims. "Ah, one second."

He hands his glass of red wine to Mike. I would hope it's wine unless vampires can get drunk off of blood. He holds up a black rose in front of me from its bright green vine. Its petals are blossomed and the thorns have yet been picked.

"The decoration," he says. "Do you know what black roses symbolize?"

"There's way too many," I say shrugging with a smile. "But tell me something new."

"Well," he says then burps. Mike tries to hold his laugh.

"Most would consider black roses to only symbolize negative things such as death, hatred, or what have you. But, for us, it means rebirth and rejuvenation. The beginning of a drastic change. Like you, Evan."

I smile then think to myself.

"Sounds my death," I joke. Abel and Mike join in laughter.

"I guess you're right," Abel responds. He pins the rose to my tux then pats my shoulders. "There. Brings out the color in your eyes."

"Thanks, uncle." He takes the glass from Mike and finishes it in a couple gulps.

"The refreshments are a marvel."

"I don't think I've ever wore a tux," I say.

Well," Abel says grabbing another drink from one of the servers, 'Thank you,' he tells him. "Now, you own one."

He tosses back the glass.

"Still won't look at good as me," Mike says as he smirks.

"Think so?" I say lifting my chin and poking out my chest.

He laughs and shakes his head.

"I'll let you win today because it's your birthday."

"You two are always competing," Abel says.

"*He* usually starts with *me*," I say giving him a playful push.

Mike bounces off.

"Well, someone's feeling strong," he says rubbing his shoulder.

"I'll allow you two to rip each other to shreds," Abel says. "The brunette over there has quite an eye for me." He holds his glass up, then tosses it back.

"Good luck," I say. My uncle dances his way to the dance floor and enjoys the music with the brunette. My mother, father, and Sarah stand next to a gift table.

"I'll catch up to you in a minute, Mike," I say giving him a pat on the shoulder.

"Sure thing," he says. "I'm going to probably still be right here. Bianca," he whispers. "Is a bit of the jealous type." He nods his head to the dance floor. Bianca stares then waves. She eyes Mike with a squint.

"Whoa, um yeah, you take care of that," I laugh.

"I shall try," he says drinking some punch.

My father and mother are dressed formal as usual. Sarah is behind them. I was unsure if she had shown up or planned to. She's dressed casually and has a large bag that slings around her shoulder.

"Happy Birthday, Evan," my father says pulling me into a hug.

"Happy Birthday, son," my mother says kissing my cheek and gives me a hug.

I look at Sarah and her scar creases with her smile. I suppose her scar was from the accident my family told me about. I had not noticed the other times she had come to visit to drop off the blood packets, but I suppose it was because I was forced to keep my distance from her.

"Happy Birthday, Evan."

"Thank you," I say.

"We'll leave you two to chat," my mother says pulling my father to the dance floor.

"I'm glad you came."

"I told you I would be back before your birthday."

I nod my head in agreement, but fail to remember.

"So, how does it feel? Being a vampire?"

"It will take some getting used to like when I want to look in the mirror, but besides that I'm adjusting."

"That will take time," she smiles as she switches her bag to her other shoulder.

"They told me a bit about what happened, but said they're leaving the rest with you."

"You lived with me most of your life. Three weeks ago, you were human. Then, you died. Now, you can live forever."

"So when I was human I lived with you?"

"Mhmm," she nods. "Sixteen years."

"Sixteen years," I repeat to myself.

"We knew when the time comes you would forget everything about your human life. That's just the way it is I guess, but it's up to you to choose what you believe."

"I believe," I say. "It's a bit difficult to feel what I believe, but I believe."

She smiles weakly.

"Good."

"What's in there? Blood packets?"

However, I can usually smell them when she's coming up the road.

"You use to be a vegetarian," she chuckles and it fades. "But no."

She walks over to the table opening the bag and I follow. She pulls out one notebook after another.

"I have much more at home, but these are your most recent notebooks I had you write in."

"Write? Like what?"

She smiles.

"Everything, and you used to hate when I was so pushy about it."

We laugh about it, but it's short-lived.

"I knew that you would forget everything, but I told myself I would try to help you remember. So every day, I had you write so when the day came and you'd change, you can read your words and hopefully they would mean something to you."

I grab one and hold it in my hands. The feel of it is familiar. The pages. The wear and tear.

"Can I have them?" I ask.

"That's why I brought them," she smiles. "I can bring more as you finish those."

I frown at myself.

"I'm still trying to remember what I wrote, but I can't. I can't see it."

"And it's okay that you don't. All I can hope is that you do believe. Believe that you were human before. You lived with me, and I --"

Her voice trails off.

"And I love you."

She kisses my forehead and turns back to the table. She closes the bag and runs her fingers across the notebooks.

"I'll leave these with you."

She smiles, but it's not convincing. She cares about me, and I am fighting myself to feel the same, but it's as though those feelings belong to someone else.

"Thank you," I tell her.

She smiles and wipes her cheek from a tear and I hug her.

"I must go. I'll see you soon alright?" she says fighting tears.

"But the party just --"

"Happy Birthday, Evan."

Without another word, she walks away. She opens the red doors, stops, and looks back. She smiles at me through her tears, then closes the door. I stare at the red wood then at the notebook in my hands.

"Can I have your attention please," I hear Abel say on the microphone, tapping his glass with a spoon. The music stops and the people listen.

"I want to thank you all for being here for my nephew's birthday," he holds his glass up to me, "and being great friends to our family over the years – well, centuries."

Everyone laughs.

"But it's been great. He's come home, he's grown up, and --" he shakes his head, "I've just waited what felt like forever for it to happen...Kaius. Valencia."

He calls them up with a hand and they join his side, smiling. I exhale deeply and look over at Bianca and Mike. Mike roots his fist in the air and Bianca waves. I couldn't help, but laugh. I'm happy for them both.

"Evan, son," my father says. "You have given us life over the years. Though you were not here, with us, you were in our hearts."

"Not a day had gone by that we didn't think of you," mother says. "Sixteen—now, seventeen years, it has been. Felt longer than all the decades and centuries I have lived. You reminded me of what is was like to be human. Constantly asking questions. Trying to find yourself and your purpose."

"We hope we can help you understand everything there is to know about yourself and our family," father says. "We look forward to teaching you more, and loving you forever."

Father raises his glass. The party turns to me and raises their glasses. I try not to blush or cry.

"To you, Evan," my father says.

"To Evan," everyone joins. They take their toast.

"Ahem," my father clears his throat on the microphone. "We have a special gift for all of you, and for you, son. Essence LaRoux,"

I flinch.

"Has agreed to play a musical selection with her violin, so in sharing her gift to Evan, with us all, I bring you, Essence LaRoux!"

Evanescence

Father claps his hands and the crowd joins in cheering. I make my way to the front as I look for her.

She steps on stage and into the spotlight. If I had a heartbeat, it'd jump out of my chest. Essence walks across the stage in a perfectly fit, black dress. It shapes around the curves of her body, and has puffs on the shoulders that are like blossomed black roses. Her red hair is big, curly, and vibrant. Her lipstick, red. Her arms and hands covered in long black gloves.

She carries her violin across the stage and stand before the microphone, in front of us. I look up to her above. When our eyes meet, she breathes through the microphone with a gasp then looks down at her necklace. It is a red heart-shaped vile with golden thorns coiled around it, and silver wings. She takes a deep breath, the crowd watches in silence, and she places the violin between her chin and shoulder and begins to play.

A few seconds in, goosebumps cover my skin. I recognize the songs she covers: *My Immortal* by *Evanescence*. The band plays along with her, the piano keys following her lead.

A few sniffles leave the crowd; the music is nothing had I expected. As she plays, here and there, she looks into my eyes, tears flowing down her cheeks. My stomach sinks into my gut. When she finishes, the crowd claps wildly. I wipe my cheek and stare at the teardrop. She takes a bow, looks at me one final time then swiftly walks off the stage. Bianca joins her and they walk to the hallway. Mike grabs hold of the microphone.

"Essence thanks you for the opportunity to play," he says. "Now let's party!" He throws his fist in the air and the people cheer and the band plays.

I head up the golden railed staircase, back to my room, and sit on the end of my bed. *This is unfair. I am hurting people I do not know or remember. Why does it have to be this way? Why can't I just remember?* I open the notebook to its most recent entry:

Fire. A 'gift,' as Essence had put it. Apart from the excitement, there is fear. Fear that I don't know how to use and control it. I wonder if the others are able to do the same, create fire, or something similar. Hopefully, they can tell me all the answers I need to know. Fire is destruction. Why would one want to possess a power that cannot be tamed?

But, when the time comes, when I die, I have to believe these words. No, YOU have to believe these words. So listen to me, Evan, writing this as a human today, reading this as a vampire, possibly tomorrow. Believe every word. Believe everything your family tells you. Believe that Sarah is your step-mother, your caretaker for sixteen years. Believe that Essence loves you, and that the human in you, loves her in return. You love her. You DO love her.

Sarah and Essence are not only afraid that you will forget who they are and your relationship with them, but they are more afraid that you will ignore these words or what they will tell you. They are also afraid, that upon reading these words, you will understand and accept them, but you will not have the emotion that your human self, me today, has for them. So be gentle.

These words will feel as though they belong to another being. A human. Not a vampire. But you were indeed human and you are loved... My breath has gone weak, and each second that passes, feels as though it may be my last.

I ask that you believe and still be there for them. I know, they are strangers, but do it for them.. Do it for me; yourself. They were there for YOU when you needed them. They helped you with the transformation you have today. You owe it to them to TRY....So believe.

I am still a part of you. Believe that your heart use to beat which was once mine. So give it to Sarah, your step-mother, and most of all, give it to Essence, your love. Believe, Evan. JUST BELIEVE."

With truth,
Me and You, to You,
Evan Macrae

P.S. Tell her, I love her.

My body populates with goosebumps. I stare at the words on the page. I toss the notebooks across the floor and shelter my face into my hands. There's a knock at my door.

"Come in," I say.

The door opens.

"How'd you find me?" I ask.

"We're a pair. I'll always find you and I'll always know something is bothering you."

I shake my head and take a deep breath.

"What's the matter brother? Why aren't you enjoying your party?" she asks closing the door behind her.

I shrug.

"Because I'm hurting people without meaning to." I lift my head from my hands. "It's—frustrating. Confusing. Painful to watch. I mean, how would you feel if Mike forgot everything about you and the relationship you both had?"

"I'd be heartbroken. Devastated."

"Right," I nod.

She joins me on the bed, gives me a hug, and rests her head on my shoulder.

"I wish this could have been easier for you. I know this is hard, but the best thing you can do is to try and cope. Take things one step at a time."

"How?"

"Well, to start, you no longer have to be stuck home. You can visit Sarah, and keep her company after school."

"I plan to."

"For her, that would mean a lot. She's used to coming home to someone. I'm sure once things take its natural course again, the bond will form for you."

"And what about Essence? What could I do or, what am I supposed to do?"

I think about the note I wrote to myself when I was human. He wants me to believe and be there for them. He says I love them, but I can't feel those emotions he had.

"Why don't you go talk to her?"

"Where is she?" I ask.

"She is in the bell tower."

We rise from my bed and Bianca follows me to the balcony doors.

"Hey," she says as I open the doors.

"Yes."

"I'm proud of you."

She hugs me and my smile was big enough for the both of us.

"Be gentle with her."

"Yes, I will," I say.

"Okay."

She fixes my bow tie and brushes my shoulders off.

"There," she says. "Go to her."

I step out and onto the balcony. Dusk is approaching and the sky is orange and beautiful. The wind blows softly above the water, and the birds fly across the sky. I look up to the top of the mansion, at the bell and begin to climb. When I reach the base of the bell tower, I peer over the edge, and Essence stands in her black dress, the sun upon her back.

I climb over railing and stand onto the platform. She turns to face me. The sun shines against her face and her eyes glow their natural color. Her hair looks more orange than red, from the sunset light. A gentle smile spreads across her lips.

"Happy Birthday, Evan."

"Thank you," I say to her. I hold my hand out for her to take. She hugs herself and looks across the valley. Then, she accepts. We begin to dance. The music from the mansion is faint and soft.

"You play the violin very well," I say. "Was that my first time hearing you play?"

She nods her head, but doesn't respond. I try to make her smile.

"I figured as much. There's no way I could have forgotten such a sound."

I hear a light giggle leave her lips, but inside, I feel ashamed. _There's no way I could have forgotten someone so beautiful._

"I'm sorry," I tell her.

She shakes her head and holds her hands on the nape of my neck.

"It's not your fault. I was told you'd forget. I guess I just miss you."

"I'm right here. I'm still here.

The corner of her lips rise then relax. She nods. My eyes lay upon her necklace which shines and glows in the sunlight. It is a jewel that dimly glows. She follows my eyes then looks away. Her hand clenches around it. She looks at it, then back up to me.

"You gave me this," she says

I hold it in my hand, gazing into the vile, as it hangs around her neck.

"I know," I say.

"You remember?"

I shake my head.

"No, but something tells me I gave it to you."

She nods.

"Your soul."

I smile.

"Whatever is left of it."

"Inside is your blood. See, it shines like--"

"Fire," I finish.

"Yes."

I then look into her eyes and she stares into mine. She looks at my lips then back into my eyes. I refrain from moving. She closes her eyes and brings her lips closer to mine. She kisses me and I kiss back. When she stops, she gazes into my eyes. She doesn't budge. Just stares as though she is trying to see through me.

"I love you, Evan."

Her eyes gloss from tears. I remember what it said in the entry. That we are lovers. I also remember what Sarah had told me. That I can choose to believe what I read is real.

"I..."

"Don't," she says, placing a finger on my lips. "You wouldn't mean it."

I nod.

"He did want me to tell you."

She looks into my eyes and a tear falls.

"He says he loves you."

She places her head against my chest and cries. I wrap my arms around her. As the music continues to play, I hold her against me, stepping side to side. I wish things didn't have to be this way. I wish I could remember or maybe it would have been much easier if I had not known or met Essence until after my transformation, to save her from the heartbreak. Essence peers over my shoulder and I follow her eyes. It's Mike. Soon joined by Bianca.

"Hope we're not interrupting," Mike says.

"Nice to see you two making the acquaintance," Bianca smiles at me and I return a smile. "Enjoying yourselves?"

Essence nods.

"We had our dance. I enjoyed it," she nods as she wipes her face from the tears.

"Great," she says. "Sorry for disrupting, just thought I let Evan know of a little family tradition."

"No honestly, you're fine," Essence says. "Please. Do share."

"What tradition?" I ask.

Abel, my father, and my mother join their side and hop over the railing. They fix their clothes and smile.

"A birthday tradition," my mother says.

"Do I want to know? You're all scaring me. I think I've had enough surprises in one lifetime," I say.

They all laugh.

"You have forever now, Evan," Abel says.

"I'll just act like that was a compliment," I smile.

"Meet us at the top," Bianca says. "Find out for yourself."

They stand on the railing and reach above, grabbing onto the lip of the bell. I turn back to Essence.

She fiddles with a black rose bracelet.

"All I ever do is lose people," she murmurs.

"Hey," I say taking a step towards her.

She looks up at me and hugs herself.

"He wouldn't want you to give up."

She shakes her head.

"I'm not…I won't."

I nod slowly.

"Good."

"Don't give up on me neither," she says.

"He—I won't. I promise."

She finds a smile.

"Until then, no sad faces."

She gasps and smiles even brighter.

"I guess you really are still you."

I shrug.

"He would hope so. I hope so. For everyone else's sake."

I look around the horizon as the water settles against the shores.

"I shall return," I say with a smile, unsure of what awaits me.

"Take your time. It was nice dancing with you."

"Dance again sometime soon?" I ask.

She blushes and looks to the ground then her eyes meet mine. She smiles.

"I'll be here," she says. "Always will be." I try not to blush, but fail.

"I have a feeling you've told me this before."

She giggles and wipes her eyes.

"Yes."

I smile.

"Have fun, Evan," she says. "And thank you. Happy Birthday."

"Thanks."

She gives me one last hug before I climb on top of the railing. I reach for the lip of the bell and pull myself up.

My family stands on the very top, and I join them, staring at the horizon and across Utica.

"Beautiful isn't it?" Mother says. We all agree with a nod.

"You guys ready?" Father says.

"What's the tradition?" I ask.

"It's a race," Bianca answers. "Down the Mohawk River Valley and back."

"Really?"

"Mhmmm," says my mother smiling.

"Up for it, son?" my father asks.

"Why not."

"That's the spirit!" Abel exclaims, throwing his fist in the air.

"Besides," Mike says. " I need a rematch. I have to remind you that even as a vampire, you will always come in second."

"Ohhhh!" the family exclaims as I laugh.

"We'll see about that," I assert playfully.

"I look forward to it."

"Okay," father says. "On go...On your mark!" my father says.

Everyone gets in their ready stance to jump.

"Get set!"

My excitement kicks in as I wait for the final call. Everyone, besides Mike, jumps, laughing, cheating. *Really?!* I shake my head as we watch them all dive and woo-hoo.

"Didn't see that coming," Mike says laughing.

"Same," I agree.

We look at the sun and inhale the breeze.

"Look at us, Ev," he says. "Best friends. Forever now."

"Even before all of this we would have been."

"Was only a couple months ago we were average high school students. Some of us having nightmares," he laughs a bit and I join.

"Yeah. Good times wasn't it?" I ask.

"The best."

He holds out his hand.

"No better way to spend eternity than with my best friend."

I clasp my hand into his.

"I wouldn't want it no other way."

He smiles and pats my shoulder.

"See you at the bottom."

Mike jumps from the lip of the bell and I watch as he plummets through the sky. The water below swallows him and soon, he is swimming after the rest of the family down the Mohawk River Valley.

My love for them is unconditional. We are a family, the Macrae clan, brought together by love. Mike has been there with me from the beginning, as I had tried to find what makes me the person I am today. He has been a brother, and though there have been times I feel he has let me down, in the end, he's always stood by my side, reminding me of how great a person he is.

Abel, my uncle, adds life to our family with his jokes and wit. He would make the perfect father someday, if he is lucky to find his lover somewhere, wherever she is now.

Bianca, my sister, my twin, my counselor, has been a second mother to me. She watched me while I was in school, and gives me the advice I need to here. She kept me calm throughout the rough times of my transformation, helping me keep a clear head.

My parents, Kaius and Valencia, I owe a debt I can never repay. The gift of life and the blessing of a parent's love. Sarah I have to thank as well, for her ability to work each day to prepare me for all of this.

Cedric, the misunderstood. Wherever he may be now, deserves a blessing. I can only hope he finds a calmer, clean self with his brother and sister. I can only hope he is not being led by vengeance.

Essence.

Essence LaRoux. The curly, redhead who's heart I broke. I am trying to remember everything that happened between us. Trying to piece together our bond, but I continue to fail. *Will I ever remember or love her in return?* I will try. There's a dark art behind love. How fatal. How beautiful.

R.J. Rogue

About The Author

R.J. Rogue *(Rafael Johnson)* is an English major at SUNY Empire State in Rochester, New York. He writes short stories, screenplays, and novels. He graduated from Bishop Kearney High School in 2008 where he wrote for the high school newspaper his senior year. During his early childhood, R.J. had an interest in dance but a passion for writing. His early inspirations included a collection of works by Stephen King, Edgar Allan Poe, and Ernest Hemingway. With a fear of sharing his writing, R.J. focused on dance, believing this was what he was called to do. After receiving feedback from a high school English teacher on his writing, R.J. was encouraged to write as a career, he learned the importance of not being afraid of your passions, to take pride in your writing, and to dream with your eyes open.

R.J. enjoys dancing, meditating, drawing, analyzing dreams, and drinking more than enough coffee while sustaining a vegetarian diet. He grew up in Rochester, New York where his mother is the Program Coordinator for the *Pathways to Success* in Rochester, and his father is the Dean of Students at Vertus Charter School in Rochester, NY. He is the oldest of five.

R.J. is co-author of *The Journey of a Teenage Mother: Struggle. Hope. Success. (On Demand Publishing, 2013)* and has recently completed, *National Novel Writing Month (NaNoWriMo) 2015,* in which he received recognition for his literary accomplishment.

You can follow R.J. via Instagram @r.j.rogue and on Twitter @R_J_Rogue. You can contact him at rjroguebooks@gmail.com.

Evanescence

'*Evanescence*' is a GenZ Publishing Book

GenZ™ is an innovative publishing platform for the new generation to have their work seen, recognized, published and read by millions. When an individual is chosen to be published on GenZ™, they can use that experience in their portfolios, for résumés, to share with friends, family, and fans. It is an accomplishment to be proud of for the rest of their lives.

We are on a mission to improve the world one word at a time. That is why we are the place for voices to be heard in a way not previously done in print and on digital media. It is a way to support young writers, our new voices.

It can be nearly impossible for young writers with promising talent to produce standout work that will be recognized, because of the state of the publishing and digital media industries. Having work recognized in a sea of so many writers is even tougher. That is why there is an underrepresentation of young and innovative voices in the publishing and print world. There are many unheard voices. GenZ is on a mission to change that.

GenZ™ provides a medium where these people can be positively recognized for their work through a professional product and supportive company.

Learn more about GenZ Publishing, how you can get involved, and all of our newest releases at GenZPublishing.org. Like us on Facebook at GenZ Publishing and follow us on Twitter @GenZPub.

CPSIA information can be obtained
at www.ICGtesting.com
Printed in the USA
LVOW04s1450250516

489934LV00021B/818/P

9 780692 634264